ROUNDING THIRD

"Another solid addition to the growing canon of gay teen lit. I've been wondering when someone would write a book about the gay teen experience for athletes—a sort of *Take Me Out* for gay teens. This just may be it!"

—Brent Hartinger
author of *Geography Club* and *The Order of the Poison Oak*

"From the opening sentence, *Rounding Third* resonates with readers. Gay, straight, young, old, avid athletes or non-fans—all will find something to relate to, and learn from, in this compelling and important story."

—Dan Woog
author of the *Jocks* series and syndicated
GLBT sports columnist ("The OutField")

ROUNDING THIRD

WALTER G. MEYER

[signature]
2009

MaxM
LTD

ROUNDING THIRD

ISBN 978-0-9825132-0-0

Cover photograph and author photograph by Joseph Panwitz.
Book and cover design by David Maxine.

First Printing
September, 2009

www.waltergmeyer.com

MaxM LTD.

Progress always involves risks. You can't steal second base and keep your foot on first.

—Frederick B. Wilcox

ONE

"Why do you even bother coming out for the team, you worthless little faggot?" Danny Taylor demanded as he slammed Bobby's head into the cemetery fence again. "You're not going to play any more than you did last year. You're just in the way!" Taylor hit Bobby again, and this time Danny's ring dug into Bobby's forehead. Bobby could feel the skin tearing above his eyebrow.

Taylor backhanded Bobby so hard his head spun into the wrought iron posts. Bobby staggered sideways, grabbing the cemetery fence to keep from falling.

Taylor slapped Corey Brickman on the arm and they both laughed. They walked back to Brickman's pimped-out Camaro and got in. Brickman spun the tires to spit gravel as the car fishtailed off the shoulder and back onto Route 303.

Bobby propped himself up against the fence and tried to catch his breath. He looked through the bars at the generations of dead ancestors and wondered if they were laughing at him, too. He picked his iPod out of the tall weeds.

Bobby didn't want his parents to see him, at least not until the bleeding stopped, so instead of heading straight home, he turned down McKinley Road away from his house and kept running.

As Bobby continued running, the sweat stung in his cuts, and once he had to use his shirttail to wipe the trickle of blood out of his eye.

He had hoped this year might be different. The new kid on the team smiled at Bobby and had actually said hello a couple of times. Today Bobby had resolved to speak to him and found the boy was friendly. It was that shred of hope which motivated Bobby to really try his best in the scrimmage game at practice.

He had been so concerned with impressing the new guy that he hadn't considered how Danny Taylor would take being embarrassed. He hadn't set out to embarrass anyone, that was just sort of a side effect, and, as bad as his face hurt, it was almost worth it to see the look on Taylor's face when, thanks to Bobby's base stealing, a runner scored.

Danny was the captain and quarterback of the football team, and although not the captain of the baseball team, he was the shortstop and unquestionably the leader of the tightest clique on the team. Danny had the movie-star kind of good looks that seemed only possible with the aid of good lighting and make-up. He attracted the attention of everyone, male or female, as soon as he entered a room. Bobby had watched people fawn over Danny since they were in the first grade together. "Oh, Mrs. Taylor, your son is sooo handsome . . ." it was the kind of adulation that had helped Danny grow into the most insufferable asshole in school, which, given some of the other competition, was quite an accomplishment.

In spite of, or perhaps because of, Taylor's arrogance, he always had a flock of disciples around him as though some of his greatness might drop to the ground and they could snatch it up. The first day of baseball practice in tenth grade Bobby had glanced over at Danny. His radiance was such it was hard not to stare, and Bobby was met with a slap to the face and the question, "What are you staring at, faggot?" There was so much threat and malice in the voice that ever since Bobby had averted his eyes in the presence of the young prince.

He had learned long before that when you were his size getting in the way of Taylor and his kind often meant kissing a locker so he stayed away from them as much as possible. As Bobby's grandmother used to say, "The nail that sticks up is the one that gets hammered down."

As Bobby ran, his face stinging, he had plenty of time to reflect on the futility and stupidity of having called attention to himself at practice. The grandstanding seemed like the thing to do at the time, but now any chance he had of fitting in on the team was gone. He marveled how he had once again managed to fall so quickly out of step. Although he often suspected that he was the only one doing the right step, and everyone else was out of sync.

TWO

"Shit sauna." It was probably not the best way to start a conversation with the new guy at the beginning of practice, but when Bobby saw him exit the green port-a-john that was the first thing that came to mind.

The new player was slipping his hand into his baseball glove as the plastic door twanged shut behind him.

"It stinks really bad," Bobby continued. "That's why we use the woods." Bobby jerked his head toward the trees beyond the leftfield fence.

"I was wondering what was going on back there." The new kid fumbled to get his glove off his right hand to shake. "I'm Josh Schlagel."

"I know." Bobby had noticed him on the first day of school last fall. New kids weren't that common at Harrisonburg High, although the new housing developments were changing that. "Bob Wardell," Bobby said at the same moment that Danny Taylor sent a ball soaring over the right field fence. Bobby had said his name so quietly it had been swallowed in the cheer that accompanied the batting practice homerun.

"Nice to meet you, Rob," Josh said.

"You, too," Bobby said, looking down. He liked the way it sounded to be called *Rob* instead of *Bob*. His parents still called him *Bobby*, and he wished they would drop the 'y' now that he was seventeen, but since his father was *Bob*, they still called him *Bobby*.

"What position do you play?" Josh asked.

"Left out."

"Left outfield?" questioned Josh.

"No, left out. As in, I don't play. That's my end of the dugout," Bobby said, pointing to the far end of the bench down the first base line. They called it a dugout although it was just a bench not lowered into the ground and lacked a covering of any kind. "I hear you might start the first game," Bobby said. "You should. You're good. I've watched you throw smoke in practice."

"Thanks."

Their nervousness was growing into a silence between them.

Both were relieved when Coach Hudson called out in his nasal Southern wail, "Huddle up!"

They trotted over to join the team. Coach Hudson announced the starting line-up for the Harrisonburg Hawks' first game: Josh Schlagel would start on the mound. There was some grumbling, mainly by Danny Taylor, that Buff Beechler should have started, but Bobby didn't hear Buff complain. Beechler was one of the few seniors on the team and certainly the largest, hairiest student at the high school, quite probably in the state of Ohio, and possibly the world. His nickname, *Water Buffalo*, had been shortened by overuse to just *Buff*.

After giving the line-ups, Hudson said, "We're going to play a five-inning inter-squad game to get us ready for Belleville next week. The starters will be the A team. The rest of you will be the B team. Since B will be a man short, Beechler, you'll play left for the A team and first for the B team; when you're batting we'll get you a sub." Josh was to play first for the A team to save his arm for the opener.

Bobby was thinking these line-ups would leave them an outfield of pitchers and him as the only semi-experienced infielder on the B Team besides Buff. Not a good thing.

Harrisonburg High wasn't so large as to require even having cuts for most of the teams. If anyone showed up for practice and tried, they were pretty much entitled to a spot, even though it might be clear that they were never going to play. The baseball team had only seventeen players, so aside from the starters and five pitchers, Bobby was one of only three extra fielders.

Hudson's next announcement caused even more concern: "To make sure everyone plays hard, the losing team will run two laps."

"Yeah!" Danny Taylor laughed.

"And since the A team should have the advantage, win or lose, for every run the B team scores, the A team will run a lap."

"What?" Danny asked.

"You didn't hear me, Taylor?" Coach Hudson demanded in his southern twang. "For you, it'll be two laps per run." Hudson appeared to be a large man at a distance, but up close, most men would have stood taller than him. Most men, but not Bobby. Hudson's age could have been between thirty and fifty and his thickness made it hard to tell if his body was muscle, fat, or muscle that had turned to fat. Rumor had it that Hudson had played minor league ball in Arizona or New Mexico or someplace out west, but Hudson never mentioned it or told any baseball stories. He never talked much more than the matter at hand so no one seemed to know if he had a wife or kids or if he had a life off the field.

The threatened laps meant laps not just around the field, but around the campus, which included the baseball field, football stadium and all of the academic buildings. And up two pretty good hills, or at least what passed for hills in northern

Ohio. A lap was just under a mile on the path worn to dirt by the many teams that used it for their training runs.

Josh Schlagel led off for the A team. The first pitch sailed by him so low and outside the catcher didn't even bother reaching for it and let it rattle against the wire mesh backstop. Josh stepped into the next pitch and connected to drive it over the leftfield fence above the fading Harrisonburg Chevrolet banner and into the woods. There was the small applause of a few guys thumping their hands into their mitts and a few calls of "Way to go!" or "Nice one!" but it was just a polite acknowledgement, not the ovation Danny Taylor got, which seemed unfair since this was a game and not just batting practice. Bobby wanted to applaud or shout encouragement to the new guy, but he didn't. He never did for anyone else on the team so it would seem strange to start now, but he felt bad that the guys were not more welcoming of Josh.

The next two batters flew out. As Bobby ran off the field, Josh stopped him. "Hey, Rob, I noticed you're the only other lefty on the team. While you're batting, can I try your glove? Mine's falling apart. I want a new one so I'd like to try yours if it's okay."

"Sure." He tossed his mitt to Josh. Bobby was flattered that Josh had noticed him enough to know which hand he used.

"Thanks!" Josh grabbed the mitt and trotted to first base.

There was a man on first base when Bobby came to the plate in the bottom of the first inning. He was so nervous, batting in a game, and trying too hard to pull the ball down the right field line, that he missed the ball entirely as it bounced in the dirt and the catcher caught it on one hop. At shortstop, Danny Taylor made a noise with his mouth like a fart. Umpiring behind the plate, assistant coach Milnes said, "C'mon, Wardell," instead of even calling the strike.

"Let's go, two!" Josh yelled Bobby's number from the infield and Bobby was so amazed that one of his teammates had actually shouted encouragement that he made it a point to plant his feet and make sure he connected. He took a full cut at the next ball, and perhaps it was an accident or subconscious aiming, but he drilled the ball to short. If Taylor hadn't gotten his glove up it would have taken his head off. Instead it bounced off his glove and into short center field.

Bobby made his turn at first and watched the other runner stop at second. When Bobby came back to the bag Josh said, "Nice hit, Rob."

"Thanks," Bobby said, smiling. He suddenly felt that maybe he could do something to help the team. Or at least help himself feel like part of the team for a change.

As they watched Buff Beechler trot in from leftfield to bat, Josh said, "It'll be embarrassing if we lose to the second string."

"I know we're going to lose, but at least I have to make sure you guys run a lap or two." Bobby wasn't sure where he found the confidence to talk to Josh, let alone act like the B team might have a chance.

Buff smacked one into deep center where the centerfielder chased it down at the fence. Both Bobby and the man on second tagged and went: runners on second and third, one out. Bobby looked over to first and saw Josh smiling at him. He smiled back.

Coach Hudson had told them to feel free to steal if they saw their chance. As soon as the pitcher went into his windup, Bobby bolted off second—towards first. The catcher came up gunning the ball to first to try to get Bobby. Hudson, coaching at third, sent the runner home from third. Bobby was almost to first when the ball arrived there and Bobby turned back towards second. Josh fired the ball to the plate, but too late to stop the run from scoring.

The catcher flung the ball to shortstop Danny Taylor, who was waiting at second. Bobby turned back to first and Taylor threw the ball to Josh. Bobby turned back toward second. Josh ran at Bobby then tossed the ball back to Taylor who started chasing him back towards first. Bobby knew from their sprints in practice that he could outrun Taylor although he had never wanted to win and risk pissing off Taylor. Taylor threw the ball to the pitcher who was now covering first. The pitcher ran at Bobby, but gave up the chase to flick the ball to Corey Brickman, the second baseman, who now was guarding his own base.

Bobby began to feel like a yo-yo, going one way then the other. The catcher was backing up first base and the centerfielder had come in to back up second. As each player charged at Bobby and Bobby outran him, the fielder would flip the ball over Bobby's head to whoever had now taken over the vacated base. If anyone had been keeping a scorebook, it would have been a ridiculous entry like 2-3-2-6-3-6-1-4-1-5-9-8-3-6-3-5-2-6 . . . , giving pi a run for its money.

Still Bobby wouldn't give up. Taylor and Brickman were getting angrier. "Just tag the faggot!" Taylor screamed at Josh.

"Get him!" Brickman yelled as he again flipped the ball over Bobby's head.

"He can't keep doing wind sprints forever!" Taylor yelled.

"Wanna bet?" Buff yelled. "Go, Wardell!"

Bobby was thinking if he kept forcing throws someone would miss. Brickman positioned himself halfway between the bases and yelled at the pitcher to do likewise. The plan was clear. They'd line the base path with men and throw to whoever was nearest Bobby. It was working. Bobby was now dodging very close tags. Coach Milnes had come out from behind the plate to make the call.

Bobby's chain was getting shorter and shorter. He lunged at first then spun and streaked towards second. The ball was there ahead of him, so he slid between Taylor's legs as Taylor swiped the glove down hitting Bobby hard in the back.

"Safe!" Milnes yelled. Bobby and the rest of the team looked to see Milnes pointing to where the ball had popped loose and was resting at the edge of the outfield grass.

Taylor looked up and yelled, "You're going to pay for that, you son of a bitch."

"Taylor, you know my rule on swearing," Coach Hudson said. Bobby was surprised to see Hudson standing next to second base. "That's a lap for the one I heard and an extra one for what I'm sure I didn't hear. Wardell, that was good hustle, but don't you know you can't steal first? If you set foot on first again, you're out."

Bobby said, barely loud enough for Hudson to hear, "I knew that, but they didn't." Hudson's thick brow creased. Bobby met the coach's eyes for the first time and added, "The run scored didn't it?"

A slight smile crossed the coach's face then vanished as he turned to the rest of the team. "These practice games are so you can practice, not screw around. Is that the way we play pickles? Eight guys handle the ball and not one of you able to make the play? There should never be more than three throws. Tomorrow, we will be working just on that. Fundamentals win ball games. Did anyone besides Wardell know there was no point in defending first base?" The downward glances answered that. Hudson shook his head. "We've got lots of work to do before our first real game next week." Hudson stalked off the field.

Taylor returned to short, bumping Bobby off the base on the way. Bobby was stranded at second as the next two batters struck out.

"Nice glove," Josh said, pulling it off his hand and holding it out for Bobby. "New." The glove still smelled like a new leather belt and had yet to start giving off the proper aura of a baseball mitt.

"A Christmas present from my dad," Bobby said. "You're welcome to borrow it anytime. God knows I'm not going to wear it out. Use it for the rest of the game and see if you like it."

By the next time Bobby batted he knew his team's loss was certain. His careful eye earned him a walk but once again he was left on base. The game ended 7-1, the lone run having come during Bobby's manic base running.

"Pathetic" was the theme of the post-game dressing down Hudson gave the A team.

As they lined up for their laps, Taylor grabbed Bobby's shirt and hissed, "You'll pay for this!" Taylor let go just as Coach Hudson arrived and blew his whistle to start them running. Bobby took off at a good clip.

Josh sprinted to catch up with Bobby then fell into stride beside him. "Did you set out to make us look like idiots or did it just turn out that way?" he asked, smiling.

Bobby shook his head, "I was dumb." Bobby could feel the anger of his other teammates drilling holes in the back of his head.

"That was amazing running. You did us all a favor. Taught us we need to practice a lot harder to win," Josh said.

"Schlagel!" Danny Taylor yelled and Josh fell back into step with the other players.

Bobby flew away, making sure to finish his laps, shower quickly and be out of the locker room before the others finished running. He had felt like part of the team for one very brief moment and he had hoped to make a good impression, but he hadn't considered how the rest of the team would react. The rage in Danny Taylor's eyes had answered that all too clearly.

THREE

Bobby's parents were willing to pick him up after games or practice, but he preferred to run the 3.8 miles to his house. He'd had his mom clock it once.

His run home gave him more time to think about how stupid his creative base running was. He ran past the sign that staked the center of Harrisonburg and gave its population as 5781. The sign had never been changed in Bobby's lifetime so he questioned its accuracy. Once town ended, he passed the entrance to the new subdivision, Quail Run, where quail no longer ran and where the houses looked more temporary than a quail nest. Until two years ago, those ten acres had been the Bauer farm. Like so many other farms in the area, it had been swallowed by a Cleveland suburb. Each year, houses ate more of the surrounding land and if Bobby gave a shit what happened to his town he might have been offended to see his town overrun by cardboard Tudor houses, but he didn't.

Next he came to the old graveyard which was home to a score of Wardells including Bobby's grandparents. The cemetery was a lopsided affair with all of the trees and the older, large marble angels and obelisks and mausoleums on one side, and the smaller, more modern flat stones baking in the shadeless sun on the other. The Wardell plot was on the edge of the old, large side, with above-ground, but not giant, monuments.

The cemetery was all the farther Bobby had made it before Brickman's Camaro had caught up with him. Danny Taylor had jumped out first and Corey Brickman had driven by and then got out so they'd have Bobby boxed in—one coming at him from each direction and the cemetery fence cutting off the only path of escape.

Over the years, Bobby had grown accustomed to being picked on and he had taken worse beatings, but he didn't like telling his parents when he got beaten up again. He had told his mom once when he was in junior high school. She called the school, but all that did was get Bobby beaten up worse for being a snitch. When his dad found out, he tried to teach Bobby to defend himself. During the disastrous boxing lesson, all Bobby could think of was how useless these techniques would be against four guys at once, each of whom was twice his size.

Bobby hated even having to be around most of the guys on the baseball team who had been tormenting him for years. But he was also so accustomed to their abuse that he refused be frightened away by them. He'd never hear the end of it in the halls of the school if he let them chase him off the team. And he couldn't add "quitter" to the list of disappointments he felt like he'd been to his father.

But Danny Taylor was right. Bobby was never going to play. Just being on the baseball team was the path of least resistance for Bobby. His father had just assumed Bobby would play Little League. For a shy boy smaller than everyone else his age, the first day of tryouts brought terror for Bobby, but he found he wasn't as big a spaz as most of the kids. He qualified at second, a position that drew way too much action to suit him, but fear of failure kept him from messing up too bad. Each year he progressed through Pony and Colt leagues until he found himself going to high school still carrying a fielder's glove.

Walter G. Meyer

He knew he was competent at best. Each year he resolved he would end the charade and stop going out for teams he had no desire to be on, but each year his father put the posters in the front window of his accounting office and displayed Bobby's team photos and trophies there as well. So each year when the day came to tell dad, he couldn't say the words.

Bobby still remembered the look on his father's face when he couldn't shoot the deer. He had fired, but at the ground. First he had shifted the rifle slightly to the left, but found he couldn't even hurt a tree. By age ten, Bobby had learned to shoot and shoot well; at 60 yards with a 3x9 scope, there was no way he'd have missed. As soon as he pulled the Winchester down from his face, he knew his father knew. Bobby was never asked to go hunting again. His dad had tried to get his sister, who was two years younger, to go. Megan also took the safety classes, learned how to shoot, but she had the guts to say there was no way she was going to get up at 4 a.m. and go freeze her butt off in hopes of slaughtering Bambi's mother.

So baseball was the one thing Bobby could give his father; the one thing he did that seemed to please him. Bobby had barely made the JV team last year and had only played two innings as a sophomore in a game so lopsided that even his presence couldn't blow their lead. He made one putout, an easy ground ball that required him to take one step before he scooped it up and shoveled it to first. He had never batted in a real game as a Harrisonburg High Hawk. Bobby did love the game of baseball, but always felt out of place in the baggy uniform, like a boy donning his father's army uniform in hopes of looking tough, but instead it made him feel conspicuous and vulnerable.

As insecure as he was about his size, Bobby had been hesitant about making friends, and in the few weeks since practice started this year, he hadn't been welcomed by the team any more than he had been sophomore year when some seemed to think that the presence of such a wimp diminished the whole squad.

After he finished his long loop around McKinley Road to let the bleeding stop, he ran back along Route 303 past the ceme-

20

tery and then Greiner's Farm Market. The market was a ram-shackle affair that looked like a good wind or snowstorm should've taken out forty years ago, but somehow it survived and even now, in the middle of spring, it still smelled of pines, pumpkins, and peaches.

Then came the Wardells' land. Bobby glanced at the white, two-story farmhouse with the wrap-around porch where he lived, but which somehow never seemed like home. Bobby's father had told him the house had been built by an ancestor, a Civil War veteran, for his anticipated large family. After the man's wife died giving birth to their second child, he had never remarried and no generation since had produced enough off-spring to properly fill the mansion.

Bobby didn't break stride until he hit the front walk. The spring sun had set and he felt a shiver. He could see movement behind the living room windows so he headed down the side of the house across the paved corner of the driveway where the basketball hoop was. He hoped he could use the kitchen door and slide upstairs unnoticed.

Bobby bolted past his mother in the kitchen and up to his room where he dropped his backpack. In the bathroom he turned on the water, stripped, and looked down at his under-sized and almost hairless body. He would have doubted he had reached puberty if other sure signs had not often shot forth. Sometimes on his runs he tried to figure out who he had killed in some former life to have drawn such a lousy hand in this one. He stepped into the water that was just short of scalding. Bobby took showers that either boiled or froze, anything to try to shock some life into his body and all thoughts out of his head.

During dinner, his mother noticed the Band-aid on his fore-head. "Slid into the catcher during practice," Bobby said. His father raised an eyebrow, but didn't question that very questionable explanation.

As usual, when Bobby woke at 3 a.m., he tried to pretend that it was really his hormones and horniness that were keeping him from sleep and that if he took care of that he would be able to sleep. And, as on so many other nights, filling a sock had relieved the tension in his little head, but did nothing to bring any ease to his big head.

So Bobby did what he had done so many other nights, he fell out of bed onto the polished hardwood floor, naked, and began doing sit ups alternating with sets of push-ups. Most nights he would work himself for hours and then crawl back into bed and sleep for another few hours. These brutal nocturnal workouts did nothing to lessen his self-doubt, but they made his body too tired to put up with his brain's nonsense.

The next morning as Bobby walked to first period, still groggy from his lack of sleep, a hand on his shoulder spun him into a locker with a bang. "You pull another stunt like that again in practice, I'll clean every toilet in this building with your head!" Danny spun Bobby around and smashed his face into the locker door; Bobby felt the pressure release and heard the receding echo of Danny's steps as he walked away. He heard Corey Brickman laughing. So much for team bonding.

Bobby looked up and saw Edward DeLallo, the office nerd, watching. Bobby felt like Edward was always watching him, but never said anything. Edward never seemed to have class. He was always working in the office or floating through the halls like Tinkerbell with a message for a teacher or a summons for a student. Edward was tall and very thin, a walking stick figure. His glasses seemed to always be sliding down his narrow nose, necessitating his constantly pushing them back up. Or picking them up off the floor when a shove from someone had knocked them off again. If Bobby was close enough, he'd silently pick up the glasses and hand them back. Bobby wished he could have done more to help Edward. Instead, they never even spoke and stayed alone in their own private torments, each too embarrassed by his own humiliations to be able to comfort the other. This misery didn't want company; it wanted to be alone in its own hell.

Bobby looked down the hall and saw many of his teammates still laughing at him.

Second period history was worse than the usual wretchedness. Mr. Welke was giving them his standard lecture of how, as a Marine in Vietnam, he had single-handedly won the war. Bobby had a hard time picturing the emaciated, balding Welke as a fierce jungle fighter, but then he could never reconcile his memory of his small, frail grandfather with the story that earned the old man a fistful of Purple Hearts during the Battle of the Bulge. Bobby wished his grandfather hadn't died before he'd ever got to ask him about what it was like to kill a man. During Welke's self-centered history lessons, Bobby was always tempted to raise his hand and remind his teacher that we sort of lost Vietnam.

At the end of class, Mr. Welke gave back their term papers. Bobby should have known better than to write his paper on Ohio's presidents; it was as dumb as stealing first. These brief, misguided moments of rebellion were not the path to a smooth high school career.

Bobby had started the paper with the town's namesake, William Henry Harrison, ninth president of the United States. He wrote about Harrison's life before his presidential term — his career as a soldier and his battles with the Indians that opened much of Ohio to white settlement. The sign welcoming visitors to Harrisonburg also focused on this, but it was an old sign, pre-political correctness, so there was no question of whether annihilating the Native Americans was the right thing to do. In Bobby's paper he didn't hesitate to include a couple of massacres. The paper noted there would be no mention of Harrison's post-presidential career, since he had none. Bobby covered his presidency: Harrison gave the longest inauguration speech in U.S. history and served the shortest term. His verbose two-hour oration in the freezing rain gave the old man pneumonia and he was dead in a month.

The paper noted that Ohio liked to brag that it had given birth to only one less president than Virginia. But in contrast to the Virginians: Washington and Jefferson, Madison and Monroe and Woodrow Wilson, Ohio could boast of Garfield and McKinley—whose only claims to fame were being shot—and Ulysses S. Grant whose administration set a standard for corruption that was not to be equaled until the presidency of another Ohioan, Warren G. Harding. Bobby noted that among the many achievements of Harding's presidency were the illegitimate children Harding had fathered before having the good sense to die while still in office and be buried in a fine funeral prior to all of the dirt surfacing. Bobby also had a side note mentioning that Grant's fellow Civil War general and later mega-loser of all of American History, George Armstrong Custer, was born in Ohio.

Bobby had seen a T-shirt once that said *Virginia is for Lovers* and thought his home state should print some that said, *Ohio is for Losers*. Or counter Illinois' *Land of Lincoln* license plates with ones that read *Land of Losers*.

Mr. Welke rewarded Bobby's well-researched efforts with a D.

*   *   *   *   *

The next few practices before opening day were especially hard. Bobby got more than a few shoves, cold stares and obscenities as the coaches made the team repeatedly practice the basics. Josh and Buff were the only ones who seemed to appreciate the extra work.

FOUR

The first game of the season made the morning announcements, but no one paid any attention to baseball except the guys on the team. Football and basketball attracted the crowds and the girls.

Josh's performance on the mound against Belleville was everything the Harrisonburg Hawks could have hoped. By the third inning, only one of the opposition's runners had reached first base on a hard-hit single on the first pitch that caused Taylor to shout from his position at short to Buff in leftfield, loud enough for everyone to hear, "They should have let you pitch—going to be a long day!"

On the bench Bobby was thinking the least the team could do was give the new guy a chance. But since that one pitch into the fat of the strike zone, Josh had shut them out at the plate, striking out six of the first ten batters.

Unfortunately, the Belleville pitcher, Derek Fujiyama, who was known throughout the league for his fireball, was equal to the challenge and no Hawk had been on base since Danny

Taylor drew a walk in the first. In the third inning, Josh, in the pitcher's traditional ninth spot, was preparing to bat.

The hoped-for friendship with Josh, small as it was, had Bobby taking a special interest in Josh's playing. Bobby realized part of the reason he had been trying a little harder at practice was because of Josh. As Josh walked toward the on-deck circle, Bobby was a little surprised to hear himself call out, "Schlagel!" Josh stopped and came over to the fence that separated the bench from the area where the batters took their warm-up swings. "The pitcher drops his shoulder if he's going off-speed or throwing junk. On a fastball, he pulls his shoulder up. Just a subtle hitch in his motion, so watch for it. If you get on, steal. He's slow."

Josh nodded his thanks and turned to watch the Blue Devils pitcher. Corey Brickman nudged Danny Taylor then yelled, "Sit down, Wardell!"

Bobby walked past the wary stares of the other players and back to his seat on the bench.

Bobby heard the boink of an aluminum bat and turned to see a weak pop-up to short that made the first out of the inning and brought Schlagel to the plate. The usual chatter went up from the bench. "C'mon, Schlagel!" "Help yourself out here!" "Let's go one-seven!"

Bobby said nothing as he leaned forward and grabbed the fence to watch Josh bat. The pitcher's right shoulder went up and sure enough, he came with a fastball. Josh was waiting for it and took a full cut but failed to get a full piece of the ball and sent it flying high up. The catcher flung off his mask and ran towards the first base dugout, but stopped when he realized the ball would clear the fence out of play. Josh picked up the mask, slapped it against his leg to shake the dust off it and held it out for the catcher who seemed a little surprised, but smiled and thanked Josh. Again Fujiyama went into his wind-up and again the shoulder hitched up. This time Josh was set and sent it sailing over the shortstop's head into shallow left.

On the next pitch, Josh was off towards second. He took

third on another stand-up stolen base. A single scored him. Josh ran across the plate and stopped to whisper to the next batter. Josh ran past the extended hands of the other congratulatory players and right to Bobby. "Good call, Wardell! Way to go!" He slapped Bobby on the back. It stung more than the slaps in the face he'd had from Danny in the past, but it felt great. Josh hurried back down the bench to whisper instructions to the rest of the team.

The rally ended with six runs in. The base runners were going on every pitch. A double steal that resulted in an over-thrown ball brought in the last run before the Hawks' catcher struck out on three straight, very hot fastballs, leaving Josh on deck.

Josh returned his bat to the rack and dropped his helmet. He looked down the bench and gave a thumbs up to Bobby then pointed at him. "You should get six RBIs for that inning."

Bobby felt the coach's hand on his shoulder. He didn't remember that Hudson had ever touched him before. "Wardell, that's smart baseball." Hudson's breathy, nasal way of speaking made it seem like he was trying to yell even when he was talking quietly at close range. Hudson looked down the rest of the bench. "The rest of you should be paying attention. You're part of this game—not spectators." Some of them shrugged, having no idea what they'd left undone.

The next inning added three more runs and Belleville pulled their starter, but by then the damage was done. Josh finished the game, his tired arm giving up two walks which led to two runs in the seventh and final inning. Josh had his first complete game and his first win as a Hawk. The team crowded around to congratulate him as much for sparking the rally as for his throwing a five-hitter, but Josh moved past them, looking for Bobby who was shoving the bats back into their bags. Bobby looked up, surprised to see Josh coming toward him.

Josh announced to the team, "Here's the guy who should really get the victory. Great job, Rob." The rest of the team looked confused. Perhaps they didn't know who *Rob* was. He wasn't sure how many of the guys knew what his last name was, let alone his first name and if they were aware of him before this, it was as Bobby. Josh slapped Bobby on the back again. "My first win, but the credit's all yours."

Bobby was as surprised by his getting all this attention as the rest of the team was. Josh turned to his teammates and told them that it was Bobby who had spotted the flaw in the other pitcher. This bit of trivia was quickly shrugged off, dismissed by the players as they went back to congratulating Josh. Josh, ignoring their accolades, hollered back at Bobby as he was getting swept away by the crowd, "I owe you one!"

In the locker room, Bobby was stuffing his uniform into his backpack when he felt a hand on his bare shoulder. "Thanks again. We couldn't have done it without you."

Recognizing the slight whistle in the subtle lisp, Bobby didn't have to turn to know Josh was at his side. "You're welcome," Bobby said, but didn't turn, and continued stuffing.

"Are you mad at me? I'm sorry, I should've made it clear to those guys that was all your doing."

"No, I'm not mad. You tried. They didn't care. But you don't have to keep thanking me. They think it's weird."

"I don't think it's weird to give credit where it's due. You won that game more than any pitch I threw or ball that was hit."

"The team won, that's all that matters." Bobby still wouldn't make eye contact.

"Thanks again. With your head for baseball and my pitching arm we make a good team." Josh again slapped Bobby's bare back and walked away.

Bobby slipped his shirt on and turned to leave, walking right into the landmass that was Buff Beechler. He seemed to always be running into Buff, but since Buff took up half the locker room, that wasn't hard to do. Buff was at least two and a half times Bobby's 110 pounds. "Sorry," Bobby mumbled as he tried to move around the large obstacle. Buff grabbed his arm.

Here it comes, Bobby thought, I've bumped into him once

too often, and now he'll pound me into the tile floor like Bobby had watched Danny Taylor do to a kid after gym class one day. Bobby had lived in fear that his time was coming and now it had.

"Hey," Buff said, forcing Bobby to look up. "That was a good catch today."

"Good catch?" Bobby stammered. "I didn't play."

"You know what I mean. Schlagel was right—you were the MVP today. It's nice to know when a fastball is coming, especially when the guy throws heat the way Fujiyama does. He's been clocked at over ninety." Bobby stood in slacked-jaw silence, unsure that Buff Beechler was really carrying on a conversation with him. Bobby could say nothing even if he'd had a clue what to say. Buff chucked him lightly on the shoulder. "Keep up the good work. And if you have any hot tips on any of the other teams we face, clue me in, 'k?"

Bobby could only nod weakly as Buff eclipsed him. Bobby tried to leave again, but this time found himself face to face with Jason Farino. "Nice going, Wardell, make the rest of us look bad again!" Farino poked him in the shoulder. Next to Bobby, Jason was the smallest kid on the team, and was by far the worst baseball player, but even he had enough size to pound Bobby and they both knew it. Bobby almost felt sorry for Jason that he was so low that the only person he was able to lord it over was Bobby. Bobby thought there should have been some bonding at the bottom, but Jason was too dumb to notice that picking on Bobby would never be enough to get him accepted by the rest of the team.

Bobby said nothing. Being the center of attention wasn't all it's cracked up to be. He popped in his earbuds and darted out the door to run home.

*   *   *   *   *

All day Saturday, Bobby and his father, and at times his mother and sister, took advantage of the warm weather to work in the fields his father jokingly called "the back forty." It was more of a hobby than work for his father. His father's accounting business and his mom's part time work paid the family bills, but they also grew much of the family's own food. Although his father hadn't gone hunting in a few years, venison used to provide winter meat. Bobby had a feeling their living off the land had more to do with some kind of tradition than economics, but he never asked. They weren't rich or poor. He didn't have his own car, but then many kids his age didn't either. And he had never even thought to ask for one since he had no place to go.

Although they often spent full days in the field, he and his father didn't talk much. Bobby thought they should be having some sort of meaningful dialogue when they spent these long days together, that a male-bonding father-son thing should be happening. He tried to avoid his father, but not any more than he avoided anyone else.

His parents weren't terribly social and sometimes Bobby had wondered if he got his lack of social skills from them. For someone who had been raised in the town and ran a business there, his father didn't seem very much a part of the town. He was not an Elk or a Lion or a Kiwani. He belonged to the Chamber of Commerce, but rarely went to meetings. Bobby got the feeling that after Vietnam and four years away at Kent State where his father met his mother, his father really didn't feel much like going home, but having no place else to go and his parents needing help with the farm he probably never questioned his duty to return home. His father was like that. Quietly doing his duty.

When Bobby was about nine, his dad had erected the basketball hoop and paved a section of the driveway into a half-court. The games were too one-sided and after a while it was clear the son was not enjoying the sport and dad stopped challenging him to after-dinner games. Now his dad played Meg or shot baskets alone. Bobby would sometimes shoot a few baskets or play Meg one-on-one, but he made it a point to never have a basketball in hand when his father was around. Dad's coaching embarrassed him since he couldn't perform as he was supposed to.

The Wardell family really did have almost forty acres. Part of the land was still in woods, and part was the large lawn for the house, although in the tradition of a century ago: the lawn was at the back and to one side, and the front of the house was almost on Route 303. They grew nearly an acre of various crops—the section his mother called their farmlette—corn, beans, tomatoes, and a large garden, plus several fruit trees of various types—which provided lots of food for his mother to can come fall. The excess produce they sold to Frank Greiner for his market. Eighty years ago, Bobby's great-grandfather had sold his produce through Frank's father. Some things never changed.

Bobby and his mother were working in the field when his father came out to them. "WTW?" he asked. Bobby's father had a habit of saying something his commanding officer used to say in Vietnam, *Ready to roll?* but before Megan could properly pronounce her Rs she had adopted her father's expression, which had become so routine a family joke it had been shortened to its abbreviation.

"Weady," Mrs. Wardell answered then turned to her son. "Sure you don't want to come?"

"Nah, I'll stay here and finish clearing these weeds."

"Think of anything else we need?" his father asked him.

Bobby shook his head. He had no desire to go to the lawn and garden center. He wanted to be alone for a bit to try to think of what he might say to Josh at Monday's game. Since Josh had tried to talk to him, he wanted to be able to have something to say in return instead of staring blankly the way he had when Buff had spoken to him.

As long as Bobby kept his body busy he could think pleasant thoughts, but once the sun was down and the world got quiet, the noise in his head started again and he would put himself through another grueling workout until exhaustion overcame anxiety and he could sleep.

FIVE

"Notice anything about this guy?" Bobby turned to see Josh standing next to him just before the start of the next game. Josh jerked his head towards the opposing pitcher.

"Like that his curve ball doesn't curve?" Bobby answered. "You guys will shell him out of there by the third inning."

"Thanks," Josh said as he started to walk away.

"Their second baseman and shortstop don't talk to each other," Bobby added.

Josh turned, smiled and nodded.

Bobby couldn't help but admire the way Josh moved on the field. Every move seemed natural. Even when Bobby was doing the right thing on the field—like getting a run in— it seemed to turn out wrong.

With the mercy rule, it was over in five innings. Final score: Hawks 14, Bears 0. The new line-up had Josh batting fifth in recognition of his hitting in the first game. Josh had gone three-for-three with two doubles, a single, and a walk. They trotted to the locker room to shower. Although there were no assigned lockers, everyone always used the same one. Josh's was in the bank of lockers with the starters. Bobby's was in another bank with the other benchwarmers.

Hudson insisted they shower and change at the gym. He thought there was something wrong about wearing their sweaty uniforms home. Although there was grumbling about this, the rule wasn't going to change anytime soon. It was just a few more minutes of agony which Bobby found pointless since he was going to run home and shower again anyway, but he went through the motions with the briefest of rinses. He was never comfortable in the shower and avoided eye contact more than usual. As he was stepping out of the shower, Taylor stepped in his way. Bobby looked up to avoid the collision. He tried not to look at Taylor, but now here they were. Taylor said, "What're you looking at, faggot?"

Bobby didn't answer and tried to step around the naked shortstop, still not meeting his eyes. Taylor shoved him the chest, which caused him to stagger back. "I asked what you were staring at down there. Looking at a real man's equipment? What you might hope to have someday if you grow up? Or do you want mine now?" he asked, grabbing his crotch and shaking it.

Brickman and others laughed. Buff Beechler pushed between Taylor and Bobby forcing both to step back. Buff's body always made Bobby do a double take—it looked as though Buff had forgotten to take off a black sweater before entering the shower, but it was all Buff's natural fur. Buff looked down at Taylor and shook his head. Bobby used the interruption to escape to his locker. He heard Buff mumble "pathetic."

Bobby was barely off school grounds when he heard a car slow beside him. Fearing it might be Taylor and Brickman, he quickened his pace. The horn honked beside him. Bobby again sped up.

"Rob! Where you headed in such a hurry?"

The slight whistle in the *S* made Bobby stop and pull off his earphones. "What?"

Bobby trotted over to the old Ford Focus where Josh Schlagel sat smiling behind the wheel. "I asked where you were running so fast."

"Sorry, I had my music on."

"Want a ride?"

"I don't want you to go out of your way."

"I won't. I live out 303."

"You know where I live?"

"Yeah, everybody uses your house and that farm market as landmarks. Whenever I ask directions, I always get 'Go past the farm market and the Wardell house . . .' Hop in."

Josh cleared some papers off the front seat as Bobby unslung his backpack and climbed in, moving the Bucks sweat-shirt off the seat.

"You from Milwaukee?" Bobby asked, eyeing the sweat-shirt. "The clothes sort of give it away."

"Do they?" Josh lifted his Brewer's cap, looked at it, smoothed his dark blond hair and replaced it on his head, this time backwards. "My father got transferred to Cleveland last summer. He commutes. Wanted us to have the small-town life." Bobby looked questioningly at Josh who continued, "He's track supervisor for a railroad. They closed the Milwaukee office and moved the few that got to keep their jobs." They had turned onto Harding Street and were driving by the office of Robert F. Wardell, CPA. "Is that your father's office?"

"Good guess."

"I figured. There aren't that many Wardells around."

They turned onto Route 303. "If you want to pull into the cemetery, I can show you a lot more." Bobby pointed to the big, wrought-iron gates rusted permanently open at the entrance.

Josh laughed. "I'll pass, thanks. That's where I live. Quail Run," Josh said pointing to the new housing development. "Do you have brothers and sisters?"

"One. Sister. Megan. She's at freshmen track practice now."

"So your whole family's fast?"

Bobby shrugged.

34

"I see you leaving Welke's classroom after second period. I had him last semester for *Between the World Wars: the nineteen-twenties and thirties*. Best sleep I got all day," Josh smiled.

"I have *Overview of American History*. We learned that ninety percent of American History happened in 1967 and '68, so I don't know what you could've covered in your class," Bobby joked.

"I learned a lot," Josh laughed. "I didn't realize how much of the Vietnam War took place during the Depression."

As Josh's tires crunched on the Wardell's gravel he asked for Bobby's cell phone number.

"I don't have a cell," Bobby answered. "Who would I call?"

"I thought I was the only guy without a cell," Josh said as Bobby wrote down his home number.

Bobby thanked him again for the ride.

"Nice hoop," Josh said, pointing to the backboard next to the garage. "You play?"

"I just shoot a little. I can't really play."

"Want to shoot a few?" Josh turned off the ignition. It was a less than subtle hint that Bobby should say yes.

Bobby got out of the car. "I'll get the ball. You might want to move your car over so it doesn't get hit by the ball and my dad can pull in past you."

"A basketball hitting this piece of junk could only improve its looks, but I'll make room for your father."

"At least you have one more car than I do."

"My parents just got me this thing because they were tired of having to pick me up all the time."

While Bobby got a ball from the garage, Josh backed the car up and pulled it forward and off to the side. Bobby dribbled across the concrete for a lay-up that bounced off the rim. Josh dashed out of the car, snagged the rebound and went in for a near-dunk. He grabbed the ball out of the net at the bottom and passed it to Bobby with the skill of someone who had done this often. Bobby dribbled twice and started in toward the basket, but Josh came in to guard him, pressing his body close. Bobby lost control of the ball; Josh grabbed it and spun to put it up and in again.

"Wow. You're good." Bobby said. "Did you play this year?"

"I went out, but then quit. Had too much other stuff going on. My father was mad. Said I should letter in all three sports. I will next year. Did you go to any of the games?"

"I've never been to any basketball or football games. I see enough of Taylor and Brickman at school and baseball." He stopped, realizing he had said too much.

"I know what you mean," Josh agreed as he did an effortless turnaround shot. The rebound took off and Bobby chased after it, dribbled once, and made a three-point swish. "Nice shot," Josh said, pulling the ball down.

"When I'd make those my dad used to say, 'even a blind squirrel gets an acorn now and then.'"

"You should practice those. With your height, you won't get much inside, but you've got a nice touch." It was the first time anyone had ever made note of Bobby's shortness without it sounding like an insult. Josh took a last shot at the hoop and let Bobby grab the rebound as Josh walked to his car. "I'd better get home," Josh said. "We can play some more next time if you want."

Bobby was a little too dazed to say anything more than, "Okay."

Josh pulled a U-turn in the large driveway and out onto Route 303. Bobby was still staring after the car when his mother pulled in. "You're home late," he said.

"Tax time, remember?"

"Oh right."

"We'll be seeing little of your dad for a while, too. But he's coming home on time tonight. He went to Meg's meet."

Right on schedule, his father and Meg pulled in the driveway. His father got out and his eyes immediately found the basketball that Bobby had under his arm.

"Must have been practicing hard, you worked up a sweat," his father said.

Bobby shrugged. His mother and sister went into the house. His father took the ball from Bobby, handing Bobby his briefcase and newspaper to hold. He took a shot that missed. "If you have any energy left, maybe we can shoot a few more after dinner."

"I have homework."

"Lots of it?"

"Another term paper since the teacher didn't like the first one."

"What's the new one on?"

"The U.S. Strategic Victory in Southeast Asia, 1964 to 1972."

His father's confusion passed quickly. "If you need any help, let me know. I was there."

"I know."

"I didn't do much, but I was there."

"I know."

"Well, let me know if you have any questions."

"That's okay, I'm making most of it up anyway," Bobby said as he turned to go into the house, leaving his father confused again.

Bobby stood under the shower. He felt bad about the way he had acted with his father. His dad was just trying to help. Like when he'd try to help him at basketball, but somehow it didn't seem like help. More like unconstructive criticism. He might not have meant it like that, but Bobby somehow always ended up taking it that way.

It still seemed a little unreal that Josh had just hung out with him. Not just given him a ride home, but actually wanted to stay. Not since Lucas had moved away when they were twelve had Bobby had a friend over to the house. And Lucas had been coming over less and less by then anyway. Something had changed between them that Bobby had never been able to put a finger on. Since Lucas, Bobby seemed to have fallen so far behind everyone else socially and physically that he had never really tried to make another friend.

Maybe Josh was too new to realize Bobby's undeserving status. Or maybe Josh was just too nice of a guy to care. Josh certainly laughed at all of his jokes. Meg and her friend Jesse were the only other ones who did. Of course they were also the only other people he ever got to be funny with.

Bobby's father had to pound on the door a second time to bring him out of the fog of his shower. "Bobby! Dinner!" Bobby shut of the water. "And try to limit the showers to half an hour."

After dinner, Bobby went into the sewing room. They still called it the sewing room, even though his grandmother's sewing machine hadn't been used for at least ten years. It still sat in the corner, its table now covered with accumulated papers, magazines and other junk that ruled out sewing. For more than a decade the room had been the computer room. Bobby looked up a few facts for his paper, stared at the monitor for a few more hours then went to bed.

SIX

The next afternoon, Meg ran in the door from practice and almost into her brother. "Oh my God! Did you see who just turned around in our driveway?"

"Who?" Bobby started towards the door, but Meg grabbed him.

"Josh Schlagel!"

"He wasn't turning around. He was hanging out here this afternoon after practice."

"Yeah, right. Like Josh Schlagel would set foot in our house."

"He did. We hung out. You know who he is?"

"Duh. Everybody knows who he is. Besides being the best player on the football team, he's the cutest guy in school."

"You think he's cute?"

"Me and every other girl in H-burg. Ash and Jess and I saw him at Manny's Pizza one night. We just stared. He has the greenest eyes. You could tell even from across the restaurant. And that dimple on just one side, and that cute way he smiles

39

so it goes up on one side and down on the other. And his voice. So soft. So romantic. And you can tell he has a perfect body."

"I see him naked in the locker room after practice all the time," Bobby said, smirking.

"Okay, now get serious. Why was Josh here?"

"I told you. To hang out. He was here yesterday, too. We're sort of becoming friends."

"You don't have any . . ." Meg stopped herself. "Wait, he was here yesterday and you didn't tell me? When's he coming back?"

"I dunno," Bobby said, "Whenever." Bobby was now finding his sister's excitement contagious and wondering when Josh might come visit again.

"Wait until I tell Ash and Jess. They will die. Josh Schlagel in my house! Twice!"

She started upstairs then stopped. "You have to let me know when he is coming so I can be here. And I need you to take a picture of us so I can email it to those guys!"

She bounded up the steps two at a time and Bobby just stood in the living room basking in his own happiness which was now enhanced by his sister's jealousy.

*   *   *   *   *

For the Saturday morning away game against Marshall High, Coach Hudson was again using Schlagel on the mound. He must have thought Josh had what it took to face the best in the league. As the Hawks took the field in the bottom of the third, there was still no score and Bobby walked over to Hudson. "Coach?"

"What, Wardell?" Hudson looked impatiently from Bobby to the field.

"I think I've got their signs." Hudson took off his hat, stroked back his hair and looked down at the small player. "From my end of the bench down there, I can see between the catcher's legs. I figured out the pattern."

Hudson was now staring intently and demanded, "You think you have the signs, or you know you do?"

40

"I do. One finger is fast ball, two is a curve, three is a change-up and four is that screwball or whatever it is he's trying to throw but missing the plate with every time."

Hudson replaced his hat and studied Bobby. "You're sure?"

"I'm sure."

The coach looked out over the field then back to the dugout. "Okay, I want you to get back down to your end of the bench. I'll tell our guys to tune in to your voice. Their first name means a fastball. Last name is a curve. Their number is a change up or other junk. If Brickman is up, yell c'mon Corey for fastball, c'mon Brickman for a curve, and c'mon one-four for anything else. Got it?"

"Sure."

"Start yelling to the defense now so the other team doesn't notice any change in your behavior when we're up."

Bobby nodded and assumed his post. When the team came in from the field after Josh put down their three batters in order, the coach called a quick huddle among the starting players and then trotted to his box at third.

"C'mon Taylor," Bobby yelled when he saw curve ball called for, then "Let's go, Danny!" when the catcher flashed one finger.

"Christ," Jason Farino said, looking at Bobby. "What got into you? Shut up."

Relief pitcher Clint Dominick looked down the bench. "That kid doesn't say a word all year, now he's a mascot. We oughta get him a costume."

Bobby ignored them and stuck to his task. Dominick replaced Josh on the mound for the last inning, but after the Hawks' runs had been posted. Final score: Hawks 3, Marshall 0.

Buff made the final catch and ran in from leftfield and right at Bobby. "Way to go! You were MVPB." Bobby looked puzzled. "Most valuable player on the bench. Good job!" He chucked Bobby on the shoulder.

When the big man moved away, Josh was standing behind him, smiling down at Bobby. "Rob, thank you. For my double.

For my single. For my RBI. And for my win. Thank you." He trotted off to line up with the other players on the first base line.

*   *   *   *   *

As Josh pulled the old Ford into the driveway, Bobby saw Meg and her father playing one-on-one on the driveway court. Josh stopped the car and turned off the engine. Bobby looked at him with a stab of fear. Josh opened the door and Bobby's panic grew.

Josh got out. Bobby scrambled to get out of the car also. Mr. Wardell held the ball under his arm and watched Josh walk towards him.

"Hi," he said to Josh.

"Hi, you must be Rob's father. I'm Josh Schlagel," he said, extending his hand.

They shook. "Bob Wardell." His dad looked a little puzzled as to who Rob might be. Meg's jaw was so slack it might drop off her face any minute. Bobby still hung back by the car, unsure what was about to happen or why he might be afraid of whatever that was.

"Nice to meet you, Mr. Wardell." Josh extended his hand again. "And you must be Meg. I've heard lots about you."

Meg's hands were as glued to her sides as her eyes were to Josh's face. Bobby couldn't watch her paralysis any longer, trotted to her side and whispered, "This is the part where you say 'nice to meet you, Josh.'" He grabbed her arm and held it out for Josh to shake.

That broke her spell and she turned and punched her brother in the stomach. "Nice to meet you, Josh," she said.

"You guys want to play?" Josh asked. "Rob and I will take you on."

Bob looked at his son, trying to confirm that Bobby was Rob, and that Rob wanted to play basketball. "What do you say, Meg?"

"Sure."

As Mr. Wardell and Josh moved away to half-court to inbound the ball, Rob whispered to his sister, "Try not to drool so much, it'll make the driveway slippery."

She hit him again and yelled, "That does it. You boys are going down!"

The game quickly became Mr. Wardell on Josh and Rob on Meg. The older man had played high school ball and was good. Meg was competitive as hell, but Josh was by far the best athlete on the court and dominated the game. Whenever Mr. Wardell had him closed off from the basket, Josh would dump the ball off to Rob who usually made the outside shot to the surprise of everyone but Josh.

Once when Meg was closely guarding Josh, he stuck his tongue out at her, got her laughing, then blew by her for the lay-up. By the end of the game, they were all sweaty, laughing and panting.

Rob's father patted him on the back. "Great game. You made some nice shots."

"Thanks," Rob answered.

"But Josh should start for the Cavs," the older man said, slapping his guest on the shoulder.

"If I were going to play basketball instead of baseball, it would be for the Bucks, not the Cavaliers," Josh protested.

"That was fun, we'll have to do that again," Meg said. Her eyes had rarely drifted from Josh.

"Mom wanted me to throw some chicken on the grill. She's working. Josh, do you want to stay for dinner?" Mr. Wardell offered.

"Thank you, Mr. Wardell, are you sure it's okay?"

"Yes!" Meg said.

"I'll have to call my mother."

"Of course. Bobby, why don't you show Josh where the phone is and where he can get cleaned up?"

"Where does your mother work?" Josh asked as they entered the kitchen.

"She does some stuff for my dad, especially at this time of year with taxes. And she does part-time bookkeeping for Trent Flooring. She usually doesn't work Saturdays, but she does some of their tax stuff, too, so I guess she went in to get caught up. I'm surprised my dad's not at work. This time of year, he usually does seven days a week."

"I worked all morning, but had to pick up Meg," his father said as he entered the house. "I just got home a little before you did. Your mom and I will both be at the office all day tomorrow."

Rob handed Josh the phone while his father got the chicken out of the refrigerator. After the phone call, the boys headed upstairs.

"So this is your room," Josh said, hesitating in the doorway before following Rob inside. The room was neat, but not obsessively so. It had all the trapping of a teenage boy's bedroom but somehow without the feeling that a real boy lived there. Josh looked at the posters of baseball players on the wall.

"Gifts from my dad. To inspire me, I guess," Rob said.

"I had this same one," Josh said, pointing. "My father tore it down. Said we shouldn't worship false gods."

Josh said it with such bitterness Rob could think of nothing to say, but "Sorry."

It had been so long since Rob had had a friend in his room, he wasn't quite sure what to do and for some reason it made him uncomfortable that Josh seemed to be looking everything over and was fascinated by it all. To Rob it all looked as drab and uninteresting as it always had.

"I'll get you a towel," Rob said and led Josh down the hall to the linen closet and then the bathroom where there were dual sinks. Josh stripped off his shirt to wipe himself down. Rob washed his face and hands then went to his room to change shirts.

Josh walked in, still carrying his own shirt. "My shirt is soaked. I don't want to stink up dinner too bad."

"I doubt Meg or Dad will shower. And we're eating on the back porch." Josh looked dubious. "I know!" Rob went to his closet and after rummaging through some stuff came out with a sweatshirt.

Josh looked at it. "I don't know if I can wear that."

"It's an extra-large. My great-aunt sent it to me. She hasn't seen me since I was like five. She must think I'm huge."

"No, I meant it's the Cleveland Browns. I'm not sure I can wear this." Josh smiled.

Rob slapped Josh's chest with the shirt then handed it to him. "You can always wear it inside out, if you don't think having the Browns' logo against your skin will cause a rash."

Josh slipped the shirt over his head. He checked himself in the mirror then looked at Rob. "Doesn't it hurt when your sister hits you like that?"

"Nah. She's been doing it for years. I'm used to it."

"She really cranks up. I think she'd kill me if she hit me that hard."

Rob shrugged.

"Are your abs really that hard?"

Again Rob shrugged.

"Let me see." Josh used the back of his hand to slap Rob's stomach. "Wow. That's like a wall." He pulled up Rob's shirt and felt the firm flesh underneath. "It's like you're wearing an iron vest under your skin." Rob still said nothing and Josh looked him in the eye, "Do you mind?"

Rob shrugged more with his eyes than his shoulders. Josh slapped Rob's bare stomach with the back of his hand. Then smacked a little harder. Then made a fist and lightly punched. "Meg hits harder than that," Rob said. Josh gave him a good jab that still didn't make Rob flinch. "You'll hurt your pitching hand," Rob teased.

Josh hit him again harder and said, "I'm impressed. I should be in that kind of shape. What do you do, sit ups all night long?"

Rob's smile vanished. "Let's go help with dinner."

Once in the kitchen, Josh and Rob made a salad while Meg attended to the other dinner details and Mr. Wardell handled the grilling chores. By the time Marilyn Wardell got home, dinner was ready. As Josh and Rob set things on the picnic table, Mr. Wardell hollered, "Bobby, the chicken's WTW, will you bring me a platter?"

The boys walked back inside and Josh asked, "WTW?"

Rob told him what it stood for and said, "It's become this lame little joke in our family."

"It's cute," Josh said. "We don't have any family jokes."

"How's the salad coming?" Meg asked as she came in.

"It's done," Rob answered.

"Yep, we're WTW," Josh said.

Meg smiled. "I see Bobby's already told you all of our family secrets."

"Not all of them," Rob said. "He doesn't know about the bodies in the basement or what you've got hidden in your closet."

Once everyone was seated at the picnic table Josh announced, "Rob won the game for us again today."

"You got a hit?" his father asked.

"He got the team eight of them," Josh answered, drowning out Rob's mumbled, "No." While adding funny little asides, Josh filled them in on Rob's signaling. "It got me a double. And my second win of the season. I'm two-and-0 thanks to Rob. Mr. Wardell, you've raised a baseball genius. He'll be managing the Indians in ten years." Josh raised his iced tea glass in salute. Rob clinked glasses, but said nothing wondering how much happier his father would have been if he had been getting hits himself.

"What do you mean two-and-0 thanks to Bobby?" Mr. Wardell asked.

Josh poked Rob in the ribs. "You mean you didn't tell them? I guess he's too modest to brag." Josh told them about Rob's keen eye in the first game, finishing with, "I hope you don't mind, but when I get drafted by the Brewers, I'm going to take him with me."

Josh kept them all laughing during dinner with an ease in talking to Rob's parents that Rob himself could only dream of possessing. "I should help you guys clean up and get going. I have homework to do."

"On a Saturday night?" Meg asked.

"Yep, with school and baseball all the time, it's hard to find time to keep my grades up."

"Do your homework at the last minute Sunday night like everyone else," she suggested.

"Can't. We have church on Sundays."

"Sunday night?" Mrs. Wardell asked.

"Yes, and Sunday morning. We go eight till noon and then seven till nine."

"That's more church in a day than we do in a year," Meg said.

"And we go Wednesday nights."

"Well," Meg said, "Then you really need to go out on a Saturday night. Don't you have a girlfriend?"

Rob laughed, "Sorry, Josh, I'll put a leash on her next time you're over."

She punched her brother in the stomach.

"This has really been fun. Thanks so much," Josh said.

They each took some things from the picnic table and carried them into the kitchen. Mrs. Wardell insisted on cleaning up and Rob walked Josh to his car. "Sorry I have to run. But I know you have your term paper to work on, too. Too bad I don't have my books with me. We could do homework together." Rob's surprised look must have confused Josh because he added, "That is, if you want to."

"Sure. Any time."

"It's hard to find quiet study time at my house."

"I can imagine, with seven kids. Meg is more than I can handle sometimes."

"She's great. Your whole family's great."

"Are all of your brothers and sisters younger?"

"Yep. The closest one is in Meg's class. I should've asked her if she knows him. Mathias."

"Six little brothers and sisters? I think I'd run away from home."

"Don't think I'm not tempted." Josh stuck out his hand and Rob shook it. "Thanks again."

Rob watched Josh flip a U-turn on the driveway and pull out.

"You working or playing?" Rob asked as he walked into the sewing room upstairs.

Meg was in front of the computer. "Chatting," she answered.

"Good, 'cause I need to work on my term paper."

Her look said she'd move but not be happy about it. "Who's Eddie Haskel?" she asked.

"I don't know. Why?"

"'Cause I heard Mom and Dad talking about how polite Josh is and Dad said, 'Almost creepy polite, like Eddie Haskell.' So I was wondering who he was."

"Never heard of him."

"I wonder if he's as cute as Josh?" Rob gave her a look. "Next time he's over, you have to take a picture of me with him. Ash and Jess are never going to believe I had Josh Schlagel's sweat on me!"

"Do you know his brother Mathias?" Rob asked. She answered with a grimace. "What's wrong?"

"That's a good question," Meg frowned. "There's something wrong with that boy. Talk about creepy, and not in a good way. He scares me."

"Josh's brother? Why?"

"He's scary to look at. Like he'd want to kill you, or bite the heads off kittens. Makes you wonder which one of them is adopted."

"Just like you and me," Rob smiled.

She stood up, gave him a poke in the stomach and left him to Southeast Asia.

SEVEN

Meg hollered from the back porch, "Bobby! Phone!"

"For me?" he asked, jogging towards the house.

She handed him the phone with her hand still cupped over the mouthpiece. "It's Josh. I'd recognize that sexy voice anywhere. He said, 'Hi, Meg.'"

"Josh?" Rob asked her.

"Schlagel. The god who played basketball here yesterday. Remember?"

Rob took the cordless from her and spoke into it. "Hey."

"Hey, how's it going?"

"Good, and you?"

"Okay. I realized I stole your shirt yesterday. I didn't mean to, I just forgot I was wearing it until I went to take it off last night."

"And I still have yours. You left it in my bedroom." Rob had picked up the sweaty wad from the floor, looked at it and hung it over his chair back where he noticed it again this morning, still smelling like Josh. "You can keep that one. It's never going to fit me anyway. And it's about time you wore something that said Cleveland on it."

"Thanks. Even without the shirt swap, I don't know what you're up to, but thought maybe we could study together this afternoon. That is, if you want to."

"Sure."

"I know your parents said they'd be gone all day so I figured it would be quiet over there." As though on cue, one of the younger Schlagels screamed in the background.

"It is. Just me and Meg. And I know she'll hate to see you." Josh laughed. "In fact, I have a favor to ask for Meg."

Rob still had his shirt off and was stacking the tools in the garage when the light coming in the backdoor of the garage was cut off. He looked to see Josh standing in the doorway blocking the sun. "You got here quick," Rob said.

"Yeah. Couldn't wait to escape." Josh looked around the room. "Big garage."

"It used to be a barn or something. Holds both cars, all the bikes, farm stuff…"

"And a gym," Josh said pointing at the weights in one section. "You must use it often to be as ripped as you are."

"I'm not ripped, just skinny."

"You're cut. What's your body fat, do you know? Like two percent, I bet."

Josh looked at the weights on the bar. "One-thirty-five. Can you do this much?"

"I don't work out in here much. Just mainly running and push-ups and sit-ups. That's from my Dad, I guess."

Josh slid under the bar. "Will you spot me?" Rob stood over Josh as he did ten reps. When Josh finished he stood up. "Now I want to see you do it." Rob hesitated. "That is, if you want to," Josh added.

Rob shrugged, grabbed a ten-pound plate, handed it to Josh and slipped another one on his own end of the bar. Rob did ten quick reps.

"That was amazing," Josh said. Rob shrugged. Josh looked

down at the outline of Rob's sweaty back on the black plastic of the bench. "No offense, but . . ." Josh stripped off his shirt and put it down to cover the wet spot. "If you can do this, I better be able to."

Rob again watched Josh's chest rise and fall this time without his shirt. Josh did his ten. "Another dime," Rob said, handing Josh another plate.

"Is this a contest?"

"If you want it to be."

"I think I'd lose." Josh smiled. "How much can you bench?"

"My highest I think was one-eighty," Rob said.

"For real?" Rob handed Josh a five-pound plate and added one to his own side. "That will make one-eighty-five," Josh said.

"You'll get to witness a new record." Rob lay down on the bench and did three sloppy reps before Josh had to help him put the bar back on the posts.

"Wow, that was impressive," Josh said, slapping Rob's pecs.

After they were done working out, talking and goofing off there wasn't time to study before Josh had to leave for family dinner and church.

Rob walked into the sewing room. The computer was on, but Meg was on the phone. "Josh is here," he said. "We were working out in the garage."

"Ash, gotta go!" She spun her feet off the computer desk and clicked off the phone without waiting for a response.

Rob came back down the steps with his digital camera.

"What's with the flags?" Josh asked, pointing to the three glass and wood triangular boxes sitting on the mantel, each of which contained a folded U.S. flag.

"They're my grandfathers'. Well, and my great-grandfather."

"You mean like their ashes are in here?"

Rob laughed. "No, those are the flags that were on their coffins. My grandfathers were both in World War II and my

51

great-grandfather was in World War I. My Dad says he's saving a spot for his flag. He was in Vietnam."

"This house is so cool. Like a museum. How long have you lived here?"

"Since I was born."

"I mean your family."

"I dunno. You'd have to ask my Dad. 1880 or '70 or something."

Pointing at the brass nameplates on the flag case, Josh asked, "So your grandfathers were Robert F. Wardells, too?"

"Yeah, I'm the fourth."

"What's the F for?"

"It's embarrassing."

"It can't be worse than my middle name," Josh said.

"Worse than Francis?" Rob asked.

Josh laughed. "You're right, it's not. Lawrence."

The noise of Meg bounding down the stairs caused them both to turn around. She had changed shirts, put on make-up, and fixed her hair. "Oh, hi, Josh," she said sounding way too casual to be casual. "Oh, I see Bobby has his camera."

Rob shook his head. "Give it up, Meg. I told him you wanted your picture taken with him. Unfortunately, he already put his shirt on."

Josh laughed and blushed. "You asked for one of me shirtless?"

Meg blushed so deeply she could have camouflaged herself against a fire engine. She gave her brother a look that said he might be in need of paramedics soon. "We should go outside, the light is better," Rob suggested. Meg followed sheepishly.

Once they were outside, Rob posed them against the backdrop of the pink blossoms of the flowering crabapple tree. Josh put his arm around Meg's shoulder and she re-blushed.

"This is really nice of you," she said, looking at him as Rob snapped another shot. "A couple of my friends sort of have crushes on you."

"Your *friends* do?" he asked. She blushed again. "So would

this make them more jealous?" Josh stripped off his shirt in one smooth motion then hugged her close. Rob snapped a few more photos. He got Meg to move and snapped a few more photos of Josh.

"Okay, enough!" Josh said putting his shirt on. "You're the one with the ripped body, not me."

"I'll email them to you," Rob said.

"We don't have email. My parents say the Internet is nothing but pornography, so we have this antique computer that is just for doing school work, but no Internet."

"That sucks. I thought we were like the last people on earth to stop using a phone modem," Meg said.

"I hate to run, but it's almost five. We never got to study," Josh said.

"There's always tomorrow," Rob answered.

*   *   *   *   *

Cuyahoga Valley's starting pitcher only lasted two innings, but their team bounced back and the H-burg Hawks were down by one run going into the bottom of the fifth. Buff's single put him on first and advanced Danny Taylor to second. Josh was up next.

Coach Hudson called time then yelled, "Wardell!" Rob ran to meet him behind home plate. "We need these runs. If Schlagel hits it, I need someone faster than Beechler on base." Hudson twanged, "Beechler!" and motioned Buff off first base.

As Bobby headed towards first, he passed Josh in the on-deck circle. Josh called in a half-whisper. "Rob, you need a helmet." Little sniggers sounded on the bench as Bobby ran back to grab one. The first helmet he selected was way too large, the second a little big. Josh handed him one. "Try this one."

It fit and Bobby trotted to first.

"Just like Goldilocks," Brickman said from the bench.

Josh, getting his fourth hit of the day, pounded one deep. Rob was sure there was no way the right fielder could catch up

53

with it and he started streaking for second knowing that as deep as it was even if it was caught, he'd still have time to get back and tag up. He was almost at second when he heard both coaches yelling, "Go! Go!" He looked at third where Hudson was whirling his arm like a full-bodied propeller. The ball had cleared the right fielder and was going to hit the fence.

Danny Taylor had hesitated between second and third and now at the urging of Hudson was breaking into a run. Rob kicked in his afterburners knowing he had to score, too; Taylor would only tie the game. Rob crossed the third base bag only a few steps behind Taylor. Danny still wasn't in full stride and slowed again to watch the right fielder pick up the ball and fire it to the cut-off man.

"Go! Go!" Rob yelled as he closed on Taylor. He was right behind him and was afraid he was going to run into him. As much as he didn't want to break stride, he did and let Taylor score one step ahead of him. Their feet hit the rubber plate: Whap! Whap! A third Whap! was the ball landing in the catcher's mitt just behind Rob. Taylor abruptly stopped to accept the congratulations of his teammates and Rob ran into him. Taylor turned and shoved Rob in the chest. "What the fuck are you doing?"

Rob stepped around the mob, one or two of whom slapped his hand or back or gave him a fist bump in congratulations.

An infield fly-out stranded Josh at third. Farino replaced Buff in left for the remainder of the game and the Hawks clung to their one-run lead to win.

"That hit wouldn't have scored me," Buff said behind Rob as they walked out to the line to say *nice game* to kids who were a little too angry at having their lead snatched away to act gracious about it. "Way to hustle!"

Hudson slapped Rob on the back. "Good job, Wardell! That's the speed I wanted to see!"

Much to Rob's amazement, two members of the opposing team and one of the coaches complimented him on his hustle in scoring what turned out to be the winning run.

After the handshake ceremony ended, Hudson yelled. "Huddle up in the outfield," then turned to their shortstop and barked, "Taylor!" The two of them went off towards the dugout. Rob could feel Taylor's eyes on him, not the coach, as he took his scolding.

As they walked toward the outfield, Rob walked up next to Josh and said, "Nice hit. Thanks for bringing me in."

"Uh, I can't give you a ride home tonight. I have church stuff with my family." Josh hurried ahead and sat next to Corey Brickman on the grass. Rob assumed his usual spot on the fringe of the group.

All during the post-game talk, Rob didn't need to look to know that Danny Taylor was still glaring at him.

Once in the locker room, Rob had barely stripped down for his shower when he saw a form standing over him. He looked up to see Danny Taylor's ripped chest blocking his vision. Each one of his chest hairs that looked as though they had been air-brushed on by an artist for *Playgirl* magazine for maximum effect stood out against his tanned pecs.

"I warned you not to embarrass me like that, you little piss-ant." Taylor shoved Rob hard in the chest and he staggered back into the lockers. Taylor closed on him and there was no retreat room left. Behind Taylor stood Corey Brickman, Shane Poulan and a couple of others. Taylor slapped Rob's face so hard Rob had to blink twice to restore his vision. His eyes cleared just in time to see a backhand about to connect with his cheek.

When he opened his eyes after that blow, he saw Josh standing among the others. It was embarrassing to have Josh watch him be bitch-slapped, but Taylor did it again and again. Poulan and Brickman each grabbed one of Rob's arms as though he needed to be restrained or might fight back. Taylor hit him in the face again, this time with a closed fist. Taylor stepped aside and Jason Farino stepped in to take his turn at bat. He hit Rob in the stomach, but his fist ricocheted off and Rob could tell it stung his hand. Omar Rivera shoved Jason out

55

of the way and took his best shot smacking Rob in the face. When Rob's eyes opened again, Buff Beechler had joined the crowd. Rob knew if Buff hit him he'd be dead.

Buff shoved his way past Josh and a few others. Rob closed his eyes and braced himself to have his nose broken by Buff's giant fist. He waited, but when no punch came, he opened his eyes and saw Buff had Taylor by the neck. "Do you have a problem, Danny?" Buff gave a look to the rest of the crowd that had the same effect as turning on a light in a basement full of cockroaches.

Rob looked at Buff who shook his head and walked away leaving Josh standing alone behind him. As soon as Rob's eyes met those of his friend, Josh put his head down and walked away.

Rob dressed. The hell with the shower at the gym rule. He ran out the door. As he ran along Garfield Street, Corey Brickman's suped-up Camaro roared by. Josh Schlagel sat in the back next to Danny Taylor.

EIGHT

As Rob ran, the sweat stung the cuts on his face. The pain was fine with him. He deserved to hurt for being so stupid. How could he have been dumb enough to think it would take very long for Josh to go back to his own kind?

The pain in his face was nothing compared to the pain of having his hopes so crushed. He almost wished Taylor and Brickman had beat him so bad he'd be able to think of nothing but the pain in his body. He had taken much worse beatings over the years, so as torments went today's physical pain was nothing. Buff's stepping in was a surprise. So was Josh's not saying anything. Or maybe it wasn't. Maybe Josh was just waiting his turn.

But it was a good lesson for Rob. Time he realized that he should keep his mouth shut, stay hidden and forget trying to make friends. He should just quit the damn team. All it meant was two or three more hours a day in a hell he could do without. He thought this year might be different, that he might help the team and help Josh. Well, fuck baseball and Josh Schlagel.

By the time he got home, the blood had dried with his sweat in streaks down his cheek. His mother flinched when she looked up from the sink, but she stayed where she was, tightening her grip on the apple she was slicing. "What happened?" she asked.

"Ran into another guy trying to catch a ball in practice," Rob answered as he ran past her and up the stairs.

He cranked the shower full blast—hot. He didn't care how bad it would scald him. Only his father banging on the door telling him again that dinner was ready made him dry his eyes and then his body.

When Rob got to the table, his father winced. "What happened?" he asked.

"I already told mom. Do we have to talk about this all evening, or can we just eat?" He wasn't sure if his parents believed his stories of all of his mishaps at school, but he also wasn't sure he cared.

That night's pain was worse than usual and all of the sit-ups he could do never put him back to sleep.

In class the next day, he was grateful for Mr. Welke's self-absorbed history so he at least got some sleep. After class he wandered bleary-eyed through the hall to third period and felt a hand on his shoulder.

"Hey." The voice was Josh's; Rob didn't need to look to know that. He kept walking. "Are you all right?"

Rob turned to him. His swollen and bruised face was all the answer anyone would need. Josh grimaced. Rob saw Josh's own face was bruised. He had a cut lip and an eye just short of black. "What happened to you?" Rob asked.

"I was wrestling with my brother. We get a little carried away sometimes." Rob recognized a bad lie when he heard one. Rob was still walking; Josh was hurrying to keep up. "Look," Josh said, grabbing his arm. "I'm sorry about yesterday."

"Why?"

Josh looked at him and Rob could see tears in Josh's eyes. "I just am, okay?"

"Whatever." Rob could feel his own tears starting and pulled his arm away.

"I'll give you a ride home after practice, and we can talk, okay?"

"Don't bother." Rob turned and went out the back exit of the school. Then he was on the road and running home.

After dinner Rob was staring at a web site about Vietnam that he had no intention of reading when the phone rang. He didn't react. It was for Meg. Ash or Jess or Stacey calling. None of the family ever bothered answering the phone except Meg anymore. It was always for her. Meg shouted from downstairs. "Rob! Phone! It's Josh!"

"I'm not here."

"I already told him you were. If you don't want to talk to him, I do."

Rob grabbed the offending instrument off its cradle. "What?"

"How are you?"

"Fine." A silence until Rob added, "Now that we've established that, I have homework to do."

"I'd like to talk to you."

"Why?"

"I'm not supposed to go out on school nights. My parents would hear my car if I start it, but I can sneak out on foot. How about I meet you in the cemetery — that'd be halfway. Please."

Rob looked around the room as though something in his surroundings would tell him why, although he didn't want to see Josh and didn't want to talk to him, he said, "Okay." He grabbed all of the paper from the printer tray, took it to his room and stashed it in a drawer.

He put on shoes and darted down the stairs. His parents sat at the dining room table, drowning in a sea of tax forms. "I need the car," he said. "We're out of paper and I need to print a draft of my term paper."

"Okay," his father said, barely looking up.

Rob grabbed the keys off the peg by the door. "Wait," his mother said.

He turned and exhaled. "What?"

"Mine's almost out of gas. Take your dad's."

He hung her keys up and grabbed his father's and opened the door again. "Wait," his father said.

Rob turned and exhaled. "What?"

"Come here a second." Rob went to the table. His father looked as his son's face. "You ought to put something on that."

"I will." He turned to leave again.

"Here," his father said, holding out money. "Why don't you take your mom's car and put some gas in it, and then the rest is for paper."

"Okay," Rob said, finally escaping. Since he had no intention of buying paper and there was plenty upstairs, he'd just have to pocket whatever he didn't spend on gas.

He pulled into the cemetery. The sign said the gates locked at sundown, but the gates had been rusted open for many a sundown. He'd never been in the cemetery at night and the car lights hitting the marble angels turned each one into a ghost. He started to drive around the loop when his lights hit a figure seated on a bench behind of the Fyfe Mausoleum, hidden from the road. The Fyfes had owned Harrisonburg a hundred years ago and now Fyfe Park, Fyfe Street and this garish tomb were all that remained of their presence.

Rob stopped the car and got out. He could smell the sweet odor of upturned earth of a fresh grave nearby.

Josh stood up and said, "Thanks for coming."

Josh motioned to a seat on the Fyfe bench and sat himself down. Rob stood.

"You're mad at me," Josh said.

"Not really."

"You should be. I should've done something. I'm sorry."

"I'm used to it."

"You shouldn't be."

"It's life." Rob shrugged.

"Can we talk?"

"We're talking. What do you want?"

"You weren't at practice today."

"I went home sick."

"Are you coming tomorrow?" Josh asked.

Rob didn't answer and instead studied the inscription on the marker of a lesser Fyfe descendant who didn't rate space inside the mausoleum. Rob shivered. He didn't realize how cold it was and wished he'd have brought a sweatshirt. A cool breeze sent goose bumps up his spine as it sent dead leaves scurrying past. Josh also shivered and clutched his own elbows, whether to hide from the cold or something else, Rob couldn't tell.

"Did you tell Coach Hudson what happened?" Josh asked.

"I'm not afraid of those guys."

"Maybe you should be." Another silence as each of them studied a grave marker. "Do you know Brittany Burnside?" Josh suddenly asked, trying to smile.

"Everybody knows Brittany Burnside. Head cheerleader. Homecoming Queen. Volleyball star. She has business cards that say that." Rob said flatly, still not looking up.

"You're too funny." Josh laughed.

"Are you going out with Brittany?" Rob was not laughing.

"No, she's been going with Brickman forever. Brittany wants me to take her friend Jenny to the prom, so we've been hanging out to try to get to know each other a bit before then."

"Have fun then." Rob was still studying gravestones instead of looking at Josh. He could sense Josh leaning forward to try to make eye contact.

"Are you coming to the game tomorrow?" Josh asked. Rob shrugged. "Please."

"I gotta go," Rob said.

Josh nodded. "Me too. I can't let them notice I'm gone. Mat usually does a great job of covering for me."

"When he's not kicking your ass wrestling?" Rob asked with too much sarcasm and it stung Josh; Rob instantly felt bad about having said it. "You want a ride?"

"It's out of your way."

"Not really. I have to go to town and get gas."

"You can just drop me along 303 so my parents don't hear the car."

They drove in silence. The car stopped and Josh patted Rob on the shoulder. "Thanks, Rob. For everything. I'll see you at the game tomorrow."

At the BP station Rob was tempted to just douse himself with the gas and light a match. Life might hurt less that way. Instead he topped off the tank, spilling a few drops on his shoe, then drove home and started doing pushups he knew wouldn't end before dawn.

*   *   *   *   *

Rob took a different route from second period. He didn't feel like seeing Josh, but the detour took him upstairs and directly into the path of Coach Hudson. "Wardell!" he honked like a foghorn with laryngitis. "Where were you yesterday?" Hudson looked at Rob's face. "You look like you been rode hard and put up wet." Hudson's Southernisms often left Rob wondering what the hell he was talking about. "What happened?"

"Wrestling with my sister." Hudson raised an eyebrow. "I caught an elbow then hit the edge of the couch."

Coach Hudson shook his head and said, "Well, good thing you're here. We'll need you today against McKinley."

"Need me?"

"It's going to be a close game, so any little edge you can give us . . ." He patted Rob on the shoulder. "Get to class. I'll see you after school."

Rob studied the exit door for a moment then headed to class.

Rob was dressing for the game when he decided he'd rather pee inside than use the woods or the green plastic sauna. He went to a stall. Stalls were safer than urinals. Less exposure. As always, the stupid stall door stuck so Rob gave it a good shove. It swung open and smacked into Josh Schlagel's bare ass.

"Sorry," Rob said. Then he noticed Josh's buttocks. They were covered with red welts. Josh spun around and covered his nakedness with his shirt as much as he could, but Rob could still see plenty of bruises on his chest and stomach and arms to match the ones on his face.

Rob mumbled "Sorry" again and left Josh to dress in the stall, closing the door behind him.

At the game, even Rob's stealing signs from the other team's coach didn't help and the Hawks took their first loss of the season. Taylor's two errors at short hurt and Josh going 0-for-four and missing a couple of plays at first didn't help. Ordinarily, Josh would have been able to grab Danny's wild throws without pulling his foot off the bag.

As they walked from the field, Josh pulled Rob aside. "I'm not going to shower here. I'm just going to grab my stuff and go home. You want a ride?"

The way he said it, it was more like asking Rob to take a ride than offering him one. As they pulled out of the lot, Rob said, "Are you going to tell me?"

"My father caught me sneaking in last night. I got a whipping."

"Did he punch your face and body, too?"

"No," Josh said, and Rob knew it was the truth. "Sorry I can't stay for hoops tonight; I have to get home and get ready for church."

"Okay, just please do me a favor and don't lie to me. If you don't want to tell me or whatever, that's fine, just don't lie."

"Like about wrestling my brother?"

"Yeah."

"We do wrestle, but he'd never hurt me. I want you to know that."

"Understood. And anytime you want to tell me, I'll listen. I won't tell anyone. I've got no one to tell."

*   *   *   *   *

After Saturday's game and Josh's third victory on the mound, Josh did stick around for basketball at Rob's, but it was

63

one-on-one. Meg was at a track meet and her parents were working. Rob was just about to suggest Josh stay for dinner since his parents were going to work through it, but Josh said. "I better get going. I have a date with Jenny. Our first real date—we've just been hanging out at school."

"Are you doubling with Brickman and Brittany?"

"No."

There was an awkward pause. Rob took the moment to try to figure out why sometimes he felt so at ease with Josh, like he could tell him anything—well almost anything—and now he felt like Josh was a total stranger. For a brief moment he had thought he and Josh were on the same page, now it felt like they were in different libraries.

"Hey," Josh said suddenly. "I wanted to ask you—we don't have a game next Saturday and the Indians do. I've never been to Progressive Field. You want to go?"

"Uh, sure."

"Okay if my brother Mat goes with us? He's never been either."

"Sure." For a second he thought about asking if he should bring Meg, then remembering Meg's opinion of Mat, said nothing and realized he wasn't eager for Mat to come along either.

NINE

Tuesday as Josh pulled into the driveway he said, "Up for a quick game?"

"Can't. Today's envelope day."

"Envelope day?"

"April fourteenth. The day before tax day. Ever since I was a little kid we've all gone to the office to help my dad. We stuff envelopes with tax returns, seal them, weigh them, put postage on them and box them so he and my mom can take them to the post office tomorrow. It makes for a pretty long evening, so we send out for pizza and make a night of it. Kind of a warped family tradition."

"Sounds fun. Can I come?"

"Uh, if you want to."

"I'll have to call my mother and make sure it's okay."

*   *   *   *   *

"We brought reinforcements," Rob announced as they entered the office. "He volunteered to help."

"Hi, Josh," Mrs. Wardell said. "What happened to your face?" Then she turned to Rob and asked, "Is he the guy you collided with?"

Josh gave Rob a puzzled look as Rob said, "Yeah."

"Thanks for coming," she said, "The more hands, the faster this will go."

They quickly settled into checking, folding, stapling stuffing, sealing and stamping.

"We should teach Josh the songs," Marilyn Wardell said.

"No!" both of her children protested.

"Songs?" Josh asked.

"Don't ask," Rob warned.

"Well, you can't just throw that out then leave it hanging," Josh said.

All of the Wardells looked at Rob. He said, "When we were little, we used to make up songs to pass the time. Stupid stuff."

Meg went on, "Like to the tune of *Michael Row Your Boat Ashore* we'd sing, *Bobby seal the envelopes, alleluia . . .*"

"The later it got, the worse the verses got, but the funnier we thought they were," Mr. Wardell said, laughing.

"I suspect this didn't end when the kids were little," Josh said, smiling.

"Mom, don't," Rob, begged.

But it was too late and his mother broke into, "*On top of the tax forms, with IRS fees, I lost the address labels when somebody sneezed . . .*"

A couple of pizzas and several dozen bad verses later, she reached for a form, but there were none left.

"Is that really it?" she asked. She and her husband looked around but could find no more work.

"It's only 8:30," he said. He looked at Josh. "We're usually here until midnight. Of course the stack gest smaller every year as we do more stuff online, but thanks. You were a big help."

"It was fun."

"You have to understand, Josh has a warped view of fun," Rob said.

"Thanks again," Mr. Wardell said. "Bobby tells me you guys are going to see the Indians on Saturday?"

"Yep, should be fun. I haven't been to a game since we moved here."

"After all your help here tonight, the least I can do is buy your ticket and give Bobby money to get you a hot dog and Coke."

"That's not necessary, Mr. Wardell."

"My pleasure. After the past few weeks of long days and long nights, I can't tell you what a treat it's going to be to get home and to bed before 1 a.m."

Rob wondered why Josh could talk to his father so easily. Why he couldn't talk to his own father that way. He was always afraid if he talked too much, he might say the wrong thing.

After Josh drove off, Mr. Wardell turned to his wife and said, "We should adopt him."

"We should," Meg seconded.

"Or just work out a trade," Rob suggested. "Josh for Meg and a player to be named later." Meg slugged him in the stomach.

"Maybe he can teach our kids to be civilized," Mrs. Wardell teased.

*　　*　　*　　*　　*

Meg was right. Mathias Schlagel did look frightening. A scar gashed his face in front of one ear. His mouth was in a permanent sneer caused by a scar that pulled one corner up. That eye drooped down as though the mouth and eye were trying to meet. Disfigurements aside, he looked like Josh, not quite as tall, and with a little thicker build, but the same hair that was somewhere between blond and brown and glistened when the light hit it. The same green eyes. But with scars that could intimidate a biker gang. Rob wondered what sort of accident he had been in. The life experience on his face made him appear older than his baby-faced brother, Josh.

As they walked behind home plate, surveying the field, Mat said, "I have this sudden urge to floss."

"What?" Rob asked.

Mat pointed to the strange-looking light poles that surrounded the outfield. "They look like giant toothbrushes."

Josh asked Mat to take a photo of him and Rob in front of the Bob Feller statue. Josh said, "He had three no-hitters. The guy was amazing."

"It was easy for him," Mat said. "He was fifteen feet tall."

"The statue isn't life-size," Rob said.

"Oh," Mat said with a wink.

"Don't listen to him," Josh smiled.

They had bought tickets on the 300 level, far down the right field line, but by the third inning had made their way to some empty seats ten rows behind the Indians dugout and from there watched the Tribe trounce the Blue Jays 9-2. They were prime foul ball seats and the boys just missed catching several that came their way — other than that, the day had been pretty much perfect.

As they drove home Josh said, "Now the bad news. My mother wants to meet you."

"Oh shit," Mat said.

"What's wrong?" Rob looked around at Mat in the back seat.

"She never likes any of our friends, and then we're not allowed to see them anymore," Mat answered.

Josh said, "Since I've been spending so much time at your house, she wants to know who I'm hanging out with."

"Why doesn't she like them?"

"Any number of reasons." Mat said. "They aren't polite enough. They look like they'd be a bad influence. They don't get good enough grades. Pick one. Pick all. Logic has nothing to do with why she dislikes people. She wouldn't let us watch *Mr. Rogers' Neighborhood* 'cause he acted too faggy."

"If she didn't pick them from our church," Josh added, "They basically aren't good enough. Comments like Meg made the other day about your family not going to church — that would be the end of it right then."

Rob looked at Josh. "So I've already failed the test?"

"Pretty much," Mat said. "No offense, Rob, but I'd give you an F right now and save you the trip to planet Schlagel."

"When is this test supposed to happen?"

"She told me to have you stop by after the game on Monday."

As good as the day had been going, there had to be something to spoil it. After the Schlagel brothers dropped him off, Rob was prepared to spend the evening sulking and working on his term paper when Meg came into the sewing room.

"How was the game?" she asked.

"Great. We had a great time. Mat is cool. A lot like Josh. You've never talked to him?"

"Nope. He sort of scares me."

"No reason he should. Nice guy. He's even funnier than Josh. You should say hi next time you see him at school."

"When are you going to upload the pics you took of me and Josh? Ash doesn't believe he's been hanging out here. She said that Josh . . . well never mind what she said. Can you do that tonight so I can email her some tomorrow? And print out the best one? For my locker."

"I guess my term paper can wait. I'll get my camera." He stood up and started toward the door.

She hit him in the stomach. "Thanks."

"But you have to do me a favor. I want to look through your jewelry box."

*   *   *   *   *

Rob found himself staring at each photo of Josh before he saved it to the computer's hard drive and wondering if Josh's Mom would say Josh couldn't hang out with him anymore.

A thousand sit-ups in the middle of the night did nothing to answer that question. As he did farm work on Sunday he wondered how Josh's Sunday afternoon of miniature golf with Jenny was going.

TEN

On Monday, Josh retired the first nine batters from South Catholic High in order before giving up the first hit.

Rob was stealing the catcher's signs and signaling his teammates. After debating whether to tell Taylor and Brickman the real signs of what pitch was coming, Rob had resolved to help them since their bats could win Josh a close game.

When Josh batted, the catcher flashed a sign Rob hadn't seen before, so Josh stepped out of the batter's box and looked at the dugout. Rob shrugged. Josh furrowed his brow then stepped back in. The pitch was a fastball—aimed right at Josh's head. Josh fell backwards into the dirt to avoid the ball. Rob winced and held his breath until Josh got back up. Josh dusted himself off and stepped in again. The catcher flashed the same sign. "Watch yourself, J. L.!" Rob yelled choosing Josh's initials since Josh's first name, last name, and number were all part of their standard code. Josh got the hint; his eyes widened and he inhaled deeply.

Rob stopped breathing as the pitcher delivered another bean-ball. Josh hit the dirt again. Beechler leapt off the bench, but Coach Milnes yelled at him to sit down while Hudson stormed up to the home plate ump. The catcher tried to argue it was an accident. The ump wasn't buying it and ejected the pitcher.

During the pitching change, Hudson came straight to Rob. "I heard the warning you gave Schlagel. You knew it was coming?"

"The second one, yeah."

"If you see that again, call time and tell me." Rob nodded. "He's not going to get away with that. After the game, I'm going to have a talk with the ump and their coach." Rob turned, but the Coach called him back. "Wardell. Good job."

The Catholic team sparked a rally and Renko, catching, had to chase an overthrown ball. Josh covered the plate and waited for the ball and runner. The runner was a huge guy who made Buff Beechler look small. Since it was obviously the opposition's goal to kill or maim the Hawk's ace pitcher, Rob tensed as the freight train roared home.

"Schlagel, move!" Hudson yelled.

Josh didn't budge. "Move! Let him score!" the Coach yelled again.

"Move!" Rob screamed and rushed to the fence to watch. Just before the crash, Rob closed his eyes and listened for the impact.

When Rob opened his eyes, Hudson was running towards the cloud of dust at the plate. Josh was flat on his back. The other player was on top of him and Josh still held the ball.

"Out!" the umpire called.

The opposing player stuck a fist into Josh's chest and pushed off to get up.

Hudson and Renko helped Josh up. They looked him over and he took a moment to check all of his moving parts. They seemed to be intact. Hudson yelled, "Don't ever pull a stupid stunt like that again. I seen mules with more sense. When I tell you to move, move. That run isn't worth losing you."

Josh nodded. "Yes, sir," and walked back to the mound.

As Rob boarded the bus after Josh's win, he felt a hand swat the seat of his pants. Rob was afraid to turn around until he heard Josh's voice, "Thanks for keeping me from getting my head knocked off."

Rob was two steps above Josh and turned around and patted him on the head. "It's a nice head and we might need it to make the playoffs."

Josh smiled. "So, are you ready to face the music?"

*   *   *   *   *

As Josh drove to his house, Rob said, "I thought he was going to kill you."

"I have been hit by bigger guys. I play football remember? I've been on pass patterns across the middle and gotten sandwiched between two guys that size. I survived."

Rob winced at the thought.

"I'm not saying I'm not going to hurt tomorrow, but I knew I could take it."

Rob reached into his pocket, pulled out Meg's gold cross and hooked its chain around his neck. Josh glanced over. It took him a moment to catch on. He smiled.

As they drove down White Tail Lane into Quail Run Woodlands, Rob noticed all of the houses were made to look slightly different, which made them all look that much more the same. The basketball hoop hanging over the Schlagel's driveway was a temporary plastic one on a stand. Most of the houses had similar appendages. Mat was shooting hoops and paused to wish Rob luck.

"I'm home," Josh announced, opening the door.

His mother entered the room. She was a small woman, Rob's height, but she had a fierceness in her eyes that Rob lacked. She looked ready for a fight, maybe with Rob, maybe with the world.

"Nice to meet you, Mrs. Schlagel," Rob said with more than adequate politeness.

"*You're* on the team?" Her question was an accusation.

"One of our most valuable guys," Josh answered. "Again today, he stole the other team's signs. He kept me from getting beaned."

She shot Josh a look that told him the question was not his to answer. "You played those Catholics today, didn't you?" She said *Catholics* the way someone might say *prostitute*.

"Yes, ma'am," Josh answered.

"It's not surprising. That's what you should expect from people who aren't Christian." Rob thought Catholics were Christian, but now he wasn't sure. She went on, "They are an evil cult. They shouldn't be allowed to play or live near normal people." Now Rob was really confused. He didn't know much about other religions. Hell, he didn't know much about his own, but he was pretty sure the Catholics were a pretty big group. "They are evil, evil people," she said. "That's why their priests sleep with boys." She turned on Rob, "You steal signs?" she demanded.

"They won't let me steal bases, so I have to steal signs," Rob smiled. She narrowed her eyes. Clearly her question was not meant to be taken lightly. "It's a big part of the game," he added, not sure why a woman whose son had played as much ball as Josh had wouldn't know that.

"When you're on the bench, you have lots of time to notice things," he continued.

"At your size, I'm not surprised you don't play." She made him a few inches shorter.

"As it says in First Samuel," Rob said, " . . .*the Lord said to Samuel, do not consider his appearance or his height, for I have rejected him. The Lord does not look at the things man looks at. Man looks at the outward appearance, but the Lord looks at the heart.*"

Her eyes widened. Josh, standing beside his mother, beamed an approving smile at his friend.

"Where does your family go to church?" she asked.

Rob wondered if she had done police interrogations before becoming a mother. "We're Methodists," he answered.

"Methodists." She said it the way one might say *Tartars* or *Berbers* or some foreign group of which one has heard but about which one knows little or nothing.

"We go to Christ Methodist on Highland Avenue." He didn't mention how often they went.

"Methodists," she said again, weighing the word as though it might give her the value of the people it represented.

"I think what church you go to doesn't matter," Rob said. "I like what it says in Deuteronomy: *But if from there you seek the Lord your God, you will find him if you look for him with all your heart and with all your soul.*"

Josh's mouth twisted as one corner went up and the other went down as he stifled a grin.

Mrs. Schlagel gave the smallest of nods. "If you're on the team," she said this as though she still wasn't sure she believed it, "You must know Daniel? Such a sweet boy," she said. "And so handsome. You can tell Christ is in him."

Rob wondered if she was now talking about the Danny he knew. He didn't remember any Bible stories about Christ persecuting the meek.

"Daniel comes over often. One of Joshua's few Christian friends. I can see you read your bible. Do you and Daniel ever have a chance to discuss the scriptures at practice?"

Rob was about to try to BS an answer to that question when two of the younger Schlagels ran into the room.

Josh caught the smaller of the two and swept her into his arms. "This is Gabriella," he said, holding her so Rob could see.

"Hi," Rob said.

"This is my friend, Rob," Josh said. "And the other one is Micah."

"Hi," Rob said again, extending his hand to the boy.

"Children, you know you are not to carry on in the living room," Mrs. Schlagel scolded. "Go back to your rooms. Your father will deal with you later."

Terror filled Micah's eyes. Josh set his sister down. "They were just . . ."

"Joshua."

Josh fell silent and swallowed. "I need to get ready for my date," Josh said.

His mother gave him another stern look. "We will talk about your disrespect later."

Josh walked Rob to the door. Rob offered to run home and save Josh the trip. The instant Rob was outside with the door closed behind him, he could hear the mother's voice raised. Rob was frozen to his spot, half expecting to hear a slap any moment.

"Don't," Mathias said, taking a shot at the basket. Rob looked at him. "It goes on all the time here. Best to ignore it." Mat shot a basket. "How did it go?"

"The word of the Lord shall be my salvation. I did my homework. I think I passed. Probably got a D, but I passed."

Mat laughed and put up another shot. "Josh said you were the smartest guy on the team."

ELEVEN

As practice was wrapping up after school, Josh said quietly to Rob, "I can't give you a ride today," then hurried off. Rob was hoping to see how Josh thought he'd done with his mother or if Josh had gotten in trouble for contradicting her. Rob also realized he had come to really enjoy his talks with Josh and missed not talking to him all day.

Rob did his quick rinse and hit the road. As he passed Quail Run he decided he'd take a loop around the complex. He turned down White Tail Lane and only took a few steps when he saw Josh's car in the Schlagel's driveway. Next to it was Danny Taylor's Jeep. Rob turned and ran back the way he had come but at a much faster pace until he got home.

As he turned into the driveway he saw Meg and Ashley shooting baskets. Knowing how much Ashley hated anything that even remotely resembled sports, he knew this must be a set-up for Ashley to see Josh.

"Hi," Meg said, trying too hard to sound casual.

"Meg. Ash." Rob said curtly.

Ashley's look made it clear she wasn't there to chitchat with him. "Where's Josh?" she demanded. "Meg said Josh Schlagel gives you rides home." She looked from brother to sister with eyes that branded them both liars.

"I wanted to run home," Rob answered. "Did you want me to play some basketball with you?" Ashley gave him another look to freeze the sun. "Didn't think so," he said and started toward the house.

"Where is Josh?" Meg asked.

"Why don't you ask him?" Rob answered without looking back.

As soon as he was inside, he dashed upstairs to drown himself in the shower. He knew he shouldn't have expected to compete with Danny Taylor for anything: a spot on the team, Josh's friendship, or the acceptance of Mrs. Schlagel. He was 0-for-three. His father's banging on the bathroom door beckoned him to another dinner where he'd have to play defense until he could retreat to his room.

The next day at school, Rob was hoping not to have to see Josh between classes, but either he was too slow or Josh was too fast and Josh, who was with Jenny, said, "Hey, Rob!" with too much cheer just as Rob was hoping to escape.

"Hi," Rob said as a barely audible breath.

"This is Jenny," Josh said proudly. "Jenny, this is Rob."

"Hi," she said, extending her hand.

"Hi," he said, barely shaking it.

"Rob and I went to grade school together," Jenny said.

"I have to get to class," Rob said, turning away.

"See you at the game," Josh called after him.

Rob wasn't able to do anything to prevent Bloomington from handing the Hawks their second defeat of the season. They boarded the bus for what was going to be a long ride home — not because of the distance, which was only about eight miles, but because of the mood. In passing Rob's seat, Josh said, "I'll give you a ride if you want."

"Don't bother," Rob answered.

Rob did his quick rinse and headed out the locker room door. Josh was waiting in his car. "Hey," he said.

"Hey."

"Hop in." Josh threw the passenger door open in a way that really didn't leave an option so Rob got in. "What's up?" Josh asked.

"Nothing. You didn't shower?"

"No."

"Did your dad whip you for the other night?"

"Do we have to talk about it?"

"No. Sorry." They rode in silence for a few blocks. "What did your mom say?"

Josh turned and smiled at him. "She's still skeptical, but I think you did okay on the midterm."

"Will there be a final?" Rob was joking.

"Every day is a test." Josh was not.

"If you want to hang around tonight, dad was going to be home early and grill some steaks."

"Sounds fun. If my mother says okay."

Josh asked Rob to get the basketball and they began a game of one-on-one. After a few plays, Josh stripped off his shirt and threw it on the grass. "It's getting warm," he said.

"You want something to drink?"

"No, thanks. Aren't you hot?"

"I guess it is getting warm," Rob said, wiping sweat from his forehead with his sleeve.

"If you're too warm, you can always take your shirt off," Josh suggested.

"I'm okay."

"You'll end up with a trucker tan," Josh smiled.

Rob hesitated a moment then threw his shirt next to Josh's.

A couple of plays later, as Rob was trying to make a shot near the basket, instead of jumping up to block it, Josh let him make the shot and dove in low tackling Rob onto the grass. They began to wrestle and Josh kept trying to pin Rob, which should have been easy with his sixty-five pound advantage, but given Rob's wiry strength, determined squirming, and the slickness of their bodies, Josh could never quite finish him off. It didn't help his efforts that they were both laughing so hard.

A car crunching gravel caused Josh to roll off Rob and sit up. Meg and her father got out. If Meg's smile burst any wider, it would have knocked her ears off her head. "Hey, Josh," she said.

"Hi, Mr. Wardell. Hi, Meg."

"How's it going, Josh?" Rob's father asked.

"Great, thanks. You ready for a rematch?" Josh asked.

"I am, but I'm not sure Meg is. She just ran the one-hundred, the four-hundred, and the four-hundred relay, and won all three!"

"Hey, congratulations!" Josh stood up to shake her hand.

"Way to go, Meg," Rob added.

"If she's as fast as her brother, she must be good," Josh said. He slapped Rob in the chest.

"I'm game," Meg said, setting her gym bag down next to the shirts on the lawn.

As Josh and Mr. Wardell took the ball down court, Rob quietly said to his sister, "You just want to guard Josh."

"You know it. Especially since you guys are playing skins!"

She broke off her whispered conversation and went after Josh. She was definitely playing the man and not the ball. With Meg glued to Josh and their father trying to block Josh's jumper, Rob was open on almost every play and able to score at will. The game wasn't close. Meg was very close.

When it was over, Mr. Wardell said, "I'll get started on dinner while you guys shower."

When they got upstairs Meg hurried to the linen closet and got Josh one of the thick bath towels that were reserved for guests, presenting it to him as though it were a pillow holding a crown for a coronation.

When Josh came back into Rob's room, he was wearing only the towel. "Did Meg try to attack you while you were in the shower?" Rob asked.

Josh laughed. "I wish! She waited and went in after I got out."

Rob laughed. "You sure take her crush well."

"It's kind of flattering."

"Do you know how many girls have crushes on you?"

"Yeah, right."

"If Meg's friends are any indication, quite a few. And I hear girls talking in class."

"I just need one girlfriend, not a whole school full of groupies."

"You have Jenny."

"Yeah, I guess we're a couple now."

During dinner, Josh again regaled the family with stories of Rob's baseball smarts, with particular emphasis on Rob's saving him from the bean-balls.

Rob woke at 2:30 and found himself on the floor again doing sit ups. Why did his happiness always seem so short? He knew the next day Josh was likely to go back to ignoring him to hang out with Danny Taylor.

TWELVE

"Wardell. Schlagel," the Coach beckoned them after everyone else headed to the locker room after practice. "I noticed you and Wardell skipped the showers last night. Three laps for each of you."

Rob had showered, such as his showers were, but he said nothing. Rob knew from being in Hudson's office that the coach had a view of the parking lot, but not the locker room, so he must have seen them leaving too quickly. As Rob and Josh started off on their penalty run, Josh said, "I'm sorry. This is my fault."

"Not a problem," Rob said. "I run anyway."

"Are you going to push me like you did last time? I need to get home in time for church."

Rob took off with Josh in pursuit. It didn't allow for much conversation, but they finished the three miles quickly. Hudson sat in his car in the parking lot to make sure they ran by him the requisite number of times.

"You set a heck of a pace," Josh panted as they entered the locker room. "You look like you could run forever."

"Some days I wish I could," he answered as he went to his corner of the locker room and hollered back. "You want to shower first?"

"We can shower together since we need to hurry."

"You sure?"

"Yeah."

Rob was prepared for the sight of red stripes on Josh's ass but there were also bruises all over his torso. Rob tried to avert his eyes as much as possible, take the briefest of showers, and dress quickly.

As they drove home he said, "You can just drop me at the entrance to Quail Run so you can get home sooner."

"You sure?"

"Yeah, I can run home from there."

"Thanks."

When Rob ran into the kitchen his mother was working on dinner. "Josh called," she said. "His number's on the pad by the phone, he said to call him."

Rob tore off the number and went upstairs to the sewing room, closed the door and punched the numbers into the phone. "Hey, Josh."

"Hi."

"What's wrong?"

"They had already left for church when I got home. My father's going to kill me. I can be late because of a game, but not from practice. And if I told him I'm late because I got in trouble at practice, it'd be even worse."

"You can blame me if you want. Say it was my fault."

"That won't help. And my mother is already suspicious enough of you."

"Suspicious of what?"

"You, well, you, I guess you aren't quite Christian enough because you don't go to our church. But thanks again for what you did with her."

All through dinner and Rob's lame attempt at his term paper, he couldn't stop thinking about Josh being beaten by his father. That as much as his usual traumas drove Rob to the floor of his bedroom in the middle of the night to punish his own body.

*   *   *   *   *

Another post-baseball and post-basketball game wrestling match over, Rob and Josh stretched their shirtless bodies on the lawn. Josh said, "Why don't I ask Jenny to see if one her friends wants to go to the prom with you? It would be fun to double date."

"Get real."

"A lot of girls think you're cute," Josh protested.

"If they think I'm cute — which I doubt — they might think I'm cute like a baby rabbit is cute, but they don't want to date them. They think you're cute the way Orlando Bloom is cute."

"I'm just saying . . ."

"I know what you're saying, and it's more humiliation and rejection than I need, but thanks."

Josh sat up and brushed the grass off Rob's back. "I'm sorry."

"I have the feeling this conversation isn't over," Rob said turning around to look at Josh.

"Well, I had a favor to ask and now this makes it kind of awkward. I, uh, that is, if you would, if you don't mind, I mean I understand if . . ."

Rob tackled Josh and knocked him backwards and pinned his shoulders to the ground. "Spit it out, Schlagel!"

"Condoms. I need them for the prom. My parents would kill me if they found out I bought some or had them in the house . . ." Rob started laughing and for a while couldn't stop.

Josh sat back up to study him. "What's so funny?"

"Nothing," Rob said, choking back tears of laughter.

"If we could stop at a store some day, and I'd give you the money, and you could go in, and then you could keep them until prom day and then . . ." Rob was still laughing. What's so funny?"

"Nothing," Rob said doubled over now in pain from laughing so hard.

Josh tackled Rob and pinned him from above, kneeling on Rob's arms so he couldn't move and began pounding on Rob's stomach. "What is so funny?" he demanded while laughing himself. Rob's face was in Josh's crotch and Rob was laughing so hard he could barely breathe. While Josh continued laughing and punching, Rob couldn't help notice the bulge in Josh's gym shorts growing. He realized his own shorts were expanding, too.

Josh fell off onto to ground, exhausted but still laughing. "So will you do it?"

"Yeah. Meg will love seeing you all dressed up in your tux."

*   *   *   *   *

Rob did crunch after crunch, the sweat running off his naked body onto his bedroom floor but the pain in his stomach did nothing to push away thoughts of Josh. It was stupid to be jealous of Jenny. After all Jenny was Josh's girlfriend. Rob was just a friend. That's all he wanted them to be, close friends. Like Batman and Robin. Ben and Jerry. Tom and Jerry. It was Josh hanging around with Danny Taylor that really pissed him off.

84

THIRTEEN

The team's fourth win in a row didn't excuse Rob and Josh from the laps that were becoming an almost daily occurrence. "Okay, gentlemen," Coach Hudson said as they finished their last lap.

"Hudson wouldn't have us doing laps if he knew we had so much fun doing them," Josh said, still laughing from the last of Rob's jokes.

It was the hottest day of the year so far, almost 80. Summer was starting early. Josh's baseball shirt was plastered to his body. Josh lifted the tail to wipe some moisture from his face. Rob watched one remaining drop run its course down Josh's temple and off his chin.

"You notice I'm keeping up with you now?" Josh's cock-eyed grin slid so far to the right it looked like it might slide into his dimple.

Rob felt the swelling in his shorts growing. Lately when Josh was around, Rob seemed to have no control over that part of his body. Josh had to notice that when they were wrestling.

Rob had certainly noticed Josh. Lately he had been watching Josh too intently and springing a woody just as it was time to hit the showers. It took all of his concentration to try to suppress it especially if he made the mistake of even glancing at Josh in the locker room or shower.

"You're definitely getting me in shape." Josh stripped off his shirt to look down at his sweat-streaked body. "And I've been doing sit-ups, too." He patted his firm, flat stomach as though it were a beer gut. "Wish I had killer abs like yours."

Rob looked up and all of his attempts to relax were useless as the blood rushed to his groin so suddenly he thought he might pass out. He gulped for air like a fish just landed in the bottom of a boat. As many times as he had seen Josh shirtless or naked, the sight never ceased to dazzle him and lately had been driving him crazier than ever.

"I wish the coach would let us take our shirts off during practice," Josh said. "Days like today. I'd like to work on my tan."

The thought of Josh's body tanned was almost more than Rob could stand. "You heard him the first day of practice — 'this is not a friggin' beach, gentlemen . . .'" Rob said, glad to be able do his Coach Hudson imitation and break the spell he felt coming over him.

"Take your shirt off," Josh said suddenly. Rob was a little startled by the request. "Let me see those abs."

Rob swallowed, but knew he wouldn't refuse any request Josh made of him. "Wish I had a washboard like that," Josh said with a low whistle. "Hey, who locks up when Coach leaves?"

"The janitors come in about six. When we get back from away games, we see them. Why?"

"Oh that's right, oh, uh, no reason. Just wondering. The place seems deserted."

The locker room did seem especially empty. Rob had been alone in it often enough with Josh, but didn't know why it seemed so different. The bulge in Rob's shorts was getting worse and not showing the slightest sign of dissolving. He had read about some guy who had taken too many Viagras and had to be admitted to a hospital; he wondered if that could be happening to him even without the drugs.

Rob and Josh each went to his locker. Rob couldn't help but stop and peek around the corner to watch Josh strip. The light shimmering on Josh's back was not helping things any, but still Rob couldn't pull his eyes away as he watched Josh stand and yank off his gym shorts. Rob didn't understand why he suddenly found the blue shorts with the gold hawk emblazoned on so sexy.

It was bad enough when thoughts of Josh just tormented him in the middle of the night but now his waking thoughts were overrun as well. Rob's eyes wandered up Josh's lightly hairy legs to the jockstrap. That small scrap of clothing. That modern day loincloth that was all that stood between Rob and all of Josh. Rob watched as Josh hesitated before pulling off the jock and Rob realized why. Josh was hard.

Josh turned and looked at Rob. Rob's gaze was so transfixed below Josh's waist that it took him a moment to realize Josh was looking at him. He was now far too embarrassed to stay in the locker room any longer with a soon-to-be-naked Joshua Lawrence Schlagel.

"Shit," Rob said, slamming his locker shut.

"What?"

"Forgot my towel. I guess I'll just wait and shower at home." Sometimes it amazed and annoyed Rob the frequency and conviction with which he routinely lied. He was accustomed to lying to his teachers and parents, but hated lying to Josh.

"No prob. You can use mine."

"I don't want to use a towel after you have wiped your scummy ass with it," he said.

Josh smiled, and still wearing only his jock, grabbed his towel and walked toward Rob. "Then I'll let you use it first."

Rob took an involuntary step backwards; Josh closed the gap without even seeming to notice Rob's sloppy retreat. Again Rob backpedaled, and Josh didn't break stride.

The sweat was still shimmering on Josh's chest. His large brown nipples were erect. The few hairs that surrounded each nipple and the few hairs in the center of Josh's chest each vied for Rob's attention. Unconsciously, Rob tried to step back again, but this time his entire body slammed into the lockers. From the sound of the collision, Rob knew that the unexpected contact should have hurt, but he was in full fight-or-flight mode and the pain didn't even faze him.

"You okay?"

Josh's voice startled Rob as though he had never heard it before. It seemed far away and very foreign. Rob was so focused on his own fear that he almost forgot that the reason for his trauma stood in front of him, less than a foot away. His terror wasn't just inside him, but in front of him, in the flesh. And what flesh. Flesh that he hated himself for wanting to touch. Flesh that he *had* found every excuse *to* touch in practice, wrestling, basketball or any other time. Now that flesh was in front of him. So exposed, so vulnerable, so alluring, so wonderful. He wanted to reach out and touch it. But if he did, Josh would hate him. Josh's girlfriend, Jenny, would hate him. Coach Hudson would hate him. His parents, the team, his sister would hate him. He hated himself for wanting to. His eyes were moistening with tears at the pain he felt trying to restrain himself.

"That must have hurt. You look like you're going to cry . . ." Rob couldn't speak. The wind had been knocked out of him, whether by the collision with the lockers or his own fear he couldn't tell. "Let me see the back of your head. Are you bleeding?"

Rob let out a sound he had only heard once before when a baby rabbit got stuck in the fence at his house. Josh reached up to feel Rob's hair. As soon as Josh's hand gently touched his head, Rob felt a shiver shoot through his body and goose bumps rise everywhere in spite of the sweat on his body and the heat of the locker room.

"I'm fine!" he blurted more adamantly than he meant to. He

broke past Josh and into the open area of the locker room. Josh threw his hands wide to let Rob pass. "I'll just go home and shower," Rob said, heading toward the door without looking back.

He was halfway across the parking lot when he realized everything—his books, street clothes, house keys—everything was still in his gym locker, which was still unlocked. His shirt was still on the bench in front of his locker. But he couldn't go back now and face Josh. He broke into a run. He headed cross-country and down the railroad tracks. He didn't want to see Josh drive by.

Rob's confusion had been so bad for so long: now that confusion had an embodiment. What would Josh have said if he knew he was partially responsible for the abs he was jealous of? Rob could hardly have told Josh that it was his lust for Josh that drove him to work his body so hard. First the workouts had been caused by nameless, faceless urges, but now there was a name to his fear. And a face and a body.

At home, he opened the back door as quietly as he could, and tiptoed up the stairs. He went into the bathroom, closed the door and collapsed against it. His legs were already cramping; he had taken the run home at a mad clip. He looked at his body in the mirror. His dark brown hair was matted in a crazy pattern on his forehead. His body was flushed from the run in the cold evening air. His tiny nipples stood out fiercely from the small firm plates of his chest. There was no way Josh would ever give up Jenny for a scrawny little body like this.

In the shower he felt the lump on the back of his head. Maybe he could blame his strangeness on head trauma. Or maybe he'd be lucky and there would be internal bleeding and he'd just drop dead.

Dinner was enough to drive him insane, expecting a question about Josh to reduce him to tears at any moment, but his flustered look must have kept any questions at bay.

FOURTEEN

Rob woke at 2:30. His legs were cramping and he tried to convince himself that it was that pain that disturbed his sleep and not the raging hard-on pressing again the sheets. The reason for his erection gave him a sudden pain in the chest. The heaviness in his chest got worse when he remembered how he had acted in front of Josh. The twitching in his legs and the twitching in his brain kept him awake until his alarm went off.

He ran to school and headed right to the gym. He went to his locker and was surprised to find it locked. He quickly did the combination and opened it to find that everything was in place. His shirt was gone, but he was lucky that it was the only thing missing considering his stupidity in leaving his locker open.

He knew he couldn't face Josh today. Or maybe ever again. If he could avoid Josh at baseball practice, tomorrow was Friday, he could dodge him again all day and he'd have the weekend to figure out a way to avoid him for the rest of the school year. He laughed out loud when he realized how stupid it sounded to drop out of school to avoid Josh.

When Josh saw him at baseball practice and said "Hi," Rob gave him a quick "Hi" in return and dashed off to the outfield. Rob always imagined that there was a special tone in the way Josh said *hi* to him that wasn't present in Josh's greeting to others. Today, in particular, there seemed to be a warmth and a depth there, or in the eyes, that made Rob tingle. But he knew it was just wishful thinking and that there was nothing special about the way Josh said hello to him.

Rob had managed to duck Josh during practice time, but the only way Rob could think to avoid the ride was to get himself laps. His legs were sore and spongy from yesterday's run, but he had no choice.

Late in practice when he saw Hudson approaching, he turned away, pretending not to see him, cupped his hands to his mouth and yelled out across the field, in the distinctive nasal twang, "That's it, gentlemen! Let's see some hustle!" Josh gave him a look to warn him, but Rob did another line of his imitation to make sure the coach heard him.

Hudson shook his head and turned to Rob, "Two laps."

"Yes, sir," Rob answered with feigned dejection.

As he took off to run his laps, he saw Josh heading for the locker room. "Rob!" Josh called.

Rob's chest tightened. "Hi," he responded. "Don't bother waiting for me. Screwed up and got myself more laps."

He glanced back to see Josh still standing outside the gym door staring at him. He felt guilty ignoring Josh, and he wanted more than anything to see him, talk to him, and be comforted by him, but instead he flew off down the trail. He took the laps much slower than usual to make sure Josh was gone when he finished.

When Rob got home, he went into his room and took off his shirt in preparation for his shower, but before going into the bathroom it hit him how much he missed talking to Josh all day. Before he realized what he was doing, he had opened the one

drawer of his desk that locked and pulled out the shirtless photos of Josh he had printed out. He sat down on his bed with the
photos of Josh.

The knock on his bedroom door startled him. He glanced at
the photos spread out on the bed and he figured he would just
have to keep Meg at the door and away from them. He crossed
the room and opened the door. The sight of Josh stunned him
into silence.

"Hey, Rob," Josh said. He took a few steps into the room
before Rob could react. Now any attempt to place himself
between Josh and the bed would look ludicrous. "You forgot
this." Josh held out Rob's baseball undershirt, which had been
laundered and neatly folded. "I locked up your locker, but did-
n't want to stick this sweaty thing in there to stink up your
other clothes, so I took it home and washed it with my stuff."
Rob just stared at the shirt. "When I locked your locker, I
noticed you did have a towel in there."

"Oh, I, uh, mustn't have seen it."

"It's red, white, and blue. It was on top."

Rob's panic level was rising again. He tried to gauge Josh's
tone. Was this an accusation? It seemed more of a question. Josh
didn't seem angry at all. He was just stating facts, and nervously probing for more. His tone seemed more one of concern.
"Are you okay?" Josh asked. Rob nodded. "I thought maybe
you hurt your head, like you had a concussion, or something,
you suddenly started acting so weird. I was going to call you
last night, but there's never any privacy to use the phone. What
are all these?" Josh asked, reaching toward the bed.

"I printed out those photos I took. For you. I made copies
for you," Rob rushed to say.

"Bobby, dinner!" Meg's voice bellowed.

"Gotta go eat," Rob said, relieved to be saved by the dinner
bell.

"Sorry, I guess I got here right at dinner time."

"I'll catch you in school Monday, okay?"

"Sure," Josh answered, disappointment evident on his face.

Rob grabbed a shirt, pulled it on and followed Josh out the door. As they hit the bottom of the stairs, Rob's mother said, "Josh is welcome to stay to dinner."

"He has to get going," Rob said.

Josh didn't answer at first, but looked at Rob, getting the hint.

Meg came over and took Josh's arm. "C'mon, Josh, stay."

Josh looked at Rob. Rob swallowed and looked away. Josh said, "Not tonight, Meg, sorry. And thanks, Mrs. Wardell." Josh looked so hurt, it was all Rob could do not to invite him to stay.

"You know you're welcome anytime," Mrs. Wardell said.

Rob walked Josh to the door. "See ya," he said as he let his friend out. Josh gave a small nervous wave in reply.

"He is so sweet," Meg sighed.

*　　*　　*　　*　　*

Rob found himself doing his usual routine at 3 a.m. and for once, it worked. He had calmed down enough to think rationally. If Josh had come to see him, he couldn't for a moment suspect why Rob had been acting so crazy. Rob resolved to act as normal as possible and pretend nothing had happened. If there was one thing Rob was good at, it was pretending to act normal when he knew so well that he was anything but.

FIFTEEN

When Rob felt Josh's hand on his shoulder on the way out to practice, Rob turned and looked at the cockeyed grin on Josh's face and knew he'd never felt so close to another human being in his life. He wanted to reach out and hug Josh and tell him how much he valued his friendship. Just his friendship, nothing more.

Josh asked Rob to play pepper and as usual their game got out of hand with Josh running like crazy as Rob sprayed balls all over the place and taunted him. Having missed the last of the balls, Josh dove at Rob's legs and tackled him. Rob squirmed to get loose.

Rob rolled over and found himself looking up at Coach Hudson. "Wardell, if you hurt him, I will kill you. You are expendable. He is not. Three laps for each of you. Stop the horseplay."

As they started their laps, Rob asked, "Didn't you see Hudson? You must like running laps."

"I like running them with you," Josh answered. Rob looked at Josh for some indication of what he meant.

They entered the locker room, laughing at another of Rob's Coach Hudson imitations. At his locker, Josh quickly stripped down to his jock. Rob took a few deep breaths in hopes of quelling the erection that had begun to grow in his jock the moment he saw Josh's sweaty chest. His furtive glances at Josh's cheeks pinched together by his jockstrap didn't help. When Josh turned around Rob could not fail to notice that Josh was also bulging in his jock. Josh grabbed his towel and walked toward Rob.

"Try not to damage any lockers tonight, will you," he said, closing on his friend with his goofy smile and dazzling green eyes.

"Try not to push me into any," Rob replied. He hoped Josh didn't hear the quavering in his voice. Rob held his ground in front of his locker until Josh was within a foot. Rob was sure Josh could see his heart pounding against his small chest. The proximity to his almost-naked friend increased Rob's perspiration more than the three laps had.

Josh hesitated for a long moment. "Rob, when I was over at your house the other night and saw the photos . . ."

Every one of Rob's muscles went rigid. His breath ceased. His heart made up for the lack of movement elsewhere in his body. He wondered if it was possible to have a heart attack at his age, and at the same time hoped he would have one to spare him whatever came next. Josh had to be able to hear the drumming against his rib cage. Rob tried to answer, but all the liquid had evaporated from his mouth.

Josh was speaking slowly as though he, too, was unsure what came next. He looked at Rob's wide fear-filled doe-eyes then looked away. He took a breath, steeled himself, and before Rob could form any sort of response went on, "I noticed you only printed out the pictures of me with my shirt off."

Rob studied Josh's face for some indication of what was to come next. Part of him feared Josh would hit him, but there was nothing the least bit threatening about Josh's nervous smile or his warm, unsteady voice. Another part of Rob feared that if

Josh wasn't about to punch him that whatever came next would be far worse. Again Rob tried to speak and again his mouth failed to make words.

"I've noticed you checking me out and I wasn't sure if it was just wishful thinking or if you really were," Josh said. It was a statement, but also a question, giving Rob a chance to refute it.

Rob tensed even tighter, clenching his jaw and feeling a stabbing pain through his chest. He'd never had a flaming arrow penetrate his body, but he imagined this was what it would feel like.

Josh swallowed, and spoke again. "I notice you get hard when we wrestle and sometimes when we shower here, but I wasn't sure what that meant until I saw all those pictures."

Rob tried to make his legs move in retreat. He tried to make his mouth form sounds. Again he heard the sick, wounded rabbit squeak out of his throat, but that was all. He feared that someone might walk in any moment. He also prayed that someone would and save him. Every warning bell was clanging like the sound effects in a movie about a sinking submarine.

"I know I get hard when I look at you," Josh said almost as though he were asking permission to.

He gave Rob a long time to object as he slowly reached out to touch Rob's stomach. Josh's hand was shaking and Rob could tell it was taking an effort for him to raise his hand across the twelve-inch wide chasm that separated their charged bodies. Rob's stomach muscles tightened even more. The tentative touch of his friend's fingertips felt like electric ice. "I've wanted to touch you since the first day I saw you in the hall, my first day at this school. And I wanted to even more after I saw you in the locker room the first day of baseball practice." Josh's voice was soft and gentle, wavering between the poles of fear and desire.

The words seem to come from very far away, and Rob was stunned to hear they were the same ones he would've been saying if he possessed the strength to speak.

"And the more I got to know you, the more I liked you, and the more I hoped you liked me. Those pictures were what gave me the guts to tell you. I couldn't believe you might like me, too." The quivering in Josh's voice made it sound like he might cry. Rob wanted to reach out and comfort his friend, to tell him it was okay. But he couldn't move, and he wasn't at all sure that it was okay.

"I've been so scared for so long to tell you." Josh ever so slowly caressed up the ripples of Rob's stomach to his small, firm chest. He let his fingers hover on the tiny, but very erect nipple. The bulge forced Rob's shorts out and he knew if Josh kept this up, he wouldn't be able to control himself. He forced himself to look down to break the spell Josh had on him, but his eyes fell upon a sight even more entrancing—Josh was poking out the top of his jock and was soaking his waistband.

"Do you want to touch it?" Josh asked, noting the target of Rob's eyes and almost pleading with Rob to do so. His voice was soft, inviting, hypnotizing.

Rob still couldn't move. He had longed for this moment. He had long feared this moment. But he never, even in his wildest 2 a.m. fantasy, thought that it would really come to pass. With a touch as gentle as a breeze Josh took Rob's hand and brought it toward his jock. Rob was too weak to resist.

Once Josh had placed the hand there, Rob instinctively took hold. He had never touched another guy and Josh was so much bigger than him. He could feel the power rushing through it. He felt electricity surging to parts of his body where he hadn't known he had nerve endings. Involuntarily he grasped more firmly. Josh recoiled and shot a hot stream that splattered over his stomach, coating the light trail of hair that ran from his navel on down. The white stream continued to spew over Josh with several warm drops hitting Rob and causing his flesh to burn as though splashed with acid.

The searing of the liquid shocked Rob enough that his mouth became unstuck. "I'm sorry," is what came out.

"No, I'm sorry. I just got too excited. I've wanted you to touch me and to touch you for so long . . ."

Rob looked into his friend's eyes and saw tears there.

"God, I have wanted you for so long . . ." Josh reached to pull Rob toward him in an embrace.

"No," Rob said as he threw his hands up as a barrier. His hands brushed Josh's perfect chest and a spark shot through him. He longed to touch that muscle, but now that he had, it terrified him and he yanked his hands away. The *no* was not loud or forceful, but it was firm enough, and Josh heeded it.

"What's wrong?" Josh seemed hurt and surprised.

"We can't do this."

"Here?"

"Anywhere. We can't."

"Why?" Josh asked.

"I . . . I . . . I . . . I've got to go."

"I want you."

"I can't."

"Yes you can. Say when and where."

"We can't." Rob's words were weak, and if either of them had really been listening, they would have wondered which of them he was trying to convince.

"Please," Josh said so plaintively that it caused tears to instantly flood Rob's eyes.

Rob had never denied his friend anything, but this time he said, "Don't." It wasn't so much an order as a pitiful plea. "Let's just go. Please."

Josh nodded. "I'm sorry."

Josh took half a step back. Rob didn't want to look down at himself still rigid or Josh, spent and dripping out the top of his jock.

"Please, could we just go?"

Josh nodded feebly. "I'm sorry, Rob."

Rob opened his locker and started cramming things into his backpack with no thought to his books, papers, or clothes.

Josh grabbed his towel and walked back to his locker wiping off the mess he had made all over himself. Released somewhat from his fear of Josh, Rob began to fear the arrival of someone else and hurried to flee the scene of the crime. They put their sweaty clothes back on, fast. Rob's shirt was on inside out, but he didn't bother to reverse it.

Josh drove with exaggerated concentration so he wouldn't have to look at Rob. Rob stared out the side window although he sensed Josh stealing glances when he would check cross-traffic at intersections.

Rob had gone from never having felt so close to someone to now never having felt so completely alone. Rob was sure he had just lost his best friend. His only true friend. The truth of what his grandmother used to say struck him: *Be careful what you wish for, you may get it.*

He had wished, hoped and prayed his whole life for someone as wonderful as Josh to touch him, and now that he had, Rob wanted to go home, get the key to his father's gun cabinet, take out the twelve-gauge, and put it in his mouth. It would have to hurt less than this.

Josh pulled into the driveway, and Rob opened the car door and started out. The sound of a voice startled him. "Rob." Rob swallowed and looked at his friend for the first time since they had left the locker room, but couldn't bear to see Josh's moist eyes and looked away again. "I'm sorry. Can we talk about this?" Josh asked.

Rob hesitated. Then he turned back so he was facing the open car door, but not Josh. "No. I don't want to talk about it. Not now. Not ever."

"Does that mean you're not going to speak to me?" Josh's voice caught in his throat as he said it.

There was a long pause as Rob contemplated the car door. "It means . . . it . . . it means . . . I don't know what it means. Goddammit." Rob slammed the car door and walked toward the house. He tried to compose himself, realized that was useless and bolted in the door, past his startled family, into the hall and up the stairs. He locked the bathroom door and cranked the shower full blast to cover the sound of his sobbing.

SIXTEEN

Rob could not bring himself to get in the shower. He stared down at the dried white spots on his stomach. He gently touched one with the tip of his finger. A jolt went through him.

He wanted to stop thinking about Josh, but here he was unable to wash this most intimate part of Josh off his body. He had hardly stopped thinking about Joshua Lawrence Schlagel since the first time he had seen him at school last September.

Josh had been walking down the hall when Rob first saw him. Rob could close his eyes and immediately bring up the image of Josh that day. Levis. A Green Bay hat, on backwards. A hank of hair that looked soft and silky, even at a distance, poked out from the opening where the adjustable band was in the back of the hat, making the hair flop onto his forehead. There was a perfectly straight line of hair across the back of his tanned neck.

His biceps showed definition even under the white Milwaukee Brewers T-shirt. The front of the shirt, where the logo was, poked out indicating there was a nice chest underneath. Rob's eyes didn't stray to check out the jeans—checking out another guy's equipment would make him gay.

The thing that really caught Rob's attention, though, was not Josh's body—as perfect as it appeared to be—it was his smile. Even though Josh was alone, and seemed to have nothing to smile about, he had a slightly crooked grin on his smooth face, creating a dimple only on the left side. Josh's nose was a just little too big and pointed, but rather than detracting from the picture, gave the almost-too-perfect face a dash of realism that made it that much more handsome.

Rob had always wished he had blue eyes, and tended to notice blue-eyed people, but Josh's eyes were *so* green, so sparkling, as though back-lit from within. As Rob got to know Josh, he actually began to see some of that inner glow that made Josh's eyes shine. Small tufts of shaggy hair flared a bit over the tops of Josh's small, cute ears. Rob instantly found the ears adorable the way they were pinned back against his head. Rob always thought his own ears were a bit too big and stuck out a little far from his thin face.

Josh's jaw tapered down to a square jaw that had a faint hint of a cleft. Rob studied that chin for the slightest hint that it had ever been shaved. A razor had still never touched Rob's face, either.

Rob didn't know who the boy was. Harrisonburg Senior High School was small enough that Rob thought he knew everyone by sight, if not by name. He had made an effort to befriend a few guys he particularly liked, but with poor results and like a dog that chases cars, he often wondered what he would do if he ever caught one. Now Rob had caught Josh—or Josh had caught and cornered Rob in the locker room—and things could never be the same. He had viewed his whole life badly up to this point so there seemed no reason to think this could possibly turn out well.

He hated Josh. For catching him. For touching him. For making him admit to himself that he liked being touched. Deny it as he might, his still-raging body told the truth. The jock he had soaked with his desires didn't lie.

Rob hated Josh for being queer. How could his hero, the man he'd longed for, be a goddamned homo? He cursed Josh with every cruel and crude name he had ever heard for *cocksucking faggots*. He suddenly stopped. He could never hate Josh. He loved Josh. No matter what Josh was, no matter what Josh did, he loved him. But why, oh God, why, was he born being attracted to guys? And worse, why did Josh have to be?

He knew he couldn't have a boyfriend or fool around with guys; that just could never happen. At best when he had fantasized about life with Josh, it was a celibate coexistence: The two of them as buds. Best friends who did everything together. They would wrestle together, play basketball together, play in a swimming pool together, even shower and sleep together, but he had never imagined himself having sex with Josh. Well, almost never. And never real sex. Just a tender touch, maybe a kiss. A hug. Like Butch and Sundance. Very close guy friends, who lived together and who never had girlfriends.

He had tried to convince himself that he never wanted sex with Josh even as he lusted after him from that first day when Josh arrived at their school. He vividly remembered every detail of every interaction he'd ever had with Josh. He didn't know what color Meg's eyes were, but he knew the location of each of Josh's few freckles.

When they had passed that first day in the hall Josh had smiled at him. The next day, as they passed, Josh said hi, but Rob had not responded. It was as though a beautiful painting or statue had spoken, a turn of events which caught Rob completely off guard and unable to speak.

He spent the next week trying to think of something to say to Josh. A few times he caught himself thinking of it as an *opening line* but that sounded too much like a *pick-up line* and he'd immediately shut out the thought. After all, he didn't want to date Josh; he just wanted to say *Hi*. Be his friend.

Rob's lack of response must have convinced the new kid to give up saying hi, because he stopped. Then Josh started hanging out with Taylor, Brickman, Poulan and the rest. Rob cursed himself for his cowardice in blowing his chance.

Rob had only wanted a friend. Someone to do things with. Rob saw his sister and mother sharing moments and at times was jealous that he lacked that sort of intimacy with anyone. He could never picture himself being that close to his father. Like the hunting incident, their few attempts at bonding had ended in disaster. Now he had bonded with Josh and that was a different kind of disaster.

Josh's voice telling him he had wanted him from that first day kept running through his head like a song. Why didn't he have the nerve to tell Josh that he had lusted for him from the first moment he saw him, and loved him more each day that he got to know him?

Rob hadn't wanted to return Josh's shirt when it was left in his room. He wanted that smell and Josh's presence to linger and now he couldn't bring himself to shower off the remnants of Josh that still clung to him. He turned off the shower and hollered downstairs, "Mom, I'm not feeling well. I'm going to skip dinner and just go to bed."

Whatever she said in reply he didn't hear since he was already closing his door.

SEVENTEEN

There was a tap at the door to Rob's room. "Yeah," he said still waking up.

"Bobby, Josh is on the phone," Meg yelled through the door.

He pulled a sheet over his naked body. "Come in."

She entered, still talking on the cordless phone. " . . . I can't wait to see you in your baseball uniform . . . " Rob reached out for the phone. Ordinarily he would have found his sister's flirting amusing, but just hearing Josh's name had caused severe spasms in his stomach and chest. " . . .What number are you, so I'll be able to spot you?"

"Give me the phone."

" . . . Cool. Do you know when you're pitching again?"

"Give me the damn phone and close the door on your way out!"

" . . . I think sick boy is saying something, hang on . . . "

As Meg got close, Rob snatched the phone from her. She gave him a dirty look, but turned and left shutting the door behind her.

"Hey." Josh's voice sounded hesitant, as though he were testing the waters. "How are you?"

"I couldn't sleep," Rob answered.

"Me neither. I'm so sorry about yesterday. I don't want you to hate me."

Rob had already decided he didn't hate Josh. Far from it. But he hated himself. He didn't answer. Josh was also silent. A car whizzing by in the background broke the silence.

"Where are you?"

"Pay phone at the 7-11. I couldn't call from home. I really need to talk to you. We have a game in three hours and I'm not going to be able to play if . . . "

"I can't," Rob cut in.

"Why?"

"I don't know what to say," Rob answered.

"You hate me, don't you?"

"I don't hate you."

"Do you still like me? Are we still friends?"

"Yeah."

"Are you coming to the game?" Josh asked.

"I dunno."

"I'm not sure if I can take seeing you there and not know what's going on."

"Then I won't come."

"I want you to."

"Then I'll come."

"Can I see you now?" Josh begged. There was a long pause then the pay phone digested the money. "I'm almost out of time. Please. The cemetery."

"Okay."

He wanted to reach out and comfort Josh, but right now he was incapable of comforting anyone, least of all himself. He pulled on some sweats and headed downstairs and out the back door.

*   *   *   *   *

Josh's car was parked next to the Fyfes' final resting place. He leapt off the bench when Rob approached. On the far side of the cemetery an old woman was placing flowers at a grave. Josh waited until Rob got close then sat back down and looked down. "I don't know why I . . . "

"You did because I wanted you to."

Josh looked up. "You did?"

"Since the first day I saw you."

"Oh, God. I was so scared. I thought I had messed up again."

"Again?"

"When I was about twelve. At Christian camp. Me and another boy. Garren Munson. We got caught. My father beat the hell out of me and they've been suspicious ever since."

"That's why they screen your friends?"

"Yeah."

"Did you think I looked queer?"

"Not at all. You freaked out so bad yesterday that I was afraid I'd guessed wrong, you'd tell the world and . . . "

"I'd never tell anyone. Who would I tell?" Rob asked.

"Have you ever . . . ?"

"No. Never."

"I was just with Garren when I was twelve. Do you want to?"

"Only with you."

Josh's grin went up and down at the same time. "Thank you."

"For what?"

"Everything. But now I need to get home, eat, sleep, shower and get ready for the game."

"My parents were leaving to take Meg to a meet in North Olmsted. The house will be empty by the time I get home."

"You want me to come over?"

Rob's voice failed so he nodded.

Nearby, four cars unloaded a dozen old men each with an armload of small flags. Rob noticed one of them was at the

Wardell plot decorating a few of his ancestors' graves for Memorial Day.

They drove home in silence. Rob was concentrating on breathing. As they entered the kitchen, Josh said, "What do you want to do?"

"I'm trying to decide if I'm hungrier than I am tired or tireder than I'm hungry."

"It's up to you." Josh said, his nervousness rising even as Rob was beginning to get his under control.

"I think I'm too smelly to eat or sleep until I shower."

Josh took a step closer. "You smell great." He leaned in as though to kiss Rob and Rob backed away. "I'm sorry," Josh said. "I don't want to rush you. We can take things as slow as you want."

Rob nodded. "Let's go upstairs."

He got Josh a guest towel from the linen closet. Rob went into the bathroom and started to close the door but at the last second decided not to shut it all the way. He stripped down and stepped into the hot stream. The water had just begun to cascade over him when heard the door hinge squeak. Rob looked through the opaque glass to where Josh now stood, shirtless. Josh dropped his pants and Rob could make out the shape of the perfect body through the frosted shower door. The door slid open and there stood Joshua Schlagel, naked.

"Do you mind?" Josh asked.

Rob stepped back to let him in. Rob watched as the water clung to Josh's body, smoothing out the few hairs that decorated Josh's chest. Rob was not aware that he had given his hands the command to rise, but he watched them reaching out for Josh's chest. He would have sworn his hands were doing this on their own, independent of the rest of him, but the message they sent back to his brain of the smooth firmness of Josh's body let him know that he was indeed touching Josh's flesh. He gently caressed Josh's chest afraid that if he touched it more firmly, like something grasped in a dream, it might wake him up and end the beautiful moment.

Josh reached up and put his hand behind Rob's head and felt his hair. "How is your head? Feels like you have a bump."

Josh used that hand to hold Rob's head still and bring it closer. Rob had no will to resist and he felt Josh's lips press onto his and was sure he had lost all feeling in every part of his body but his lips. Josh's lips were so much softer than he could have imagined. Like lambskin stuffed with cotton, they were so gentle. Rob involuntarily opened his lips for Josh.

After a long, long shower during which they silently explored each other's bodies with their hands and mouths, Josh broke the spell. "I hate to spoil this, but we really should get some rest before the game."

Rob nodded. After toweling off, Rob took Josh's hand and led him to his bed. They curled up in bed with Rob spooned against Josh's back. Rob was exhausted. Drained in ways he never knew he could be. Josh quickly drifted off to sleep while Rob held him.

Rob realized he hadn't set an alarm and as tired as he was knew if he fell asleep they might not wake in time for the game and now he couldn't pull his arm out from under Josh without waking him. But Rob also didn't want to sleep. He was perfectly happy just holding Josh. As wrong as his life had been to this point he never dreamed he would have ever felt so right. He slowly caressed Josh's chest and lightly kissed and licked Josh's shoulder.

He was sure he could never be as happy as he was in this moment. Josh Schlagel was in his bed, asleep in his arms. Heaven could not compete with this. Rob savored the feel of Josh's body. The smell of his skin, the softness of his hair. The warm, rhythmic sounds of Josh's breathing. The way his shoulders rose and fell with each breath.

Rob had to sit up partway to check his clock and after Josh had slept for an hour, he slowly rolled Josh over and kissed him on the lips. "Game time," he whispered.

It took Josh a moment to wake enough to realize where he was, but as soon as he had, his beautiful smile burst across his face. "Good morning, Robby," he purred.

"Did you sleep well?'

"The best sleep I've ever had. Did you?"

"I didn't sleep at all."

"I'm sorry."

"I'm not. I've never felt so well rested." For the first time in his life, Rob felt at peace. "I'll make us some breakfast."

Rob tried to rise, but Josh pulled him back down to the bed. "Have you ever been to Cuyahoga Valley National Park?"

"Yeah, of course," Rob answered.

"There's a trail there to a waterfall. And everyone always stops at the waterfall so I like to hike beyond it and be completely alone. It's kind of my private world. After the game, I thought maybe we could go out there."

"Sounds fun."

"Do you still have the leftover condoms?"

"You want to . . . ?" Rob asked.

"Only if you do. I don't want to rush you."

Rob got up and walked to his desk, unlocked the drawer, pulled out the condoms and tossed the box to Josh. "Get dressed," he said.

*   *   *   *   *

Rob had always admired the way Josh fit on the baseball diamond. He was as much a part of the field as the pitcher's mound or first base. He moved with a grace and sureness of knowing that this was the space he was made to occupy; as natural a part of his element as a dolphin in the ocean. He wore his uniform with such ease that it was a part of him. Rob liked watching the way the sun sparkled in the blondish hairs on Josh's forearms and the way his sweat seemed to run down his face in perfectly shaped drops. Rob never tired of watching Josh's every move and today he was even more fixated. Josh played better than Rob had ever seen, as though his feet didn't touch the ground. Josh went four-for-four including two homeruns and four RBIs.

After the game they drove out to Cuyahoga Valley National Park. There, out beyond the waterfall, in Josh's private world, they made love. They walked back through bushes almost as green as Josh's eyes and past the small waterfall which at twenty or so feet was dwarfed by the view Rob had seen of Niagara Falls as a kid, but Rob wondered if he had ever seen anything so beautiful as this small Ohio waterfall and this trail to paradise. He was really seeing the world for the first time. A world where baseball diamonds and waterfalls were more wonderful than he had ever known them to be. He thought of *The Wizard of Oz* when suddenly everything was in color.

Rob invited Josh for dinner and they giggled all through the meal, much to the confusion of the rest of the family. It was Rob instead of Josh who regaled the family with tales of his friend's ball field heroics. After dinner, Rob walked Josh to his car. "Thank you," Rob said. "For the most amazing day of my life."

"Let's have lots more days like this." Josh gently touched his arm, got in his car and drove away.

Meg touching Rob's shoulder finally awakened him from his stupor. "Are you just going to stand here all night?"

Rob realized the sun had set and he still hadn't moved from the driveway.

EIGHTEEN

Josh pitched and won on Monday then the team dropped the next two games, meaning they'd have to beat the Vikings on Thursday to make the playoffs. With only two days rest, Coach Hudson decided to use Josh on the mound. Josh was still playing as though he was on a cloud of invincibility and going into the fifth inning he had a no-hitter working. The rest of the Hawks were playing well, but had only two runs on the board.

As Danny Taylor batted, a pitch came way inside; he tried to dodge it, but it caught him full on the hand. He hollered in pain as the bat shot from his grasp. Both coaches ran to him.

They conferred quietly with Taylor then Coach Milnes started walking him toward the bench. "Farino, get some ice," the coach yelled. Jason did as he was told and Milnes attended to Danny.

Hudson looked down the bench. "Wardell! Take Taylor's place on first."

Rob hesitated. He was never really sure he wanted in a game and now he was positive he didn't. With a slim two-run lead and Josh's no-hitter at stake this was just the sort of responsibility he'd been determined to avoid. He looked around. What were the alternatives? He'd trust himself to play before he'd put Farino in. Hudson had made the only move he could.

"Today, Wardell," Brickman yelled.

Rob started toward the field. "Wardell," the coach said, beckoning him over. "If Beechler hits one, you've got to get around those bases. Listen to me and watch for my signs."

Rob could only nod. The look on the coach's face said Rob's lack of response wasn't exactly inspiring confidence. Rob forced a smile and tried to find a voice to reassure him. "Got it."

Buff did his job and sent the first pitch into right field, just fair. As soon as Rob could see there wasn't a chance of it being caught, he was running. An instant later he heard Coach Milnes behind him shouting, "Go! Go!"

Rob glanced at the fielder who now had the ball but ran into foul territory before he could stop his momentum. Rob didn't even think about stopping at second, but looked to third just to make sure. Hudson was yelling and waving his arm. The play would be at third and Rob sensed the ball coming in somewhere behind him. He hadn't slid since Little League and back then no one played for keeps. If he had to force his way to the bag, he was sure the large third baseman would crush him.

Rob tore towards third and suddenly the Viking player moved aside. Rob saw Hudson holding his hands up as though to stop Rob. Rob hit the bag and stopped just as the third baseman caught the throw which had gone wide.

"Time," Hudson yelled. He motioned for Rob to come to him. The coach put his arm around his shoulder and steered him away from the field. "How would you feel about a suicide squeeze?"

"Huh?" Again Rob regretted his less than inspirational reaction.

"You know Schlagel can lay it down and I know you've got the speed. I'll have Schlagel take the first two pitches so you can time your move, then I want you to go."

Rob shook his head. "If the first two are strikes he can't bunt on third. I've been watching this guy all game. Have Josh take the first pitch, I'll go on the second." Rob was surprised at how confident he sounded. He knew he couldn't be the cause of losing Josh's no hitter but Hudson was right, it was the perfect situation for a squeeze. "I'm sure. I'll get there."

"You can't go into their catcher; you'll have to go under him."

"I know."

Hudson slapped Rob on the butt as he returned to the base. Rob felt the need to try to provide himself with a bit of smoke-screen, so began to yell, "C'mon one-seven, hit one out of here! Knock it over the fence! C'mon Schlagel, you can blast one!"

The pitcher wound up and delivered. To Rob and Hudson's surprise, Josh took a full cut and missed. Had he missed the sign? Then Rob realized Josh had read his mind. He was swinging for the fences and deliberately missed to let Rob get ready and also to fake the opposing players into thinking he was going after the long ball. It worked. Both the infield and outfield backed up and into an even more pronounced left-handed batter shift.

Rob looked at Hudson, who looked nervous. Rob was afraid Hudson would call time to make sure Josh knew the sign, but that would call more attention to the upcoming play and Rob's life might literally depend on how well they pulled this off. "Coach, I'm sure Josh can smack one just where we need it," he said. Hudson seemed to be considering this, so Rob winked at him. Hudson smiled and started flashing signs at Josh. Most of them were nonsense signs, but there, just after the belt, Hudson went to his cap then his shoulder. The squeeze was on. Rob took his lead a little farther than last time, but not so far as to draw a throw. The pitcher went into his wind-up and Rob was gone. He had never willed his legs to move so fast and for a moment it seemed he might arrive at the plate the same instant the ball did.

Josh stuck out his bat and made contact. He dropped the ball about ten feet in front of the plate, just inside the third base line. Rob knew he was far ahead of the third baseman so there was no way he'd make this play. Out of the corner of his eye he saw the pitcher charging the ball, but Josh had bunted the ball so dead it was barely rolling and was still closest to the catcher. The catcher started to come out after it but the pitcher called him off. The pitcher got to the ball as the catcher headed back to the plate. It was going to be a three-way tie between Rob, the catcher and the ball. Rob picked the back corner of the plate as his objective. As soon as he was close enough, he dove head-first, arms extended. Josh was the only person on earth he'd do this for.

Smack! Rob heard the ball hit the catcher's mitt, he saw the mitt swinging towards him, and he could only try to dive lower. The mitt came around and caught him hard on the left thigh just as his left hand found the rubber edge of the plate and he got a mouthful and two eyes-full of dirt.

He kept sliding until the catcher toppled backwards onto his legs which brought his slide to an abrupt halt. Through the dust and pain Rob heard, "Safe!"

The catcher was instantly off him, screaming, "I tagged him! I tagged him!"

Rob rolled over to take inventory. He felt no pain. The elation that he had scored to help cinch Josh's victory was a great anesthetic. Hudson was standing over him now and the opposing coach had joined the argument with the ump. Corey Brickman was standing over Rob, his bat on his shoulder. "You okay?" It was Corey who asked first.

Rob smiled. "Never better."

Much to Rob's shock it was Brickman who held out a hand and Rob used it to get up. His leg hurt and his chest ached from where the wind was knocked out of him when he bit the dust, but he just smiled.

"Way to go," Brickman said. He slapped Rob's biceps, for the first time in a gesture of camaraderie, not evil.

As Rob's head cleared a bit, he realized most of the team was up and waiting for him. He had never felt such adulation before. But all he could think about was the one person he had done it for. He looked to first base where Josh was beaming at him. Josh touched his hand to his helmet brim in salute. Rob touched his own helmet in return.

Brickman and Acosta both struck out ending the inning far too quickly and now they had to take the field. The idea that he might do something in the field to mess up Josh's no hitter had Rob's guts tied tighter than the laces on his spikes.

Hudson pulled Brickman and Rob aside, "Brickman, you're moving to short. Wardell, take second, but let Brickman cover the bag. Take all of the practice throws now. Brickman, throw him some and let him warm up."

Rob was relieved that no balls came to him in the inning: Josh struck out the first and third batters and the number two man hit a grounder to short that Brickman handled smoothly. Rob was glad he had time to adjust to being in the game before he actually had to do anything. The Hawks also went three-up, three down in their half of the inning. The Vikings had their last shot in the bottom of the seventh.

The first pitch Josh threw was a mistake. A fat slider down the middle that failed to slide much. The batter caught the meat of it and smashed it just over Josh's head. Josh leapt but it was too high. Brickman was way out of position toward third so Rob took two giant steps and dove. His second dive of the day and coming down from this one would hurt even more than the first since there was no way to brace himself and he was flying parallel to the ground at a much greater height than the surface dive that had taken him into home. He had his eyes focused on the ball and just prayed his glove would get there.

The ball hit his glove and Rob squeezed tight. He gripped hard as he prepared for his emergency landing with no gear down. His body slammed into the ground. What ribs weren't broken in the play at the plate had to have been now. He was sure he'd lose consciousness any second, but before he did he had to do one thing. He rolled over and held up the glove with the ball still in it to prove to any doubters that he'd held on.

115

"Out!" The umpire yelled.

"Yes!" Rob recognized the whistled *S* as belonging to only one person.

Rob felt the ball yanked from his glove. Corey Brickman stood over him. "Nice catch."

"Thanks," Rob wheezed.

Brickman threw the ball to third then extended his hand again. "I don't want to spend the whole game picking you up." Brick smiled.

Rob slowly came to his feet. He saw stars for a moment and as they cleared, he saw Josh coming off the mound and toward him. Rob had never seen so much love and gratitude in his life. He knew if they got close he'd want to kiss him. Rob held up his hand to wave Josh off.

Josh stopped, smiled and said, "Good catch." But there was so much more behind those words that Rob glowed.

"Thanks," Rob answered with a smile and tone that echoed Josh's sentiments.

"Bobby, you okay?" It was Buff coming over from first to check on him.

"Yeah, fine." Actually he wasn't sure he was physically fine, but he was too high to care about minor things like broken bones or the need for oxygen in his collapsed lungs.

"You okay, Wardell?" This time it was the coach.

"Fine!" After being touched with their concern, he now wished they would quit treating him like a little kid. He was fine, he was a ballplayer and he was ready to play ball. He slapped his glove against his leg to send up a cloud of dust and walked back to his position shouting over his shoulder, "C'mon one-seven. Two more outs!"

Another strikeout and a sorry excuse for a ground ball to the mound that Josh flipped underhand to first and Josh's first no-hitter was in the books. Josh was already to the first base side of the mound so he just turned and made a line right for Rob. He grabbed him, picked him up and kissed him. Rob was shocked and wanted to tell Josh to put him down before the whole team came down on them, but it was too late. The whole team did swarm them, but with shouts of joy. The kiss must've been seen as the crazed exuberance of a guy who just played the most amazing game of his career and had his no-hitter saved by a spectacular catch. A solitary walk and an early error by Taylor had allowed the only two Vikings on base. Two runners short of a perfect game.

Rob felt himself being pulled away from Josh and for a moment he wondered if this was when the tarring and feathering began, but instead he was lifted in the air and found himself atop Buff Beechler and a moment later Josh joined him on high as several other teammates hoisted their pitcher in the air. Above the team, Rob smiled at Josh who smiled back.

The opposing teams lined up for the handshakes. Rob heard several of them congratulate Josh. He was surprised when several said "Nice catch" to Rob. As he was walking off the field a middle-aged man, probably the father of one of one of the opposing players, hollered to him from behind the backstop, "Nice slide and nice catch. You're a helluva ballplayer. I'm surprised you don't start."

NINETEEN

Josh and Rob went out to dinner to celebrate, then to Cuyahoga Valley National Park. Josh took Rob's hand as soon as he put the car in park. He turned to him. "Thank you."

"You didn't believe me when I said I would do anything for you?" Rob beamed.

"If I ever doubted it, I don't now. You were amazing."

"You were pretty good yourself."

"We make a great team."

"We do," Rob smiled. "But you know Strongsville is going to kill us on Monday?"

"They won't. But if they do, after today I'd die happy." Josh's sideways grin lent proof to the statement then they finished the kiss they had started on the baseball field.

*　　*　　*　　*　　*

By the time Rob woke up, his parents would have long been at work. Rob loved teacher *In Service* days. In fact he loved pretty much every day these days. He immediately called Josh who was eagerly awaiting his call and came to get him. Josh had told him his mother would be gone with the younger kids until dinnertime. They spent another day *hiking* in Cuyahoga Valley; Josh had to be home for dinner so he dropped Rob on the fly.

Rob was on the porch when he heard a honk and turned to see Josh waving at Meg who was getting out of Ashley's mother's car. Meg gave him a big smile and waved back. Ashley stared in awe. Rob went inside where his dad was setting the table while his mom was in the kitchen putting the finishing touches on dinner.

"Hi," his dad said, setting down the plates. "I saw the headline in the paper that Josh had a no-hitter, but I didn't have time to read the article. He must've done well yesterday."

"You should've read the article," Megan smirked. She turned to her brother and slugged him in the stomach. "Everyone was talking about you at the mall."

"Talking about you?" his mother asked, putting the salad on the table.

His father unfolded the *Harrisonburg Herald* and flipped to the sports page. "Nice photo!" he said and quickly skimmed down the columns then read, "*Schlagel helped his own cause with a perfectly executed bunt in the fifth inning which scored second baseman Bobby Wardell on a squeeze. Wardell slid in under the tag of Viking catcher Bryan Murray to add to the Hawks' thin lead.*"

He stopped reading and Rob saw him looking over the paper at his son.

"Keep reading," Meg urged.

Mr. Wardell mumbled as he skimmed another paragraph or two, then read, "*Schlagel's no-hitter was in jeopardy in the seventh when Viking shortstop Jeremy Clark ripped a shot up the middle. Hawks' second baseman, Wardell, a junior playing in his first game of the season, made a dramatic dive to stab the ball out of the air and cancel the sure single. A strikeout then a groundout to Schlagel ended the inning. The two heroes of the day, Schlagel and Wardell were carried off the field by their teammates. The*

Hawks must face Strongsville on Monday to advance to the Regionals."

Rob liked the way that sounded, *Schlagel and Wardell.* His father stopped reading and looked at Rob again. The article wasn't quite accurate—it wasn't his first game of the year, but his contribution in the other game was so minor that the paper could be forgiven that mistake.

His mother hugged and kissed him. "Why didn't you tell us?"

"I got in after you were in bed and got up after you left."

"Ashley said her brother said everyone was shocked. No one had a clue Bobby was that good." Ashley's brother, Clint Dominick, was a relief pitcher who rarely got to relieve.

"Sit down," Mom urged. "I want to hear all about it."

"I would've loved to have seen that!" his father said, folding back the paper to show his wife the photo of Rob and Josh on their teammates' shoulders.

It hadn't occurred to Rob that there might've been reporters or photographers at the game. He wondered if they caught the kiss as well.

Mrs. Wardell grabbed the paper. "I'm going to have to run out after dinner and buy twenty copies of the paper."

Rob said nothing, but he wanted a few for himself. Him and Josh basking in their shared glory. If his life ever sank into its former nothingness, that photo and the memory of that moment could sustain him forever.

*   *   *   *   *

Fame is fleeting, as Rob was quickly reminded. On Monday when Rob saw Corey Brickman in the hall, Corey smiled. Rob smiled back and said, "Hi, Brick."

Taylor stepped from behind Corey and said, "Only his friends can call him that." Taylor pinned Rob against a locker. "And don't think 'cause you made a lucky catch and got your face in the paper that you are taking my spot in the line-up!"

"I don't," Rob murmured. It had never occurred to him that one stellar day would qualify him to permanently replace Taylor.

Taylor let go of him and Rob started toward his locker listening to Taylor and Brickman laugh in his wake.

*   *   *   *   *

The Strongsville game ended 15-1; the Hawks' score coming from a solo homerun by Josh Schlagel. Everything that could go wrong went wrong as though H-burg had saved all of their mistakes to make in one day. Buff was shelled off the mound by the second inning. Andrews, Virtusio, Dominick and even Schlagel had each taken an inning in relief but none of them had been able to stop the hemorrhaging. Seven errors in the infield — none of them by Josh — was a team, if not a league, record.

"There's always next year," Rob said as they drove home. "You were just starting to hit your stride. You're going to do great next year."

"So are you. We need to practice over the summer and you'll have Brick's spot at second."

"I dunno about that."

"Or you can take third since Rydell is graduating."

"I have a hard time with the throw."

"We'll work on the throw. But if you prove yourself at second, maybe Coach Hudson will move Brick to third and put you at second. It would be fun to have our own half of the infield."

"That'd be great," Rob said. "It's going seem strange to have all this extra time. You getting a summer job?"

"I've got one. My father got me one doing track maintenance for the railroad. It's grueling, backbreaking work in the hot sun, but he said it'll make a man out of me."

"You're already a man," Rob said, sliding his hand into Josh's lap. "Too bad you have a job. I was going to try to get you one with me. My mom got me a job where she works. I'll be doing warehouse stuff. Loading trucks and pulling orders, I guess."

"So you'll be getting all buff, too?"

"But not tanned like you."

"Are you going to be working Monday through Friday?" Josh asked.

"Yep. You?"

"Most of the time, unless there is an emergency or something, but that's great. We'll have our weekends free together." Rob looked at Josh and smiled. Josh smiled back and continued, "I have lots of plans for us. I've never been to Cedar Point. Or the Rock and Roll Hall of Fame. And the Brewers are playing the Pirates in three weeks. I thought we could drive down to Pittsburgh . . . "

"You've been thinking about this a lot. How did you know I'd say yes?"

"I was just hoping," Josh answered. "And we can work out this summer. I can get you to bulk up a bit and you can get me to run."

"Okay, starting tomorrow after school, we lift in my garage then we run."

"Promise me you won't wear a shirt for either, and you're on."

"I was thinking Friday night . . . " Rob began, but stopped when Josh shook his head. "What?"

"I have a date with Jenny."

"You're still dating her?"

"Yeah, I guess so. I think it's best. It keeps my parents..."

"I thought we . . . " Rob began.

"We do. We are. But I have to keep up appearances."

Rob nodded, accepting. In spite of the inconvenience of sharing Josh with Jenny, Rob knew it was going to be the best summer of his, or anyone's life.

TWENTY

Rob had always looked forward to the end of school, but more so now that the summer meant time with Josh.

Not that they needed anything to make their time together more special, but they were always doing something wonderul. The trip to the amusement park at Cedar Point. To Pittsburgh for the Brewers' game. To Toledo to catch a Mudhens game.

Each day that Rob spent with Josh he was sure was the happiest day of his life, but then the next day they were together was even better. Each night he got what he was sure was the best sleep he'd ever get, but the next night would be even more restful with seven or eight hours straight through without the need of a nocturnal workout. He saved his workouts for the daylight hours with Josh. The camping trips, when they could sleep nestled in each other's arms, were beyond heaven.

Rob found himself needing condoms so often he was embarrassed to buy them locally and would have Josh stop at one of the big chain drug stores where no one knew him.

When no one was home, or sometimes even if someone was, they'd fool around in Rob's room or go into the woods on the Wardell property. A few close calls with the unexpected entries of other Wardells often just added to the excitement. And every chance they got, they went to Josh's secret spot out beyond the waterfall.

As they drove home after one such evening, Josh said, "You don't know how hard this is on me. I spend this time with you and I'm so happy. I can just be me and be with you and then I have to go home and become this completely different person, watch everything I say, every move I make. Sometimes I feel like I'm becoming schizophrenic, splitting into these two different people who barely know each other anymore."

"I know what you mean. Ever since the first time you kissed me, I've wanted to tell Meg, my parents, everyone. I've wanted to climb out my bedroom window and hang a banner saying how happy I am. But I have to shut it all down and say nothing."

Josh looked at Rob. "I don't think you really do know what it's like. Life at your house is nothing compared to mine. If your parents found out, they wouldn't kill us."

*   *   *   *   *

It was a typical Monday with Rob awaiting Josh's nightly visit. As far as the Schlagels knew, more than half of these visits were to Jenny, but in reality it was more like a 90-10 split in Rob's favor. But the evening wore on and Josh didn't show. Rob started getting worried, but he knew he wasn't supposed to call Josh's house. He had been there a few times, but the place creeped him out and he felt on trial the whole time he was there. He never called Josh, but never had reason to; Josh was either at the Wardells or calling Rob.

Tuesday Josh called from a pay phone on the way home from work and asked if he could come over. "Do you have to ask?" Rob replied.

Once they were in Rob's room with the door closed, Rob asked, "Where were you yesterday?'

Josh looked away before he looked back and answered, "Danny Taylor came over."

"Why do you hang around with him?"

Josh hesitated. "My mother thinks we're friends."

"Are you friends?"

There was a longer hesitation. "No."

Somehow just asking the question had changed the mood in the room and when Rob moved in to kiss Josh, he moved away on the bed — the first time Rob had been rejected by Josh. When Rob tried to move closer, Josh stood and walked to the window.

Meg knocked and shouted through the door. "If you two are done making out in there, dinner is ready!" she teased. Josh and Rob tensed.

Saturday they were to go to see Erie's minor league team, the Sea Wolves, play — part of Josh's goal to hit every ballpark within a 300 mile radius — and hang out at the beaches on Presque Isle, but Josh never showed up. Rob's parents asked several times what was up, but when, an hour past the appointed time Josh still had not showed up, Rob couldn't take their stares any longer and went for a run.

He knew he wouldn't hear from Josh Sunday morning while he was at church, but he expected a call and explanation during the afternoon, but none came. Rob spent the day working out and running and working in the fields trying not to drive himself crazy.

He had been neglecting the fields, but he sensed his parents were so happy to see him happy that they didn't care. He still did his share of chores on Sunday mornings and on the evenings when Josh was out with Jenny.

A few weeks earlier Meg had said to him, "Mom asked me if you were in love."

Rob's eyes burst wide. He took a moment to catch his breath before he asked, "Why would she ask that?"

"She said she's never seen you so happy."

"What did you say?"

"I said, 'Bobby in love? Get real.'"

"Thanks."

"What are sisters for? And I told her that if I was hanging around with Josh as much as you are, I'd be happy, too."

Rob turned away for fear his face might give something away. "What did she say to that?"

"She just laughed."

Now Rob was wondering if he was falling in love with Josh. Or Josh with him. As close as he felt to Josh, on days like this, with no phone call and no explanation, he wondered if he knew Josh at all. He sometimes thought Josh could look into his eyes and see right into his soul. All of his thoughts, fears and desires. But when he looked into Josh's eyes, he saw a luminescent green curtain pulled down that admitted no one.

Monday at work, Rob was having a hard time concentrating. He hated his job. He had hoped he might be able to do a real man's work, loading heavy boxes of floor tiles, but on the first day of the summer job, Mr. Trent had taken one look at Rob's size and gave him a metal clipboard and told him he was to check all of the orders against the invoices as they went on the trucks. If a box was missing, he had to tell these older men who had been there for years that they forgot something. Every time he had to do that, he was met with a look that told him how out of line he was thinking he could order them around. He always tried to ask as nicely as possible, but they took it as badly as possible.

He was happy to have survived another day to head home and see Josh, but again the evening brought no phone call, no visit. He wanted to call and make sure Josh was okay, but he didn't want to risk having to talk to either of Josh's parents: his mother, who was a known terror and his father, who was still an unknown one. Rob was tempted to ask Meg to call thinking a phone call from a girl might sit better with Josh's family, but he could think of no plausible reason for asking her to check up on Josh.

Since they had been together, he'd never had to go this long without Josh. His life had sucked for so long, he figured it was only a matter of time until it returned to sucking. Josh was bound to come to his senses sooner or later and realize he belonged with Jenny or even Danny, but not Rob. Rob found himself doing his first middle of the night sweat session in weeks.

Tuesday at work was another day of having to will himself to really look at what he was doing. He didn't want to hear it from Trent or the ignorant gorillas of the loading dock if he was the cause of an order mis-shipped.

Over dinner, Mr. Wardell asked the family if any of them had been in the garage as he was leaving for work. They all denied it and he was just about to explain why he was asking when the phone rang and, as always, Meg answered it. "Hey, Josh," she said, her face lighting up.

Rob was out of his chair and running upstairs. "I'll take it in the sewing room," he yelled.

He picked up the phone and Meg was chattering away to Josh. "I've got it," he said into the phone. Meg kept talking, but getting monosyllabic answers from Josh instead of his usual teasing.

"Hang up!" Rob barked.

"Geez," Meg said, "What got into you? I'll talk to you later, Josh."

"See ya, Meg," Josh said and she hung up.

There was silence.

Finally Rob could take it no longer and said, "Well?"

"I'm sorry."

"Where were you?"

"Away. Rob, please don't be mad at me." Josh's tone was pitiful. "I really can't talk now. I'm at a pay phone. My time is almost up."

"So come over." As angry as Rob was he still wanted an explanation and he still wanted to see him.

"Not now. I'll call you."

The line went dead.

All the sit ups and push-ups Rob could force his body to do did nothing to bring sleep. The next night there was no word from Josh and Rob could feel his life slipping back into days of grief, nights of agony.

TWENTY-ONE

The next night as Rob and his mother pulled into the driveway, he saw the side door to the garage was open just a crack. Rob looked at his mother. She shook her head.

"See where Meg is," he said. He stood back to watch the garage door as his mother went into the house. His mother returned a minute later. "She's watching TV. She hasn't been in the garage."

Rob grabbed the shovel that had been left leaning against the back porch.

"Should I get your dad's gun?" she asked.

"I'm sure it's nothing," Rob said. "Dad probably left it open."

"Be careful," she said as Rob walked in the door and flipped the light on.

There was a noise beside him and Rob turned, the shovel poised.

"Hey, Rob," Josh said.

"Schlagel! What are you doing?"

"I figured you'd be home any minute so I just came in to get the basketball," Josh lied.

Rob threw down the shovel and demanded, "What the fuck?" Josh tried to smile, but it didn't work. Rob stuck his head out the door and said to his mother, "It's only Josh."

She was saying something, but Rob closed the door. Rob turned to face his friend.

"Sorry," Josh said. "Didn't mean to scare you."

"Where have you been?'

"I was away."

"Where?"

Josh turned away. "I went to Brickman's father's hunting cabin with the guys."

"Why?"

Josh still would not face him. "It's kind of a team tradition thing. A football thing. It was really last minute." Rob wasn't sure what to say. Josh filled the gap. "Please don't be mad at me. I really need a friend right now." He turned back to Rob and was crying. As angry as Rob was he wanted to rush to Josh and hug him but the force field of pain around Josh made him want to keep his distance even more. "I got fired. I missed the last two days of work and didn't call in until this afternoon. My father is going to kill me."

"What did you do, drink all weekend?"

"No. Josh pointed to a spot on the floor of the garage. "I've spent the last two nights here. I'm afraid to go home."

"Why didn't you come to the house?"

"I couldn't."

The answers were making less sense. "Josh, please. Tell me what's wrong?"

Josh flung himself at Rob and buried his head on the smaller boy's shoulder. Just seeing his friend in such agony reduced Rob to tears as well and he held Josh until his breathing returned to something close to normal.

"Tell me what's going on," Rob pleaded.

"I can't."

"You can tell me anything."

"No, I can't."

"I have to go," Josh choked.

"Where?"

"Home. Every day I stay away will just make it worse."

"Where's your car?"

"I left it in the cemetery."

"Do you want a ride?"

"No, I need to run." Josh looked at Rob. "Now you have me trying to run my problems away, too."

"If things are too bad, you know you can always come back."

Josh turned to leave then turned back. "Thank you. Goodbye, Rob."

Before Rob could respond, Josh was gone, and Rob had the horrible feeling that he might have seen Josh for the last time.

Rob got no sleep once again and, come morning, his chest and abdominal muscles pained him as much as the ache in his head.

*   *   *   *   *

The next few days at work were worse than usual and Rob did mess up a couple of tile orders, but with no sleep and his mind only on Josh, it was impossible to focus on trivialities like which customer got Navajo Sunset and who got Arizona Sand.

When the phone rang Sunday afternoon, Rob lunged at it ahead of Meg. A somewhat familiar voice said, "Is Rob there?"

"Speaking."

"Rob, it's Mat. Mathias Schlagel. Josh's . . . "

"Yes, Mat. How are you? How is Josh?"

"I'm fine. Josh's so-so. He asked me to call you and I have to make this quick, but he didn't want you to worry. He's grounded, but said he'll try to call soon."

"Thanks. Tell him I said hi." Rob wanted to tell Mat a lot more than that, but didn't dare. He hung up the phone and went out to run.

The next two weeks were hell without Josh, but at least he knew where Josh was—stuck at home. Or thought he knew.

Rob found himself back working the fields more than he had been all summer and when he harvested the first corn of the season and knew it would be way too much for the family he took the excess to Greiner's Market.

"Hey, Bobby," Frank Greiner said when Rob got out of the SUV. "Haven't seen you all summer. Have you grown?"

Rob shrugged. "It's been a while."

Frank had always said to call him Frank, but considering Frank was old enough to be his grandfather, Rob tried to avoid calling him anything. Frank had known him since before he was born and as close as their families had been for generations, Frank almost was his grandfather.

"How much are the beans?" a woman shouted. Rob went to her aid.

It was an hour later when Frank noticed Rob was still working and said, "Are you still here?"

"They won't let me leave," Rob said, indicating the line of customers that had formed around him.

"I could use you, if you can stay," Frank said. "That stupid Vaughn kid quit on me so I'm short-handed."

"I can stay." Since age ten, Rob had worked from time to time at the market.

"Want a fulltime job?" Frank asked as he rang up another sale.

"I have one," Rob answered, not missing a beat in waiting on his own line of customers.

"You like it?" Frank said, before turning to the man in front of him. "That will be fourteen-thirty-seven."

For a moment, thinking about how much he hated the flooring business, Rob was tempted, but then thought of something else. "I know someone who is looking."

"Who?"

"Josh Schlagel."

"The football star?"

132

Rob had forgotten how closely Frank followed the H-burg Hawks. Greiner's Farm Market always had the full-page ad on the back of the football programs.

"Yep," Rob said. "He's a friend of mine." At least Rob hoped they were still friends.

"Hi, Bobby." Rob looked up to see the next customer waiting was Mrs. Dominick, Ashley and Clint's mother. "How are you?"

"Good, and you?" he asked.

"Fine. You've changed so much I almost didn't recognize you," she said. "I haven't seen you in months. Not since you had your picture in the paper. I guess you're turning into quite the baseball star."

*   *   *   *   *

When Rob opened the wooden screen door of the house, Meg was waiting. "Where've you been all afternoon?"

"Working at Greiner's."

"Josh called twice. He said he'd call later if he could. What's the deal with that?"

"His parents go to that whacked out church and have more rules for their kids than you'd believe."

"No wonder Mat is so weird. I'm amazed Josh turned out so well."

"Stop saying Mat's weird. He's a nice guy. He just looks weird. How would you like it if people thought you were weird after you had an accident and got all scarred up?"

"Sorry."

"But you're right. I'm amazed Josh isn't weirder than he is given that family's strangeness."

"Josh isn't weird," she protested.

The phone ringing ended their argument as they both lunged for it. Rob grabbed it and Meg punched him in the stomach. "Hey, Josh," he said. Rob could feel his innards turning to Jell-O at the sound of the voice he had missed so long. "I'll take this upstairs. Hang on."

He turned to Meg. "When I get it, hang it up. And I mean, hang up!" He dashed out of the room and up the stairs. Three hours later, after ignoring numerous calls to dinner, Rob came back down, smiling for the first time in weeks.

"What's up with Josh?" Meg asked.

"He's un-grounded. And he's happy I got him a job. That should help smooth things over with his parents."

"You got him a job?" his mother asked.

"Yep, at Greiner's. Frank asked me, but I figured it wasn't fair to quit Trent's with only a few weeks left in the summer."

"I'm glad you didn't," she replied. "I know you're not happy at Trent's and you get along so well with Frank."

Rob wondered how she knew he wasn't happy at Trent's since he had never said anything to her about it.

Her husband looked at her and smiled, "Is it really possible, could our kids actually start acting responsibly?"

*   *   *   *   *

After his first day of work at the market, Josh came to the Wardell's for dinner. He was his usual polite, funny self and Rob thought things were back to normal. After dinner they went upstairs and once the door was closed, Rob grabbed at Josh's shirt to pull it off.

"Don't," Josh protested.

"Why not?"

"Your parents might hear."

"They're downstairs with the TV on. We've done it before." Rob again pulled at Josh's shirt and Josh slapped his hand away.

"What's wrong?" Rob asked.

"Why do you have to grab at me like that?"

"Huh? You damn near rape me every time we're alone. I just wanted to hold you. I missed you."

"And I missed you."

"You're not acting like it," Rob said.

"I missed you more than you could know." Josh threw himself at Rob and clutched him close.

Rob guided him to the bed and silently held him for a while. "Do you want to tell me what is going on?"

"I can't."

"If you're embarrassed 'cause you've got bruises from your dad, it's okay, I've seen them before."

"Would you do me a favor?" Josh asked.

"Sure, anything."

"Don't ask. Stop asking. Just hold me."

*   *   *   *   *

After another week of strangeness, life with Josh soon fell back into its old pattern. He was not only willing to have Rob touch him, he was giving him every opportunity to do so. Now that he was working adjacent to the Wardell farmlette he came over almost every evening. He and Rob could work out and hang out. If Josh had to work Saturday, Rob would work with him at the farm market and they could still spend the day together. As school approached, for the first time in his life Rob found himself not dreading it.

Whether it was the working out or the hard work, both of them had become taller and more buff over the summer. Rob felt that now the weight of his lonely world had been lifted from his shoulders he could finally grow unhindered.

As they lay entwined on Rob's bed after a long day at the produce stand, Rob said, "You know, I was thinking, I should go out for football."

Josh sat up. "Are you crazy?"

"I just thought, I've been working out, put on some weight . . . "

"No."

"It would give us a chance to spend more time..."

"No."

"Don't you think I could handle it?" Rob asked.

"Football, yes. The football team, no. They'd kill you. Please don't." Josh pinned Rob to the bed. "This is the only tackling I want you to get."

They rolled around wrestling on the bed until they fell off and crashed to the floor laughing.

TWENTY-TWO

Football practice started a week later and since Josh was off at practice, Rob had volunteered to take Meg back-to-school shopping.

"You are such a liar!" Megan yelled at her brother as she ran in the door of their house ahead of him.

"I'm never taking you anywhere again!" Rob said as he shoved past his sister.

Their mother, who had been listening for the car to pull into the gravel drive, stood up. "What happened?"

"Your daughter," Rob pointed an accusing finger, "Was trying to pick up the guy at the Gap!"

"I wasn't trying to pick him up," Meg replied. "I was just flirting. He was cute."

"He had to be twenty years old!" Rob taunted.

"So?"

"You're fifteen!"

Turning back to his mother he said, "Your daughter. The slut." Meg slugged her brother in the stomach.

"Josh is going to be jealous." Rob grinned.

She pinned him against the gun cabinet next to the door. "And for the last time, I do not have a crush on Josh."

"Megan, stop." The use of her full name and his tone made it clear this was not going to be their father's usual injunction to stop teasing. Meg and Rob stopped laughing. Rob noticed that his parents were in the center of the large living room—the good couch and chairs reserved for entertaining in between the informal seating areas facing a fireplace at one end and a TV at the other.

Their mother sat back down and pointed to the large footstool halfway between her and her husband. "Bobby, please sit down," she said.

Meg cast Rob a *whatever you did, it sounds serious* look.

"I was kidding about her being a slut . . . " Rob started to apologize.

His father quickly shook his head like a pitcher shaking off the wrong sign. "Bobby, er, uh, Robert . . . Rob, there's no easy way to say this."

"Your mother . . . well . . . tell him." The distraught man looked at his wife.

One small antique lamp lit only the immediate vicinity occupied by his parents. His mother's glasses lay on the table next to her. Rob now noticed she was crying as she began softly, "I got a call from Wendy Dominick." It took him a moment to register that she meant Ashley and Clint's mother. "Today, after practice, Josh . . . Josh is in the hospital. Wendy said he's in 'serious but stable' condition. They said he's going to be okay," she tried to reassure him.

"What happened?" Rob asked.

His parents gave each other looks that left Rob feeling that the news he'd just heard was not the worst news they'd had that evening. Rob's lungs didn't seem to be functioning and he found himself taking small gulps of air.

Bob Wardell looked at his son then looked away as he said in a voice that fought for control with every word, "Clint told his mother there was an incident in the locker room after practice . . . "

He didn't need to hear more. He could guess the rest. He nodded his head to make the words stop and they did.

His father looked past his son's head at a spot on the wall and sighed, "Afterwards, Josh tried to kill himself."

Rob's eyes and stomach instantly launched into a competition as to which would burst first.

"What?" Meg asked. "He's like Mr. Perfect, why would he . . . ?

Rob's look at Meg told her to stop talking and she did. Both parents looked at Rob. He knew why. And they knew why. Rob tried hard to stifle tears and looked up with the same mask of terror he had seen on the one and only deer he'd ever had in his sights. He hadn't had the nerve to fire then, but he knew the look of impending death. Somehow Rob found the courage to say, "I need to see Josh."

His father shook his head. "Not now." There was no anger in his voice at all. It was said matter-of-factly, leaving no room for discussion. "Robert." There was another long pause. Saying the name was completely unnecessary since the son was hanging on every word, but he repeated it, "Robert." There was another pause. "Please go . . . please go upstairs. Your mother and I . . . would you please just go upstairs. We'll talk in the morning."

Rob walked towards the stairs but stopped, turned and said something he rarely said, "I love you guys. Good night." There was no response from either parent. He waited a moment then began climbing.

He heard Meg's fast footsteps gaining on him.

"Bobby," she said. "What . . . " she started to ask, but when he turned to look at her, she stopped.

Rob walked the last mile to his room. As he was closing the door Megan said, "Good night, Bobby."

Rob fell on his bed burying his head in his pillow to muffle his sobs.

He didn't know when he fell asleep, but he was still clothed and his body wet with sweat and the pillow damp when he awoke. The sun was up and shining through the window. There were sounds downstairs.

He lay in bed a moment and tried to clear his head of the raging nightmares that failed to vanish when he awoke. His best friend was in the hospital and his parents now knew he liked Josh. Really liked Josh. They probably thought he was ___. Even now Rob could not bring himself to say the word.

Those two pillars of horror brought him fully awake. He sucked in a deep breath that exhaled as a cough. He felt awful and was sure he had cried more than slept all night. He stood and almost immediately teetered over. He yanked off his shoes and socks and ripped off the shirt that was stuck to his body. He hoped a warm shower would rinse away some of the terrifying haze that engulfed him. Maybe when he was fully awake he'd realize it had all been a bad dream. It had to be. There was no way Josh could be hurt and their secret could be out.

There was a very soft knock at his door. Someone had been listening for him to stir. His father's voice said quietly, "Bobby?"

He glanced at the clock. It was past time for his parents and him to be at work. He crossed the room and opened the door. He was still shirtless and shoeless.

"Hi, Dad," he said with a forced calm, although his voice crashed and caught in his throat.

His father stepped into the room. His tone was as slow and low as it had been the previous evening. "Your mother and I didn't get much sleep last night." Rob nodded silently. "It's going to take us a while to . . . " he searched the wall as though he would find the right word there. Not finding the right one, he threw out a few " . . . come to terms . . . accept . . . comprehend . . . "

Rob again nodded. He waited for a minute for his father to go on, but there was nothing further, so Rob said, "I need to see Josh."

"We understand. We're very concerned also. We called the hospital. Josh was in surgery."

"Surgery? For what?"

"One of his eyes was badly damaged." Mr. Wardell winced. "He could lose the sight in it." Queasy, Rob staggered to the bed to sit down. "There was also internal bleeding. They had to go in to stop it. In his . . . " Mr. Wardell paused. No words that he could find seemed to be finding their way out. "They apparently kicked him, uh, down there."

"Jesus," Rob said as the room began to spin.

His father went on, still studying baseball posters instead of looking at his son, "Josh made his way home and took an overdose of Tylenol. They said he took everything in the medicine cabinet, but what did the most damage was the Tylenol. Apparently a large dose does terrible things to your liver. They had to stabilize him over night before they could operate."

Rob looked down and covered his mouth. He was afraid he was going to vomit.

"Bobby, are you okay?" It was his mother's voice, but it took him a moment for him to look up and recognize her in his doorway. "Did you tell him?" she asked her husband.

"Tell me what?" Rob asked.

His mother sat on the bed next to him and put her arm around him. "Bobby," she took another breath before she could go on. "Bobby . . . "

"What?" he asked, still staring at his hands in his lap.

"He has several broken ribs and his left wrist is broken. It might be a few days until he can walk—his legs are very badly bruised from where they kicked him." Rob winced and his mother went on as gently as possible. "Josh is in pretty bad shape. He has a broken nose, and a broken orbital socket, you know, eye socket . . . " Rob looked up as his mother drew a line with her finger around her eye. " . . . Broken cheek bone, concussion, fifty-some stitches for various cuts, multiple bruises, particularly in the groin area. There was internal bleeding, they did surgery to drain some blood . . . "

"Enough. Is he going to be okay?"

"The good news is if the eye surgery goes okay, everything else should heal. He should be okay in a few months."

Rob thought, but did not say, *not quite*, knowing the internal scars may take even longer to heal. Instead he asked, "Can I go to the hospital?"

"I'm not sure there's much point," his mother said. "I imagine he'll be under sedation most of the day."

"I still want to be with him. See him."

His mother nodded. "Get showered and your dad and I'll be downstairs."

The shower did nothing to wash away the pain. When Rob came downstairs, his parents were at the kitchen table. His father had grip on a coffee cup so tight that it looked like he might shatter the ceramic.

"Shouldn't you be at work?" Rob asked.

"I took the day off," his father answered.

His mother added, "I called Mr. Trent and told him you were sick and I was staying home to look after you. I'll make it up next Monday. Sit down and I'll make you some breakfast."

"Monday is Memorial Day," Rob said. "They're closed. And I'm not hungry, I just want to go."

"It's Labor Day, but you're right they'll be closed. And you have to eat something. I'll call him later and tell him I'll make it up sometime."

"If I eat anything, I'll throw up. I just want to go."

His father barely moved his head in the slightest of nods. His eyes met his son's. "Several guys beat up Josh because . . . he's . . . I don't want you going alone. I'll drive you." Rob didn't like the idea of the long drive to the hospital with his father, but also knew it wasn't a matter open to discussion. "If you go to see him, you know what people will say about you. This is a small town. Someone will know, and everyone will know."

Rob hadn't thought about that, and what it would mean, but he also knew no matter what the consequences, he was in earnest when he said, "I have to go."

Like his father's statement, this was not something to be debated. "I'll take him," he said to his wife. "Why don't you wait for Meg to wake up? After last night she'll be wondering where we are and what's going on."

Once they were in the SUV, his father cleared his throat several times and then quietly asked, "Is it true?"

Rob hesitated too long before saying anything and the silence answered the question.

His father drove a mile or two and then cleared his throat several more times before he asked, "Are you sure?"

"What do you want me to say?"

"I mean, I know you like Josh, he is a good guy, but . . . "

Rob just stared out the window, first at farmland, then at suburbs and strip malls, and couldn't even begin to form an answer when so many larger thoughts rocketed through his mind. He was still trying to grasp the truth. Josh had tried to kill himself. If someone with as much going for him as Josh couldn't hold his own in this world, what chance did Rob have? Rob glanced over at his father; his father's clear discomfiture wasn't helping. But how could his father be surprised? His father wasn't stupid. His whole life, from deer hunting on, there had certainly been enough signs.

TWENTY-THREE

"Do you want me to come up with you?" his father asked at the hospital. Rob shook his head. "I'll wait here," his father said, pointing to a seat in the lobby.

Rob inquired at the reception desk, stepped away, hesitated, then stepped back and hesitated again. The gray-haired woman with a tiny face asked, "Was there something else?"

"Is he alone? Does he have visitors?"

She replied, "No, he hasn't had any visitors."

Rob didn't want to see the Schlagels but found it odd that they weren't in Josh's room. He said nothing and followed her directions to the room.

Rob pushed open the door and, in the first bed, saw a young man who looked like he might be suffering from a tattoo overdose. Except for his face, every part of his body not covered by the hospital gown and sheets was covered with swirls of ink. Rob smiled and in return got a head nod and a "Wassup!" that sounded much too cheerful for someone in a hospital. As the man went back to watching a game show on the TV, Rob slowly inched forward anxiously moving around the curtain toward the bed nearer the window.

This patient had half of his head bandaged, including his left eye. His nose wore a large wad of bandages as well. His mouth looked like a whole, peeled tomato, red and raw. The rest of his face was disfigured and discolored.

Rob looked down at the number on the card the woman had given him, sure that he had been given the wrong room. At the sound of Rob's step, the poor kid turned so his good eye could see who had entered.

The damage to the guy's face was so grotesque Rob wanted to run from the room, but standing this close to the bed he felt he had to say something so he stammered, "Hi. I'm really sorry to disturb you. They said my friend was in this room. I'm sorry."

Rob took a step back to turn to leave and he heard a small voice croak, "Rob."

Suddenly Rob recognized the green glint in the eye. His knees buckled and he grabbed the foot of the bed to steady himself. His horrified reaction caused Josh to flinch and Rob instantly regretted losing his composure.

He took a breath and tried to smile. "Hey," Rob said with the little cheer he could force into his voice.

Josh opened his mouth, but said nothing. Rob could tell that the slightest movement of his face muscles pained him.

"How ya doin'?" Rob asked as his voice broke as it competed with the sob that tried to escape at the same time. He contorted his face into his best goofy smile, the one that had never failed to get a reaction. It failed this time. "Yeah, I know, stupid question, but I gotta say somethin'."

Josh just stared and blinked the one swollen eye.

"Can you talk?" Rob asked quietly so the boy in the next bed couldn't hear. Josh nodded. Rob said, "It must have been awful."

"I survived," Josh mumbled through his swollen lips.

"Don't talk if it hurts."

Josh shrugged and the shrug seemed to hurt worse than the talking. "The worst was when I realized my parents would find out. After the guys finished with me, they just dumped me along 303 and I stumbled home and took every pill in the medicine cabinet. You know my parents. They'd kill me as soon as they found out, so I tried to do it myself." Rob struggled to think of what he could possibly say and Josh filled the silence. Rob had to bend close to hear the whisper. "And couldn't even do that right. Mat found me and called 9-1-1. My parents would've liked it better if I'd died." He said it so dispassionately it was as though he were reciting sports scores to someone who was not a fan.

Rob was shocked. For a few more minutes he stared at Josh's chest as it rose and fell under the faded blue hospital gown. Josh's green eye, so dazzling to Rob across a baseball diamond now blinked dully.

Rob checked to make sure the curtain hid any sight of them. Reaching out, Rob took Josh's hand and held it gently for fear of disturbing the IV tubes that fed his arm. He leaned in close so his head was almost on the pillow, and he could smell Josh's hair.

"Joshua, do you love me?"

The wounded boy turned so his eye locked on Rob's. He seemed too startled to respond. "I love you, Josh. More than anything in my life. More than I ever have anyone. I never understood why people much cared about much of anything until you came along. If anything happened to you I'd have no reason to go on living, either. I don't want to kill myself. But if you died, I would. So if you love me, please promise me you won't ever try to hurt yourself again."

Josh reached up with non-tubed arm, pulled Rob's head to his, and kissed his hair. The door to the room flew open and Rob recoiled from the bed. A posse of teenagers descended on the next bed. Rob turned his head to the window when one of the shaved heads stuck around the curtain and said, "Wassup, homies?"

146

When the boy was gone, Rob went back to Josh's ear. "I love you. Get well. I want you back. I'll come again as soon as I can."

He quickly kissed the moist, swollen cheek. Josh grabbed and squeezed Rob's hand in reply. Rob took a moment to compose himself then quickly strode out of the room. "'Sup," Rob said to the guys on the way out of the room in his best imitation of street-wise hipness.

His father sat in the lobby with a sports magazine open on his lap which he wasn't reading.

"I'm ready to go," Rob said.

"How is he?"

Rob could not answer, but his face and shaking limbs told the story. His father swallowed.

"I'd like to come back tomorrow."

His father didn't answer, instead he stood up and they walked together to the SUV. The trip home seemed longer than the drive to the hospital. Rob stared out his window, staring at Josh's mutilated face.

Meg ran to the SUV as it pulled into the driveway. "Is he going to be all right?" she asked.

"Yeah," Rob said relieved he would not have to go into detail. "He'll be okay, I guess." He wasn't sure himself if this was true since the doubt was evident in his voice.

TWENTY-FOUR

The next morning Rob's father had to go to the office so his mother insisted on driving Rob to the hospital and accompanying him to Josh's room.

Her reaction to seeing Josh was worse than Rob's. As soon as she rounded the corner of the curtain and saw Josh, she fainted. It was all Rob could do to brace her so her fall to the floor was a gentle one. He turned to the tattooed kid and said, "Would you call a nurse, please!"

"Sure, bro," was the reply and soon an overweight black woman in scrubs adorned with multi-colored bunnies was helping Rob lift his mother into a chair.

"Your bud must be hella messed up," Josh's roommate said as Rob fanned his mother's face.

By the time the nurse returned with smelling salts, Marilyn Wardell was coming around.

Rob and his mother kept a vigil at Josh's bedside for almost three hours but Josh never woke up. A nurse came in and said they would have to leave; they had to prep Josh for his next surgery. Rob would have spent the day if his mother would have agreed, but she insisted they head home.

Saturday morning Rob went to the hospital with his father, but Josh was still asleep. Rob covered for Josh at the farm market. He wanted to hold Josh's job until he was well enough to get it back. He had missed the last two days at his own job, but he was glad the summer was over and he didn't have to go back ever again.

While Josh could do nothing but sleep, Rob could find no way to sleep. All night he tormented himself with images of Josh, wondering if he would ever awaken. Wringing all of the sweat from his body gave him no peace and the next day he stumbled to the breakfast table.

Sunday he planned to work the afternoon shift at the market and visit Josh later when he might be awake. Rob got up early with his parents to harvest corn so he could take it with him when he went to Greiner's.

The sun reached its height and heat early, and Meg and Rob went back to the house to go to the bathroom and get sunscreen and a pitcher of iced tea for their parents. The phone rang just as he hit the first step.

"Bobby," Meg called with a volume that indicated she must have thought he had already made it upstairs.

He came back down a step and grabbed the extension in the living room. Josh was the only person who ever called him so he said a tentative, "Hello."

"Rob, it's Mat. I can't really talk. My parents would kill me if they knew I was talking to you."

"Mat! What's wrong? How's Josh?"

Mat let loose with a flood of words so fast Rob had a hard time hearing them, let alone digesting their meaning. "The hospital called yesterday. They said they're releasing Josh Tuesday morning. My mother told them to tell him, 'The next time he tries to kill himself to do it right,' and hung up. They aren't going to pick him up. I'm at a pay phone at the Mini-Mart across from the church. I told them I was going to the bathroom, and dashed over here to call you. They'd kill me if they knew. They said we are never to speak to Josh or mention his name ever again. I'm so scared, Rob. This is so fucked up. Tell my brother I love him, and I'll figure a way to stay in touch. But you gotta help him. You're all he's got right now. Please."

The phone went dead. Rob put a hand on the back of the nearest chair to steady himself. Anguish was rapidly replaced by a hatred of Josh's parents so intense that for a moment he studied the gun cabinet. His concern for Josh quickly pushed out the violent thoughts. Rob sat for a moment to think.

He stood and walked to the kitchen. Meg had already left with the jug of iced tea for their parents in the back forty. He had completely forgotten his need for the bathroom and sunscreen. He walked to the area where his family worked.

"Meg, could you give us a minute?"

She looked up, and Rob could tell she had a smart-ass answer poised, but seeing the pain on Rob's face, she swallowed it, and said, "Sure."

His parents looked at him.

"Mom. Dad. I know this is hard for both of you. I know we still have a lot to talk about, but . . . " Rob paused, unsure how to continue.

"Go on . . . " his mother said with less than full encouragement, since most of the news of the last few days had not been good.

"Mat Schlagel just called. Josh's parents have disowned him. They told the hospital they won't pick him up when he's released on Tuesday." The Wardells exchanged a look. Rob went on, "I know this is asking a lot, but Josh has no place to go. I was wondering, if it would be okay . . . that is . . . could he have Nonie's bed on the sun porch until we figure something out?"

His parents looked at each other. "They aren't going to pick up their son?" his mother said as much to herself as to anyone else. "That's just not right," she said. She grabbed her son and hugged him to her, spilling out, "Whatever happens we love you."

"I think your mother and I better talk about this one," his father said.

"I understand. I'll give you guys a few." Rob and his mother broke their clench and the young man turned and walked to the house.

Megan was nervously pacing in the kitchen. She almost jumped Rob when he came in the door, but his face broadcast, *don't ask*. She tried to let him pass, but then blocked his way, "I know you don't want to talk about whatever it is that is going on around here," she said, clearly agitated, "But please tell me everything is going to be okay. I have never seen Mom and Dad act so freaky. They won't let me go out or talk to Ash or Jess. What's going on? Are you in some kind of trouble?"

"No, Meg. And I hope things will be okay soon." She reached out as though to hug her brother. "I'm all sweaty," he warned. She clutched him to her anyway. Rob wasn't used to hugging his sister, and the unexpected closeness made him uncomfortable so he whispered, "Thanks, but I gotta pee."

By the time he returned to the kitchen, his parents were there. Indicating the chairs around the table, his father said, "I guess we all need to talk. Meg, we're trusting that you're mature enough to handle what we're about to say." He looked pointedly at Rob and then added, "Honestly, I'm not sure I can handle it, so bear with me."

Meg looked desperately to each of the family members for some hint of what was coming, but found none.

"Megan. We love you and your brother, and nothing will ever change that," their mother said. Rob could feel his eyes swelling up. "And we hope you will always care for him."

"Is Bobby dying?" Meg blurted, on the verge of losing control.

"No! I'm sorry, no," their mother quickly said.

"I'm fine! I am!" Rob grabbed her hand.

"You don't look fine," she said. "Okay, we have established I can handle the news, and he's not dying, so it can't be that bad, so please, tell me what is going on."

"Josh Schlagel will be moving in with us for a little while . . . "

"He will?" Rob asked.

"Temporarily. Until we can sort this all out," Mr. Wardell said.

"No one is going to have to sleep in the street while I'm around," his wife added. "It seems that it's all over town that Josh, that is, Josh Schlagel, that is, there are rumors . . . "

"Josh got beat up by some guys who thought . . . " her husband wasn't getting to the point any sooner.

Rob could no longer tolerate watching the struggle and said, "Meg, Josh and I have a relationship."

Rob's father did a half-gasp at hearing it stated so bluntly, but tried to cover his mouth to stifle it. Suddenly he seemed self-conscious of a rather effeminate gesture and quickly converted it to stroking his chin.

"Yeah, you guys are friends. So?"

Their mother was still trying to finish the sentence she had started. "The rumors are that . . . that Josh . . . "

"We're more than just friends," Rob finished.

Meg let out a laugh. "What? Like you're gay? That's so stupid. Josh and Bobby? That is so lame, I can't . . . " Suddenly the silent looks on the other three faces at the table registered with her, and she said, "Oh my God."

"The Schlagels won't let Josh come home again," Rob said. Megan looked puzzled. "They go to that whacked-out church, remember?" Rob added.

"Some members of the football team beat Josh up," their father added.

"That's what you meant 'he had an accident'? But you said he's going to be okay, right?"

"Yes. But there are some very small-minded people in this town," their mother went on. "So we're concerned what will happen when Bobby goes back to school. Or what anyone might say to you." This was the first Rob had heard his parents voice these concerns. "So neither of you are to go out alone around town until we see how things go."

The family meeting went on for some time longer before his mother insisted it was time to start lunch. Rob volunteered to gather up the tools that they had left out in the sun before they got too hot to touch. Rob was surprised when Meg volunteered to help him.

They were a hundred yards from the house before she spoke. "There are so many things I want to ask you."

"I'm not sure I can answer them."

"You mean you don't want to talk about it?"

"No, there are so many things I haven't answered for myself yet. Just now, in the kitchen, that was the first time I ever even thought about us having a relationship. We never talked about it. We just were with each other. But neither one of us ever called it that."

"You don't say 'I love you,' and kiss?"

"We kiss, but at the hospital was the first time I ever told him I loved him. I don't think we wanted to admit it, even to us." Megan suddenly laughed. "What's so funny?" Rob asked.

"I just realized why you found it so hilarious when I flirted with him. You both knew it'd never happen!"

"Actually," Rob said, laughing also, "We joked that he could marry you so we'd have an excuse to stay close for the rest of our lives."

She slugged her brother in the stomach.

TWENTY-FIVE

Whatever joy Josh felt at knowing he was going to be able to move in with Rob was overshadowed by the news that his parents weren't coming. Nothing Rob could do could get him to smile or give more than the briefest response. Rob hoped it was just the painkillers and the hospital atmosphere and that when he got him home he'd be better.

As Rob was leaving, the tattooed guy called, "Dude."

Rob looked at him and the guy motioned for him to come closer. Rob stood next to his bed and was motioned even closer. Rob didn't want to lean too close for fear some of the numerous piercings in the man's face might come loose and send shrapnel flying. When Rob was within whispering range the boy said, "I saw your homey the other day when they were wheelin' him back in." Rob nodded for him to continue. "If I ever looked like that bro, I wouldn't want to know it. You might wanna get rid of all the mirrors before he gets home."

Rob hadn't thought about that. He nodded. "Thanks. Take care. I hope you get out of here soon, too."

Rob finally managed to convince his parents that it would be better for him to miss the first day of school than for them to miss more work and that he should pick up Josh alone.

Rob entered Josh's hospital room with the brightest smile he could muster plastered on his face. This should've been the happiest day of his life. Josh was moving in with him, but he couldn't find much joy in it.

Josh sat on the edge of the hospital bed. His feet dangling above the floor made him look like a lost little boy. A large bandage still covered half his face. The other half still bore the black, purple and green of the bruises. His mouth was still swollen. He was dressed in scrubs with a small plastic drawstring bag next to him. His head was down. He looked helpless and homeless.

"Hey Josh-u-a!" he tried to chime, but his voice broke more than it sang.

Josh moved, but didn't look up far enough to meet Rob's eyes. He tried a smile, but the muscles around his mouth never got the message and the corners of his lips just twitched. His young athletic form was now frail, as though he had lost twenty pounds in the last few days. Rob thought of the black and white photos in his history book of men during the Great Depression who had seen too much sadness for one lifetime.

"Weady to woll?" Rob asked. Again he tried to inject some joy into his voice and again he failed.

Josh's head bobbed in a slight nod. He mumbled something about the nurse and checking out, but it was so soft Rob couldn't catch it. With great effort, Josh reached for the phone and dialed a few numbers. He spoke gingerly to someone about being discharged. He placed the phone back on the cradle as though it was fifty pounds of fragile glass and turned toward Rob, still not meeting his eyes. "They have to wheel me out. They said my father came this morning to settle the bill and left. He told them to tell me not to come home."

"I'm sorry," was all Rob could say knowing it sounded small and inadequate.

Rob was grateful when the nurse arrived with the wheel-chair. "Hey there! Liberation day!" she beamed. The clowns on her scrubs were obviously geared to the younger kids at the other end of the pediatrics ward and seemed particularly out of place in this room. "I'll bet it feels great to be going home."

Rob wanted to tell her to be quiet. To quit reminding Josh that he had no home to go to. She wheeled the chair into place and Josh took his seat. Rob reached for the bag, but she got it first and placed it in Josh's lap with an exaggerated flourish, "Here's your goody bag!" Rob wanted to stuff something in her smiling face to shut her up. Didn't she know that small piece of hospital-issue, throwaway luggage was a symbol of the mea-gerness of Josh's existence right now? Her cheery flow of words was no match for his silent flow of tears and by the time they reached the lobby, she had admitted defeat with her silence. When Josh stood, she hugged him and said with none of the forced humor, "It'll get better."

They walked in silence to Rob's mother's car, Josh clutching the bag in front of him as though it could protect him from all of the evils of the world.

They were out on the highway before Josh spoke and when he did the voice was thin and far away. "You won't want me coming to your house after I tell you what I have to tell you."

Rob turned to Josh and looked so hard for some hint of what Josh meant that the car dropped onto the gravel shoulder and Rob had to wrench the wheel to veer back into his lane. He glued his eyes to the road and hands to the wheel to counteract the lack of control inside.

"There's something I need to tell you," Josh croaked.

"K," Rob answered, his eyes still a part of the white lines, his heart pounding.

He fought to maintain control of the car and his emotions as the silence in the car grew, punctuated only by the feeble sounds of Josh's crying.

When Rob saw the exit for Lake Isaac, he looked at Josh. "Is this okay?"

It took Josh a moment to realize what Rob was asking and he made a small sound that Rob took as agreement, so with keen concentration Rob guided the car through the turn. Rob's hand was shaking badly when he turned off the ignition key in the parking lot overlooking the lake. Rob looked left and right to confirm that the area was deserted. Rob put a hand on Josh's shoulder, but Josh pulled away, pressing himself against the car door.

"You're going to hate me," Josh said.

"I could never hate you." Rob hoped what he was saying was true, but he dreaded to think of what Josh could be on the brink of telling him that might change that. Josh gasped for breath like a fish with a hook still in its gills. "Just tell me what it is. Whatever it is, it'll be okay. Just tell me."

"I lied to you. And I've been cheating on you."

Rob felt his heart, which had been in his throat plunge hard into his stomach. Waiting for Josh to speak again was like waiting for the guillotine blade to make contact after hearing it start to fall.

"I've been having sex with Danny Taylor for the past year."

TWENTY-SIX

The news about Danny Taylor made Rob's gag reflex instantly kick in and he had to suck air to keep from vomiting. Rob was still reeling from the news when Josh drove more nails into his gut. "And Corey Brickman. And Shane Poulan."

Rob felt the car lurch forward and grabbed for the parking brake only to discover the car had not moved; it was just the ground shifting under his world. Rob waited for Josh to say something more but heard only Josh's crying. Finally Rob said, "I thought . . . "

"I didn't want to." This remark puzzled Rob, but before he could decipher it, Josh added, "I understand you don't want me at your place. I don't blame you." He reached for the door handle.

Rob clutched Josh's arm. "Why?"

Josh was speaking, but crying so hard Rob couldn't make anything out. Tears continued to drown some of the words, but Rob was able to piece together the story. Josh had only been in school a few days — the new kid last year — and had noticed Rob and had tried to get his attention. When it didn't happen, it dashed Josh's hope of finding a friend.

Then Danny noticed Josh checking him out in the locker room at football practice. It wasn't the first time their eyes had met and held a little too long. Danny came on to Josh and Josh thought he had found a kindred spirit. Not since he was twelve years old and experimented with the guy at Christian camp had Josh had the chance to touch another boy. Rob remembered Josh telling him about his sexual experience; when they got caught and their parents told, the other boy blamed Josh and left Josh to feel he had done something unforgivable. That one time had left him scared and confused, but every time he thought about being with the boy, he knew he wanted more. To have a stud like Danny Taylor checking him out was more than Josh could resist.

"But he's an asshole," Rob blurted into Josh's story.

Josh nodded. "You don't even know," he sobbed. "After practice, we drove off in Danny's car." Josh thought he was finally making a friend. He had never been offered a ride by anyone before. Had never been in a friend's car. Rob certainly knew how thrilling the feeling was the first time Josh had given him a ride. Danny touched Josh, stroked his hair and suggested Josh go down on him. Josh continued, "And I wanted him so badly, I did."

Once Josh was done, Danny completely changed. He grabbed Josh's hair and yanked his head up. "You liked that, didn't you, fag boy?" Josh was too stunned to answer and Danny continued, "You really didn't think I was going to suck you, did you? You didn't really think I was a faggot like you, did you? God, fags like you disgust me!" Josh said that being so used and rejected devastated him and he started to cry and Danny said, "That's right, cry, you little cocksucker. And you aren't going to mention this to anyone, 'cause if you do, I will kick your faggot ass, and then tell the whole school what you wanted to do to me. How do you think the rest of team will like having a queer receiver? They'll stomp your fag face in. And you know they'll believe me—I grew up with those guys. And your parents go to the same Jesus-freak church as my parents. They'll love hearing their son's a homo!"

Before Josh could even register all of this, Danny ordered him out of his car and left him shaking in the parking lot behind Trent Flooring. He shivered behind the shipping racks for hours. Then he had to make a major effort to compose himself before he walked back to school, got his car and drove home.

Rob felt the horror surrounding him and also it hit him—if he had befriended Josh earlier—when Josh had first smiled at him in the hall, none of this might have happened.

"I thought that would be the end of it," Josh choked. "But two days later, after practice, he cornered me and said, 'We're going for a ride.' I knew what he meant. I was too afraid not to. It went on for weeks. Finally I told him I couldn't do it anymore and he hit me. I couldn't even defend myself. Just a bunch of fast punches."

Rob remembered seeing Josh at school with a black eye and swollen lip. The story was he caught a shoe during a pile-up at football practice. Rob remembered feeling so bad to see Josh's cute face marred, and now even more so that he knew the real reason.

"He told me if I didn't get down on my fag knees and do what I was supposed to, he'd really hurt me. And tell everyone about me."

"Hello." The deep voice of authority startled them both. Rob looked up into the window of a four-wheel drive.

"Something wrong?" The voice of the park ranger was something between concern and an accusation; that professional tone adopted by peace officers until they're sure who or what they're dealing with.

"Yes, something is wrong, but nothing you can really help with, sir," Rob replied. Rob could feel Josh's eyes on him. Rob went on smoothly, "We just got a call at school. My friend's father just died. They were both in a bad car wreck. I offered to drive him home, but he wanted to try to calm down a little before seeing his mother."

The ranger nodded gravely and offered generic words of condolence. He wished them well, pointed out an emergency callbox if they needed it, and drove off.

Rob turned to see Josh's eyes still on him. "You lie so well."

"I've had a lot of practice."

"So have I. I hate that I lied to you."

"I understand why you did."

"You haven't heard all of it."

"I'm not sure I want to."

"Danny got me to do the other guys as well. If I ever resisted, they'd beat me up. Usually just body punches so the marks wouldn't show." Rob winced at the thought of Josh's fine body being battered and bruised. "They didn't care how much they hurt me, or how much I cried, as long as I sucked them. One night they took me to Brickman's cabin, held me down and took turns using me and hitting me. Especially my balls. They kept pounding and pounding my balls. Their fists, their feet . . . "

Josh was convulsing now, reliving the agony. Rob, too, was cringing in sympathetic pain.

"I pissed blood for a week, but couldn't tell anyone. I was so scared. I didn't even want to go out for football this year. I knew what would happen. My father made me. Said it would make a man out of me. I worked hard to avoid them all summer. I didn't completely. That weekend at Brickman's cabin . . . " He was sobbing so badly now, Rob had to lean close to understand the words. "I couldn't take it anymore. And once you came into the picture, lying to you . . . then football started up again and Taylor wanted to pick up where we left off . . . I should've known I couldn't avoid them forever. "

Rob could resist no longer. Whether the ranger was watching or not, he took Josh in his arms and buried his face in his neck. "I had to tell them no. I had to. And you saw what they did. But I just couldn't do it anymore." His story finished, he became a limp doll in Rob's arms.

When Josh could finally breathe enough to speak he said.

"That's why I insisted we use condoms. I told you it was 'cause I was fooling around with Jenny, but I haven't, not since prom night. So I've been cheating on you and lying to you, so I understand if you never want to see me again. No one else does."

Rob looked into Josh's red and bruised eye. "I want you to come home with me now."

"But . . . "

"You did what you had to. It wasn't by choice and it wasn't your fault. So let's not talk about this anymore. Let's go home."

"You forgive me?"

"There's nothing to forgive."

"So you're sure you want me to come stay with you?"

"I've never been more sure of anything in my life. I feel like it's my fault that you went through all this."

"It's not your fault. In fact ever since I met you, you were the only reason I made it through. I saw a thing on TV once about POWs in Vietnam and they said you just had to focus your mind elsewhere so it really doesn't hurt that much. So I just focused on you and it made it bearable."

Rob had only driven only about a hundred feet when he stopped the car again.

Rob could see the fear on Josh's face. "I haven't changed my mind," Rob said. "I almost forgot my parents' rules. My mom and dad are okay about you staying and all, but just still a bit weirded out—dad especially—that you and I are, well, you know. So he said there was to be no touching. So we have to really play it cool around them. We managed to not let anyone know for this long we just have to keep acting like there is nothing going on between us. You'll be sleeping in my grandmother's room downstairs, okay?"

Josh nodded.

"We're expected to do all the usual stuff—make our own beds, take out our trash, and stuff. Till you're well enough, I'll take care of that stuff for you, but let me know if you need anything so my parents don't have to do much. I don't want dad to have the slightest reason to want you out."

"I want to be the perfect guest."

"I'm sure you will be. I love you. They love you. Meg really loves you." Rob hoped this last would get a laugh, and as distraught as Josh was it did bring a partial smile.

"Does Meg know about us?"

"Yeah, so teasing her won't be quite as much fun."

TWENTY-SEVEN

By the way his mom casually noticed their arrival, Rob knew she had been watching and waiting. She had said she was only going to work a half-day. She came swinging into the living room to welcome Josh, but flinched when she saw him. Tears immediately formed and she looked away. She forced composure back before she said, "Josh, it's so good to have you here. Welcome."

Rob was surprised to see the daybed newly arranged on the sun-porch-turned-bedroom and that some of the figurines, porcelain flowers and other grandmotherly items had been removed. They still referred to it as the sun porch although it had been enclosed as a bedroom for his grandmother more than ten years ago, and they still referred to the furnishings in the room as his grandmother's, although she had been dead for over five.

There was a stack of gift-wrapped boxes on the bed and fresh flowers from the garden on the window ledge.

"Is it someone's birthday?" Josh asked.

"Those are for you," Rob said. "Meg's idea, so she wants to be here when you open them. We wanted you to feel at home." He reached out to hug Josh, but his friend stopped him with a look.

"Right, sorry," Rob smiled.

They went back into the kitchen where the table was nicely set complete with more fresh flowers.

"Thanks. This is all . . . " Josh broke down again.

Mrs. Wardell grabbed him and held him in a motherly hug and cooed, "It'll be okay. You're safe now. It's okay. Let it out."

When Josh could compose himself enough he said, "Excuse me," and left for the bathroom.

"I think there's going to be a lot of that for a while," Rob said.

"I think you're right," his mother nodded.

Rob wondered if Josh would realize why they had taken down the mirrors in the sun porch and living room and taken the door off the medicine cabinet in the powder room.

Meg burst onto the sun porch as soon as she got home from school. Rob and Josh sat in front of a video game. Rob had brought his TV, DVD and Xbox down from his room so that Josh would have a better set to watch. Josh protested but Rob said, truthfully, he rarely watched TV in his room anyway.

"Mom said you'd . . . " upon seeing the mess that was Josh's face, Meg lost her words in instant tears. She swallowed a few times to try to find her voice. All of Rob's and his mother's attempts to prepare her had apparently failed.

When Meg could speak she said, "Are you ready to open your presents?"

"You shouldn't have," he protested.

"Yes, we should," she said. "And we wanted to."

"We went shopping yesterday," Rob said. "It was her idea. C'mon."

"Open mine first," Meg commanded, handing Josh a box.

"Get mom," Rob suggested and Meg disappeared then returned in a moment with their mother.

Josh was still staring at the first package. "I can't, I mean, you shouldn't . . . " the tears were starting again.

It took a major force of will for Rob not to reach out and hold Josh. When Rob could stand it no longer, he grabbed Meg and thrust her at his friend so she would have no choice but to hug him until he calmed down. "You, okay?" she asked tenderly. Josh sniffled and nodded. "Here," Meg said again handing him a box.

His hands were shaking so badly she sat next to him on the bed to help him open it. Inside were a pair a jeans and a shirt. "We figured you'd need a few things."

"This is so nice of you." He gave Meg a peck on the cheek. "Thank you for thinking of me."

"She thinks of you a lot," Rob joked. "She said she thinks you'll look sexy in the shirt."

"If those aren't the right size, we saved the receipt" their mother said to change the subject.

"I know his size," Rob said with more sureness than was prudent.

Josh looked at the label to confirm that the jeans would fit. Meg handed Josh the next box. "From my mom and dad," she said.

He had relaxed to the point that he could open this box without help. Inside were briefs and undershirts and socks.

"Just like a mother to give you underwear," Rob joked.

"He'll need it," she said.

"Yes, I will, thank you. They gave me these scrubs at the hospital. They cut away my clothes when they took me in."

"I knew you'd need a bunch of stuff, so I went for quantity, not quality," Rob said handing Josh the final box from the bed. As Josh opened it, Rob continued, "So it's not Abercrombie and Fitch." As Josh opened the box, he went on, "I got the three-for-ten-dollar T-shirts, the two-for-fifteen shorts, the cheap sweat pants . . . "

"These are great. Thanks," he again hugged Meg.

"You're closer to Bobby's father's size than his, so I'll get him to go through his closet with you and see what you might be able to use that he doesn't wear anymore."

Once again the emotion rushed over him and he excused himself and fled for the bathroom. Meg followed, but Rob caught her in the living room. "Let him go," he said. "He's going to be like this for a while. It'll just take time."

"He seems so broken," she said.

"Wouldn't you be if mom and dad threw you out and told you that you could never come home again? He's going to need lots of hugs, and I know you won't mind this favor a bit. Since I'm not allowed to do it, will you?"

Meg smiled. "You always stick me with the rotten jobs!"

"I knew you'd hate it."

"That was really sweet of you to think of all that stuff. For a stupid little sister you can be kinda smart sometimes."

Meg slugged him in the stomach. "Well, he'll need clothes to go back to school."

Josh was coming out of the bathroom as she said it and answered, "I'm not going back to school. I can't. They'd kill me."

Rob hadn't thought about that. Nor apparently had anyone else.

"Well, you're no condition to go anywhere for a while anyway," Mrs. Wardell said. "So we can wait until you're feeling better to figure it out."

*   *   *   *   *

After Mrs. Wardell had helped Rob get Josh settled in for the night, they rejoined Meg and her father in the living room. The uncomfortable silence only lasted a few minutes before Meg suggested a movie and pulled a comedy from their selection of DVDs.

The movie was nearing the happily-ever-after ending that no one was really buying when there was the sound of glass shattering, followed by a voice screaming "Fucking faggots!"

and the sound of a car speeding off. There was the squeal of tires and the sound of car tires racing back toward them.

"Get down!" Mr. Wardell yelled as he shoved Meg off the couch from where she had been sitting next to him. He darted to the gun cabinet and fumbled to get his keys out as the sound of several more glass explosions on the porch joined with more shouted obscenities. By the time he had his pistol in hand, the car had sped off.

Rob started to get up from the floor where he had dropped next to his mother.

"Stay down," his father ordered and Rob stayed on his knees. "All of you, just stay put." He headed into the kitchen and a moment later they heard the kitchen door open.

Rob looked into the frightened eyes of his mother then the angry eyes of his sister.

His father returned, his gun still in his hand. "They're gone. No real damage, just some broken beer bottles."

Rob suddenly jumped up. "Josh!" He ran into the sun porch. By the time he returned to the sun porch door his family was behind him. "He's still asleep."

"Good," Mrs. Wardell said. "The drugs must have kicked in. He doesn't need to be any more frightened than he has been."

They breathed a sigh in unison.

"Bobby," Mr. Wardell said, "What about school tomorrow?"

"What about it?"

"Are you going?"

"Don't I have to?"

"I'm not sure I want you to. Not after what happened to Josh. And what just happened tonight."

"What am I supposed to do? Drop out?"

"You could get hurt. Very hurt. You saw what they did to Josh."

"I have to go back to school sometime."

"I'm not sure about tomorrow . . . "

"Then when? Just hide for a year or two?" Rob was surprised to hear himself arguing to go to school rather than be allowed to skip.

The next morning, Mr. Wardell insisted on taking his children to school. Rob felt like he was entering a maximum security prison. With each step he felt his legs get a little shakier. He could feel his father's eyes on him and he didn't dare turn back.

Rob and Meg parted at the front door and she headed down the hall toward the sophomore homerooms. She looked back, smiled and winked.

The school looked no different, but the insidious creepiness he had always felt in these halls had crystallized into an ominous presence. He heard several mumbled comments as he walked the halls all day, but the only words he heard distinctly and often were *queer* and *fag*.

Rob ran home after school to find Josh still asleep. Rob went outside to do a little yard work and his heart sank when he saw FAGGITS painted across the garage door. He didn't know when that had happened; he hadn't seen it when he left for school.

As his first chore of the day, he got out the white paint with the intention of just painting over the graffiti, but when he did, the blotch was still noticeable so painting the entire garage door was pretty much all he got done all afternoon. He didn't want his father to see it and be more upset or have any reason to throw Josh out. When he went back in the house he found Josh laying on the day bed, just staring at the ceiling.

"Hey," Rob said, but the reunion was quickly quashed by Meg's bolting in the front door and coming directly to Josh's room. Her chipper smile faded fast when she saw Josh's sad condition again and she had to work hard to re-implant her happy face.

After trying to cheer Josh up for a few minutes, an attempt which made as much headway as a cup of water poured on a blistering hot sidewalk would have at cooling the concrete, Meg left to start dinner.

"Soft stuff, okay?" Rob suggested.

"Gotcha. How about mashed potatoes and I'll make pudding for dessert?"

It was a sad dinner with every attempt at livening the mood evaporating before it could take hold. Meg again was ready with a fun movie, this time insisting Josh join them. The movie was half-over when the sound of a speeding car caused the family to tense and Josh to look at them in surprise. A bottle shattered against the front porch and the cry of "Goddamn queers!" echoed in its wake. Rob ran to the front window and, standing off to the side, peered out.

"Get down!" his father ordered.

"I want to see whose car it is."

The car did a return pass as it had the night before and several more beer bottles again splintered as someone shouted, "You should've died, fag!"

"It's Brickman's car," Rob said.

"I'm calling the police. We should've last night," his father said. Rob noticed his father had the .22 in his hand, but was holding it down at his side away from Josh and the family.

Mrs. Wardell grabbed the phone and dialed. After she hung up she said, "I used to think this was a nice little town."

"I'm sure that is what Matthew Shepard thought about Laramie," her husband said.

"Who?" Meg asked.

"A student at the University of Wyoming who . . . "

"Oh Christ, Bob, don't even think that!" his wife cut him off.

"I'm not sure it's safe with him here," Mr. Wardell said.

"I'm not sure it would make any difference. We're in this now," his wife protested.

"I should go." Josh said and all eyes turned to him.

"Go where?" Mrs. Wardell asked.

With a firm look, she implored her husband to say something and he said, "You're not going anywhere tonight. Marilyn, why don't you help Josh get to bed."

The police took a report, but seemed relieved that Rob didn't have a license number for Brickman's car, which gave them an excuse to do nothing. Mr. Wardell demanded, "How many '67 Camaros are there in this town that have flames painted on the hood?"

Rob didn't sleep well, and apparently neither did the rest of the family, because he heard lots of walking in the halls as he performed his nocturnal work out.

TWENTY-EIGHT

Rob was staring out the window when Edward DeLallo, the office nerd, came into his homeroom. Rob's thoughts had taken him so far away that it took Mr. Hacker's calling his name a third time to rouse him. When he did look up, Hacker beckoned him to his desk, handed him a hall pass and said, "Mr. Hudson wants to see you in his homeroom. Now."

Rob glanced at the pass that granted him permission to go to room 110. Edward gave Rob a curious looking over and then flipped his hair back out of his face and, with his usual flourish, exited the room.

Rob had no idea what Coach Hudson could want this long from baseball season, but Rob wasn't in the mood to talk to anyone. He was no sooner in the hall than the bell sounded sealing the rest of the students in their rooms. As Rob walked the empty halls they rang with echoes of the Pledge of Allegiance rasping from tinny speakers in every room. The morning announcements were underway when he reached 110 in the freshman wing. He hesitated for a moment outside the door unsure if he should knock or just enter. While he was considering this, Coach Hudson looked up from his desk and saw Rob through the wire-mesh window. The coach rose and came out into the hall, letting the door close behind him. The teacher looked solemnly at the student. Rob had seen many of the coach's moods and looks, but couldn't place this one.

The older man almost pinned the boy to the wall with his body, so close Rob could smell his shaving cream and coffee. "I want you to tell me what's going on."

"Coach?" Rob asked, surprised and a little scared.

"I've been hearing stories. Schlagel hasn't come back to school yet and you missed Tuesday. I saw Taylor in the hall yesterday and when I asked him what was up, you'd have thought I'd caught him raiding the chicken coop. Now you're going to tell me what's up." The coach leaned even closer. His nose was almost touching Rob's. "Homeroom is almost over. When it is, you and I are going to my office and we're going to talk."

"I have European History first period."

"History will wait. I'll give you a pass. Wait here. Don't move."

The coach didn't seem to be angry with Rob, but there was a firmness in his tone Rob had only heard once before, when the opposing pitcher had thrown a bean-ball at Josh. Hudson returned to his room, and Rob's back which had been held rigidly to the wall, now slumped. Homeroom ended in a nanosecond and Rob hadn't had time to think of what to tell Hudson. The halls flooded with students walking past where Rob tried to fuse into the wall.

Hudson was the last out of the room. "Come," he said, and Rob did, walking with the sinking feeling that he was on his way to a lethal injection. He didn't know what, if anything, he should tell the coach, or what, if anything, the coach already knew. As skilled as Rob was at lying to everyone, Hudson always seemed to see through the lie even if he never called Rob on it.

A few heads turned, and Rob thought he heard someone murmur "Wardell" as he walked through the locker room with the coach. Hudson unlocked the office, switched on the light and moved some books and shirts off a chair to give Rob a place to sit. He closed the blinds.

To Rob's surprise, Hudson didn't take the seat behind the desk but instead cleared off the other hard metal chair to sit next to Rob.

"Okay, Bobby, tell me what's going on."

The coach rarely called him — or as far as Rob knew — anyone else by a first name and that further impressed upon the young man the gravity of the situation.

Rob could think of no better way to stall than to say, "About what?"

Hudson took a deep breath. "Bobby, sometimes it amazes us teachers to have you kids think we are all as stupid as y'all seem to think we are. We have eyes and we have ears and we know a lot more than we let on most of the time. I appreciate that we're the enemy and there are things that you're not supposed to tell us. But some things are too important for those games. So let's take this one step at a time. Where's Josh?"

"I don't . . . I mean, I . . . "

"Don't tell me you don't know. That kid hasn't farted since he's been in this school without you knowing about it."

The blunt statement acknowledging that the coach knew of Rob's infatuation cut through his defenses like an armor-piercing bullet. The dam holding his tears in was rapidly crumbling. His head started swimming. He had never fainted before and wondered if this was what it felt like just before one did. If the coach knew, did everyone know? If so . . .

Before he could even begin to sort this out, he felt the coach's hand on his knee. "Bobby, I'm not mad at you. Or at Josh. You're not in any trouble that I know of. So, please, be honest with me. I'm concerned about you, and I'm concerned about Josh. Tell me what's going on. Maybe I can help." Rob was still too overwhelmed to answer. "Okay, let's start with an easy one.

174

Is Josh okay?"

Rob nodded, then said with less conviction, "I guess."

"What happened? How bad is he?"

"He should be able to pitch by spring."

"Dammit, Bobby, this isn't about baseball. What happened to Josh?"

Rob, his last defenses broken down, started to cry. The coach moved his hand from Rob's knee to his shoulder. "Take it easy. I'm sorry. I don't mean to yell at you. What happened? Please tell me everything. I've heard the rumors, I'd like to hear the truth and I think you know that." Rob looked at the coach. "Let me help. Josh got beat up after football practice. Taylor, Brickman, Poulan, Semianski, Rivera. Probably others. How bad was he hurt?"

Rob inventoried Josh's injuries then paused for breath. "Oh God, Coach, you wouldn't recognize him."

The coach held Rob for a few minutes until Rob got hold of himself.

"And the rest?" the Coach asked even more gently. Rob formed the question with his eyes. "The pills? He tried to overdose?" Rob could only nod. "And the why?" Rob just stared through tear-streaked eyes. "So it's true?" Rob could still only stare.

"God," The coach said and rose from his chair. Rob saw Hudson form a fist and for a moment thought the man was going to hit him. Instead he delivered a sharp jab to the metal file cabinet, the sound of which echoed in the small office. The coach sat back down; the file cabinet was still rocking and a large dent remained. "Where's Josh?"

"My house."

"So it's true his parents don't want him back?" Rob nodded harder, spilling teardrops onto his lap. "Is Josh going to press charges?"

Rob shook his head. "He's afraid to. They told him while they were beating him that if he ever told anyone who did it that they'd kill him. They hurt him bad, Coach. He believes them."

Hudson stood and paced back and forth in the small space before turning and viciously attacking the file cabinet again, leaving another dent. The sound and fury frightened Rob. "They're not going to get away with this," the coach hissed.

Hudson tapped his front teeth, thinking. "I'm guessing it's a lie that Schlagel came on to Taylor. Grabbed him in the shower is what supposedly started this." Rob shook his head. "I didn't think so. So what did start it?"

"I know you're trying to help, but . . . "

"Okay, okay, I won't go there. But what I think keeps you and DeLallo and a few others about whom there are rumors safe is that you keep a low profile and fly below the radar. I suggest you keep doing that. I have to figure out how best to handle this."

Rob was stunned. "There are rumors?"

"Only guilt by association because of Josh. Everyone knows about DeLallo and a few others. I don't have to tell you who."

Rob didn't have a clue who else might like guys and he didn't really appreciate being lumped in with someone as feminine as Edward DeLallo.

"Do you know what Schlagel did that made Taylor go after him . . . you don't have to tell me why, but do you know?" Rob nodded. "Is it something you can avoid doing?"

Again Rob nodded. "Tell Josh when he comes back to school to come and see me first thing."

"It'll be a while before he comes back," Rob said. "He's afraid to. And says he has no reason to."

"I want to talk to Josh. Would it be okay if I visited him?"

"Not today. He's still pretty out of it."

"I understand." The coach looked at him again. "Are you okay, Bobby?" Rob shrugged. "Anytime you need me, call and leave a message at the office. Use this number. And I'm putting my cell on here as well. Please don't give it to anyone." The coach grabbed a scrap of paper from the desk and scribbled the number.

Rob started to leave then turned. "Thanks, Coach."

"I wish I knew what to do, but I'll do anything I can to help."

As Rob walked back to class, he looked at the scrap of paper on which Hudson had written the phone numbers. It was a line-up card from last season bearing the names of Acosta, Poulan, Taylor, Beechler and Schlagel as the top of the order.

TWENTY-NINE

As Rob went to his locker the next morning he realized the new route he had taken was not a good one. Brickman and Poulan were coming towards him. He glanced behind him for a possible path of retreat, but Danny Taylor was there. It didn't look or feel like a set up, just poor planning on Rob's part.

Rob tensed. He thought he had a better chance escaping Taylor alone than trying to get past the two guys in front of him. He did a U-turn as casually as possible, but someone grabbed him from behind. He was spun around into a locker and Brickman's fist slammed into his face. Taylor's voice demanded, "Where's your boyfriend?"

Poulan grabbed the longer, spiked-up hair above Rob's forehead and smashed Rob's head into the locker. "Since he's not around these days, maybe you can take his place. Do you like it up the ass as much as he does?"

"What's going on here?" For the first time in Rob's high school career he was grateful for the sound of Mr. Welke's voice. The history teacher strode into the crowd.

He turned to Rob. "You get to your homeroom. The rest of you . . . " he hesitated, "Clear out of here."

Homeroom was almost over and Rob was still staring out the window ignoring the morning announcements when Edward DeLallo came in. Mr. Hacker looked at the pass and said, "Wardell, the principal's office."

Rob wondered what the problem was now. Europe was going to run out of history by the time he got there. In the hall, Edward said, "They can't keep doing this shit to us."

Rob was again a little disturbed by being included in an *us* with Edward, but lacking any other allies, he nodded. Edward went on, "I'm so sorry to hear about Joshua. I had no idea about you guys."

Rob wasn't sure what the appropriate response to that was so he just nodded again. They got to the office just as Coach Hudson did. He stopped to look at the bruise on Rob's face. Hudson ushered him into the office. The secretary looked up and seemed surprised by the trio.

Hudson said, "We need to see Mr. Frost. Now."

"He's on the phone . . . "

"This is more urgent. Interrupt his call."

"I . . . "

Hudson walked past her and opened the inner office door. There was quick, quiet conversation that Rob couldn't quite hear then Hudson motioned for Rob to come. Rob went into the office and Hudson pointed him to a chair. Rob had never been in the principal's office before and expected it to be imposing to somehow make up for the small man who occupied it, but Mr. Frost was more threatening than his surroundings.

Hudson was saying to Frost, ". . . and this is the student who was assaulted. There were witnesses."

"Assaulted?" Frost questioned. "I wouldn't use that word. There are bound to be . . . "

" . . . Assaults? I don't think so. This school has a zero tolerance policy on bullying and fighting. It's about time you enforce it. I want all of the boys involved in this suspended."

"Mr. Hudson, I don't think you understand..."

"I understand perfectly. You may be willing to sit back and watch your students being attacked, but I'm not."

"Mr. Hudson . . . "

There was half a knock then the door opened and the secretary stuck her head in. "Mr. Frost, sorry to interrupt, but the police are here."

Frost stood up and turned to Hudson, "You called the police?"

"I didn't," Hudson said. "But I'm glad someone did."

"I did," a small voice said from the doorway.

They all turned to see Edward DeLallo standing there. "I saw the attack. I called the police before I went and told Mr. Hudson."

Edward stepped aside to let the police enter. Edward followed them in and closed the door behind him. He turned to the police officers, "I saw Daniel Taylor, Corey Brickman and Shane Poulan attack this student." He pointed at Rob. "Mr. Welke was also a witness and could testify against them."

"Testify?" Mr. Frost almost shouted. "We're talking about a little high school fight, not a criminal proceeding."

Hudson turned to the policemen. "Officers, if I punched Mr. Frost here in the mouth, what would you do?"

"Place you under arrest."

"So as far as you know there's nothing in the law that excuses assault if it occurs on school grounds?"

"No, sir."

Hudson walked to the door and said to the secretary, "Pull the schedules of Corey Brickman, Shane Poulan, and Daniel Taylor. Find out where they are this period." He closed the door and turned back to the police. "I want them arrested and taken out in handcuffs."

"What?" Frost demanded. "We're talking about a little school matter."

"We are talking about crimes being committed."

The two men stared at each other until there was another

half knock at the door and the secretary entered carrying a piece of paper.

One cop looked nervously at the other. "Uh, we only have two sets of cuffs. We'd have to go to the car and get more."

"Then do it," Hudson demanded.

The cop looked at the list. "Isn't Danny Taylor the quarterback?"

"Yeah, even quarterbacks commit crimes. Let's go." Hudson opened the door to leave.

Frost tripped on the corner of his desk hurrying to get around it. "You can't." But it sounded like less of an order than a plea.

"Why not?" Hudson demanded looking as though he might make good on his threat to hit the principal. "Officers?" he said, prompting them to leave.

One of the policemen turned to Edward. "You say a teacher witnessed this?"

"Yes. Mr. Welke."

"We'd like to talk to him."

*   *   *   *   *

Hudson spoke to Rob and Edward outside the principal's office while Frost made frantic phone calls inside. "When they come back to school, if they come back, I'm going to have a talk with each one of them and tell them that if anything happens to you, they will each answer to me. Not as a teacher, but as one pissed-off sonuvabitch. Both of you, watch yourselves. Don't be alone at any time and stay away from Taylor and those bastards. If any of them comes near you, you come to me. Find me. I don't care where, when, the middle of class, doesn't matter. Find me."

Rob, Edward and Hudson stood aside as the three students were led past in handcuffs. Each of them gave Rob a fierce look.

Frost came out of the office. "I called the boys' parents."

Hudson asked, "Did you call the Wardells and tell them their son had been attacked?"

"Mr. Hudson, I don't think . . . "

"That's exactly right, you don't think." Hudson snapped back. "But think about this: school districts and school principals have been held liable for failing to protect their students. You better hope the Schlagels don't sue you. And since you've been given more than fair warning, you know the Wardells or DeLallos will, if anything happens to their children. I'm asking you to do your job, that's all." He turned to the boys. "Are you guys okay? Do you want to go home?"

Rob didn't answer. He was still too stunned by the past hour's events which had spun his head more than the slam to the locker.

"I'm fine," Edward said. He touched Rob's arm, "Are you okay?"

Before Rob could take inventory and answer Frost said, "You realize of course, you boys bring a lot of this on yourselves?"

"By trying to go to school and get an education?" Hudson yelled. "Yeah, that provokes a lot of trouble!"

"Mr. Hudson, we can talk privately later, but I don't think this is the place to have this discussion."

"Where would you rather have it? The police station? A court? A hospital? The morgue?"

"Oh stop!" Frost yelled. "You're being awfully melodramatic."

"Mr. Wardell," the coach said, turning to Rob, "How would you characterize the nature of Joshua Schlagel's injuries?" Rob blinked, but didn't answer. "From what you told me, they were just short of life-threatening, aren't they?"

Rob blinked again and said clearly, "They almost killed him."

THIRTY

Rob had only been in class for a few minutes when Mr. Frost appeared at the classroom door. After whispered words to the teacher, Frost said, "Mr. Wardell."

Rob got up and went with him. As they walked to the office Frost said, "Your father called. He wants you to call him immediately. He says it's an emergency. I tried to assure him that everything was fine, but he insisted."

Rob's heart flipped inside his chest. What had happened to Josh? Or had someone attacked the house while no one was around? Rob quickened his pace and Frost almost had to jog to keep up. Frost showed him into the inner office and handed him the phone.

"Dad?"

"Bobby, are you okay?"

"Yeah, what's wrong?"

"I got a call from Bill Taylor, Danny's father. He said you're pressing charges for assault against Danny. Did he assault you? Are you okay?"

Rob didn't appreciate that Frost was standing right next to him listening to every word. He wanted to downplay the attack so as not to worry his dad, but didn't want Frost to think nothing had happened either.

"Yeah, I'm okay. Some guys roughed me up a little this morning, but they got arrested."

"Did you hurt Danny?"

A laugh burst from Rob. "Me hurt Danny?"

"His father was all upset like you did something to him."

"Hardly."

Rob's father sat in his SUV in the driveway that circled the flagpole on the east side of the school. His father looked at the bruise on Rob's face and shook his head. "You didn't have to come," Rob said.

"I talked to your mother," his father said. "We're thinking you should stay home until things calm down a bit. Take a few weeks off."

"I'm not going to be scared off by them."

"We just thought . . . "

"Dad, do you remember when I was little and asked you why you went to Vietnam?"

There was a silence until Bob Wardell realized this wasn't a rhetorical question. "Honestly, no," he answered.

"You said 'to fight for freedom.' Was that the truth?"

"Yeah, I guess, sort of. But more realistically because I was drafted."

"So was the freedom line just some bullshit you handed your little kid?"

Mr. Wardell seemed a little startled to have his son swear at him. "No. I believed that then. I've been confused since about why we were there, but at the time, I guess I believed that. What does this have to do . . . "

"This is about freedom. Mine and Josh's. The U.S. went over there supposedly to bring freedom and security to Vietnam and Josh and I aren't even free to walk the halls of our own school and feel secure."

"This is very different. I was in supply, miles from the action. I never saw the enemy. You'll be on the front lines every day with no one watching your back."

"Coach Hudson has my back. And after the stink he made today, I'm sure it will be a while until anybody tries anything."

His father shook his head then nodded, "Now I know how my parents must have felt." For the first time in a long time Rob really looked at his father and noticed his father had gray hair.

His father dropped him at the house, went back to work for a few hours, then picked up Meg as soon as school was out. His mother had taken Josh into Cleveland to get his eye, wrist and other injuries checked. It was going to be a full round of doctors and they would be gone most of the day. When his father came in with Meg, Rob was asleep on the couch and woke with a start.

His father motioned for Rob to come over to the gun cabinet.

"I'm not sure how long it'll be until things settle down. And you saw the attitude of the police when they came. In the meantime . . . " He handed Rob and Meg each two small keys. "I had these made for each of you today. Keep them on you." He walked to the gun cabinet and used a matching gold key on his own key chain to open the drawer. In it was a large .45 caliber revolver. Rob wondered where the .22 was that his dad had grabbed two nights ago. "You guys are old enough now to be trusted with keys to this. I think it would be best if Josh didn't know what was in here or that you had keys." The older Wardell looked pointedly at his son who got the message and nodded. "The little silver key opens the lock box in my nightstand. My .38 is in there. Both of those guns are kept loaded." He pointed back to a box of bullets in the drawer. There are more shells for this one in here. And . . . " He held up a set of keys from the drawer. "This is the key to the rifle rack." He tapped the locked doors of the cabinet. "The rifle and shotgun shells are in the second drawer." He showed them another key on the ring. "The rifles and shotguns aren't kept loaded, so if you need them, you'll have to load them. You both remember how?"

Rob looked at Meg. She was as frightened as he was and swallowing hard. Their father caught their worried looks. "Don't be frightened. I really don't think you should ever have to open this drawer. But like knowing how to use the fire extinguisher, it's something you should know. You remember what I taught you about gun safety?" Rob and Meg nodded as gravely as they knew their father wanted them to. "I know it's been a while for both of you, so if either of you don't feel comfortable, we can go to the shooting range and practice."

Meg nodded and Rob shook his head, both meaning the same thing; they didn't want to go.

Rob watched his little sister swallow hard again. They watched their father return the keys and the bullets to the drawer, lock it, and pocket his keys.

"I have some work to finish up, so I'll be in the sewing room. That great smell is chocolate chip cookies your mom baked before she left."

After their father went upstairs, the kids headed into the kitchen for their snack. Meg opened the Tupperware and offered it to her brother. He took a cookie but just stared at it.

"Bobby, I don't think I could shoot anyone," Meg said.

"Neither did I until a few days ago, but when I see what they did to Josh, I want to track down each one of them and kill them. And his fucking parents!" Rob, finding his stomach suddenly churning, put his cookie back into the container.

Meg set down the container and took her brother's arm. "I'm sorry I upset you."

"You didn't. They did. You've been great, Meg. Thanks. Just one more thing to be pissed at them about. A few years ago I couldn't shoot a stupid deer and now they have me wanting to commit murder."

Meg hugged him. "You're not a murderer. You just love Josh."

He hugged her back then broke the clinch. "I'm going to take out my frustrations on some weeds."

She patted his shoulder as he left the kitchen to go upstairs to change. Instead of going to the yard, he put on his sneakers and ran and didn't come home until he was completely drained.

That evening's movie was uninterrupted although they all sat in tense poses. They had gone to bed but Rob wasn't sleeping when a car racing by made him sit up. Shattering glass and obscenities spoiled the warm, peaceful night. The car did a high-speed U-turn returning with more bottles and epithets. But then the car stopped. Car doors opened.

Rob grabbed his pants off the floor, not bothering with underwear or a shirt. When he got to the hall, his father was already there wearing nothing but boxers and carrying a pistol.

"I'll check on Josh, you stay up here with your mother and sister. Your mom's calling the police."

His mother came out of her bedroom with the snub-nose .38 in her hand. They stood at the top of the stairs and heard the front door open and his father in a sterner voice than Rob had ever heard him use yell, "I'll shoot the first one of you that sets foot on this property!"

There was scurrying of feet and then the car doors opened and the car sped off.

By the time Rob got downstairs he was surprised to see his father sitting on the bed on the sun porch holding a trembling Josh.

After much hemming and excuses, the police agreed to ". . . look into the matter."

"Just so we get clear here, officer," Mr. Wardell said as they stood on the front porch, "I have filed two complaints. If I end up shooting anyone for trespassing or attacking any members of my household, I want it in writing that you were warned this was going to happen. Next time they come by, I'll shoot out their damn windshield before I call you."

"Mr. Wardell," the younger of the two policemen began, "I don't think you should be making threats . . . "

"We're the ones who are threatened here. If you won't do your job and protect us, I will."

THIRTY-ONE

The weekend was awkward for all of them. The good news that Josh's eye was healing, although he'd need to keep it bandaged a while longer, did little to cheer any of them up. Rob worked at Greiner's Farm Market and found himself the subject of whispers and stares from several customers.

Rob felt bad that he was working and leaving the task of trying to brighten Josh's mood to his family, but since he seemed to be making no more progress than they were, he was glad to escape the funereal house. Meg's attempts at being the entertainment committee had all fallen flat.

Josh remembered his car was still at school and Rob and his father went to get it half expecting it to be vandalized, but it was still there, intact.

Rob and his father helped Josh climb the stairs to take a shower. When Josh was done and helped back to his room he said, "You can put the mirrors back up. I've seen myself."

"Oh shit. I forgot about the ones upstairs," Rob said.

"It's okay. I was going to have to see it sometime."

"Once the swelling goes down and the bandages come off, I'm sure you'll be good as new." Rob checked the door to make sure no one was near and gave Josh a peck on the cheek.

*   *   *   *   *

Monday morning Rob again felt like he was entering enemy territory. He had driven Josh's car to school in case he had to escape. When he passed Edward DeLallo he got a "How's it going?"

"Hey," Rob answered, returning the smile.

"Have you seen Taylor and those guys today?"

"Thankfully, no."

"You won't. They each got two-week suspensions. Taylor is protesting his 'cause he didn't actually lay a hand on you."

"A technicality. He was just too slow," Rob smiled. "At least we'll have two weeks of peace."

"Don't count on it. Those guys have lots of friends."

"Let's be optimistic."

Rob was waiting to meet Meg after school when he saw Ryan Tattorelli coming toward him. Since Buff Beechler had graduated, Ryan was the anchor of the offensive line and unquestionably the biggest kid in school.

Rob looked around for an escape route. He could head back inside, but that meant possibly being trapped. Where the hell was Meg? At least a witness might discourage what was about to happen. Ryan was getting closer and Rob was trying to get his fight-or-flight response to make a decision.

"Hey," Ryan said with no threat at all in his voice. Ryan stopped at a safe distance and looked up to where Rob stood a couple of steps above him. "I don't expect you to believe this, but I just wanted you to know not all of us on the football team are assholes. I think what they did to Josh sucks. I'd have stopped it if I'd have known."

Rob nodded but was still too shocked to speak.

Ryan went on, "I can't expect you to want to trust any football players, but we aren't all bad." He turned, walked down

189

two steps then turned back. "And for the record, Josh wasn't the only gay guy on the team."

He turned and walked away. When Meg came up Rob was still staring at the space Ryan Tattorelli had vacated.Meg burst into the house and Josh's room ahead of Rob. Josh was watching TV, although from his posture and the bleariness of his one good eye, it appeared that he wasn't so much watching it as staring at it. "Hi, Josh. How's it going?" He shrugged. There was no good answer to that. "I have something for you," she continued. "I hope you don't mind, I already showed it to Bobby, er, Rob." She handed a note to Josh. "Your brother slipped me that in the hall today."

Josh unfolded the piece of notebook paper with the ragged torn-out edge.

Josh — I can't believe how bad this sucks. They told me I can't see you, but I have to. If at all possible, please meet me behind the football stadium at 1:10 tomorrow. With all my love, your brother, Mathias.

Josh looked at Rob. Rob smiled and said, "He said on the phone he'd stay in touch."

"Will you go with me?" Josh looked scared.

"Sure."

"It's not that I don't trust my brother, it's just that the idea of going near the football stadium or locker room . . . and . . . "

"What, Josh?" Rob was leaning forward. Josh hesitated. "Do you want Meg to leave?"

Meg gave her brother a look that said she didn't want to leave, but turned to Josh, "I can go, if you guys need to talk."

"No, that's okay, Meg, thanks." Josh paused a little longer. The two Wardells stared, waiting. "I, well, I know my parents, that is Mat would never willingly be a part of anything, but God only knows what's going on at that house." There was a long pause before the next sentence. "They had these friends. Their son was gay. They sent him to a camp. To be deprogrammed. I'm just afraid that they beat Mat into . . . "

"Can I take your car again tomorrow? I'll park it nearby, out of sight, over on Clover Street. And I'll scout out the stadium before you get out of the car. I'll come home and get you during lunch."

"You'll miss English."

"I won't *miss* it," Rob smiled.

"I don't want you getting in any trouble."

"I won't, I've skipped it before. Besides Coach Hudson said he'd help anyway he can. He'll give me a pass if I need it."

Josh nodded and Rob noticed for the first time that Josh's hands were shaking. Another episode was coming on. Josh headed for the bathroom.

Rob looked hard at his sister. "Mom's at work, right?"

"Yeah, why?"

Rob quickly went to the gun cabinet, pulled out his keys and unlocked the top drawer. He could feel her eyes upon him as he quickly slid the large .45 pistol out of the drawer and slipped it into his backpack on top of his books. Once done, he turned to face his sister.

She was now shaking too, and a quiver was in her voice when she said, "Bobby, be careful."

"Do you know what they do at those deprogramming places? I've read stuff on line about them. He's not going."

"Just be careful, please."

THIRTY-TWO

Rob ran into the house, "Hey, Josh, WTW?" he called as chipper as he could as he sprinted to the bathroom. When he burst back out of the door, Josh was waiting nervously by the front door. "It'll be great to see Mat, won't it?"

Josh mumbled something, but looked more scared than thrilled at the impending meeting.

The drive was tense silence. He always saw Josh as the big, strong one of their relationship and now here he was prepared to die or, even more frighteningly, kill to protect Josh. He tried to be as casual as possible as he drove, but when Josh pointed out that Rob had completely ignored a red light as they cut through town, his cover was blown and he gave up any attempt at acting cool.

As promised, Rob parked on a side street out of view of the school and any passing traffic. He did a U-turn to have the car facing out of the street for a quick getaway. He patted Josh's arm, grabbed his backpack and got out of the car.

"You're taking your books?"

Rob knew he looked and felt guilty. "Uh, yeah. If someone sees me, I can say I was on my way to class or something." Rob knew Josh knew him well enough to see through the lie, but Josh was too nervous to question it.

Rob nervously slung the pack over one shoulder. Once he started walking, he spun it around in front of him, unzipping it halfway. He started looking around, checking for the Schlagels' cars in the lot by the stadium or in the drive that circled behind the west stands. He peeked under the stands and then stood back to look down the long drive. Mat stood alone, shifting nervously under one of the girders that supported the bleachers. Rob checked again behind him then broke into a trot. At the sound of feet on gravel, Mat started running toward him, but then slowed when he saw it wasn't Josh.

"Hey," Rob smiled.

"Where's Josh? Is he okay?" Rob noticed Mat also had a backpack.

"Yeah, he's okay. Are you alone?" Rob continued to look around to confirm this.

"You guys thought I'd . . . ?"

Rob could see the hurt look in Mat's eyes. "Not you. Your parents. Josh wouldn't put anything past them at this point. He wasn't sure what they had forced you to do."

Mat nodded. "They're crazy over this."

"C'mon," Rob started jogging toward the car. He checked the parking lot and the street one last time before turning down Clover Street.

When Josh saw his brother he leapt from the car. His battered body caused Mat to stop in his tracks. "He looked so bad when I found him in the bathroom, but all the bandages . . . "

Josh came forward and gently gave a one-armed hug to his brother.

"Oh, God, Josh," Mat blubbered. "You okay?"

"I'm going to be, yeah."

"Mom and dad have been insane."

"I'm sure they're taking it out on you, bad."

Mat smiled. "I can handle it."

"You always did, better than I could."

"You had something to hide, I didn't."

"You knew?"

"Duh, I figured you and Rob out the first time I saw you two together."

"You never said anything."

"What was I supposed to say, 'Hey, bro, you boinking Wardell?'" Mat was doing his best to be nonchalant, but Rob noticed the tears never stopped streaming down his cheeks. Josh bore matching wet tracks. "Hey, I brought you something." Mat headed toward the car and the other boys followed him. Mat opened his backpack and dumped its contents into the open back window. Out tumbled shirts, a pair of jeans, some underwear, socks and a couple of books. "I figured you could use some stuff. I gotta keep my backpack, though."

"This is awesome, thanks, Mat."

"No prob. I laid dibs to all your stuff, so I can just sneak you a few things now and then."

"Be careful. I don't want them to banish you."

"Fuck them!" Rob was stunned, and the vehemence of Mat's anger obviously startled Josh as well. "I'm tempted to tell them to eat shit, and just leave."

"Where would you go?"

"The streets of Cleveland would beat that psycho ward."

"You can't leave. You're the only sanity left in that house. Who would protect Jeremiah, Ruth, Sarah, Micah . . . "

"I know. I'm not going anywhere. I just said I want to."

"Thanks. You were a good brother. And my protector, too. You saved my life and are still risking trouble for me."

"What are brothers for?"

"I should leave you guys alone," Rob said.

"Nah." Mat touched Rob's arm. "I need to get back. I can't get caught skipping." Rob nodded. "I guess it worked okay to slip a note to your sister? We pass each other every day. So if you need to get a hold of me, have her get me a note. And as soon as I can, I'll try to meet you again. Is she okay with this, being our messenger?"

"Yeah, she'd do anything for Josh. Sorry about the cloak and dagger shit, but we didn't want to take chances."

"Now that I think about it, I don't blame you. I forgot about the Gibsons and Brandon."

"I didn't," Josh said, shuddering. "They told that story around me a lot as a warning,"

"What they left out is what a mess that kid was after," Mat said bitterly.

"Hug the kids for me," Josh said.

"I can't. I mean I can't tell anyone I saw you."

Josh grabbed his brother in a tearful hug. "So just hug them and don't tell them why."

"That I can do. I love you, Josh."

Mat finally pushed him away. "I gotta go. Hey, since you guys are so paranoid—not that you don't have reason to be—any notes from me will be addressed to Joshua Lawrence. If you get a note or message from me that's just to Josh, that means they forced me to write it and don't trust it. I'm on your side, and you know I'd do anything for you, but God only knows what they might try to pull." Josh and Rob nodded. Mat turned and hugged Rob, "Take good care of him, please."

"I will. I promise. Meg was all worried about how things would go. When you see her, can you just give her a thumbs up or smile or something so she knows it's all good?"

"Sure. Tell Meg it's nothing personal, but I can't risk being seen talking to her. All we need is for one of those Christian freaks to tell my parents . . . "

"I understand. She understands."

"I'll see ya. Bye."

Mat turned and sprinted off toward the school, his empty backpack slapping him as he ran.

THIRTY-THREE

As Rob drove, Josh looked at him, "Your parents are being amazing about this."

"My dad is still sort of freaked, but I think he'll calm down."

"My father would've killed us by now, so yours is a saint by comparison. You know what I was saying to Mat about being my protector?" Rob nodded. "My father used to beat us for anything."

"Yeah, you've told me a few stories."

"Not a tenth of what he did. I was a pretty good kid, so didn't give him much cause, for breaking the rules or whatever, the way Mat did and Jeremiah is starting to. What I got most of my beatings for was 'acting girlish.'"

"I never noticed that."

"That's because my father beat it out of me. If he saw me doing anything he thought was girlish, he would get the belt. One day, I was about thirteen, so Mat must've been eleven, and I crossed my legs at the knee, instead of the ankle. We were just watching TV — football — one of the few things besides Bible hour and the Republican Convention we were ever allowed to watch — and I crossed my legs. I barely knew what happened. My father grabbed me, yanked my pants down, ripped off his belt and started in. It was brutal. I was screaming, asking what I'd done, and he just kept whipping me and whipping me. I had blood soaking my underwear and running down my legs. Finally Mat couldn't take watching it anymore and grabbed my father's arm. No one had ever interfered with one of his punishments before and he went berserk. He grabbed Mat and turned on him. He beat him and beat him, and I was too scared to stop it. He smacked him a few times with the belt — the one caught him full in the face — that scar Mat has next to his ear is from the buckle."

Rob could barely keep his eyes on the road, trying to also watch Josh pour out his story.

"He dropped the belt and started punching and punching; it was awful. And I didn't have the guts to do anything. My father's right, I'm a pussy. Mat would take that beating for me, and I didn't have the guts to step in for him."

"You were a kid. A scared and beaten and bloody kid."

"I should've done something."

"You couldn't. Obviously Mat doesn't blame you."

"He's still willing to risk pissing off my father to come see me. I was his hero, if you can believe it. He was in the hospital for two days after that beating. I can't look at his crooked nose — broken by my father, that mashed-up lip — or that scar and not want to cry. You always tell me how cute I am. Can you imagine how cute Mat would be if my father had kept his hands off him? He's had his nose broken a few times by my father. You always say how cute it is that I smile down on one side instead of up. What I never told you is that my father hit my so hard when I was about twelve, I cut my mouth on my teeth so bad I had to get stitches inside my mouth. It did nerve damage. I can't raise the right side of my mouth."

"So every time I mentioned your smile, it brought back those memories? I'm so sorry."

"No." Josh sniffled. "I liked that you even liked all that was wrong with me."

"You never had him arrested?"

"Get real. My father would always tell the hospital we hurt each other, 'boys will be boys,' 'they did it wrestling,' whatever. A teacher reported it in Minnesota. My father took a demotion at work so he could move. That's when we went to Wisconsin. He beat me bad because he thought I told."

Rob made a sudden right turn and drove into the cemetery and stopped behind the Fyfe mausoleum. Rob put the car in park and turned to hug Josh. "I'm so sorry."

"Easy, easy," Josh pleaded.

"Sorry, I just wanted to hug you so much. My poor baby." Rob kissed both of Josh's cheeks and then gingerly touched his lips to Josh's still swollen lips. "No one will ever hurt you again, I promise."

"I wish you could protect me forever. But I'm not sure anyone can."

"If I can, I will. I love you, Josh." Rob was surprised how easily he was now saying those words and how right they sounded. Josh tenderly touched Rob's face and neck. He still had not said the words, but Rob got the message. He watched as Josh suddenly winced. "The ribs?"

"Yeah."

"We need to get you home, get you some pills and a nap."

"Yeah." Rob reached to start the car. "Wait," Josh added.

"What?"

"Lean over here again."

Rob complied and Josh leaned forward and kissed Rob long and hard, his sore lips pressing onto Rob's. "That hurt, but it was worth it. As bad as things are right now, I'm lucky to have the best brother and the best friend in the world." He stroked Rob's hair. "I'm sorry I almost hurt you. I didn't even think about you when I tried to . . . " he couldn't say the words . . . "I'm sorry. You mean everything to me, and if I ever doubted I had a reason to live . . . " again he couldn't finish the thought.

"Josh, do you love me?"

"I don't know. I mean, I think so." Josh looked down. "I'm not sure what love is. My parents told us they loved us and then beat us. They'd preach about God's love. The God who's going to send me to hell for eternity for being who He made me. I've never heard your parents tell you or Meg they love you, but they don't have to. So if I told you I loved you, I'm not sure whose version of love that would be."

"It can be ours, if you want."

For the first time since that horrible Thursday, Josh had really smiled and Rob began to hope that the worst was behind them.

Josh took his pills and went to lie down. Rob made sure his mother was at work and then returned the gun to its drawer, breathing a deep sigh of relief as he did so. He felt so guilty about even having taken it, he was tempted to wipe the prints off before he closed and locked the drawer.

Rob walked into the sun porch and as quietly and gently as he could, slid onto the bed next to Josh. He intended only to stay a moment, but he was awakened by Meg whispering in his ear. "Bobby, wake up." He grunted, unsure where he was but knowing he was sorry to be waking from the most peaceful sleep he'd had in a week. "Bobby, now!" his sister hissed. He wanted to tell her to get lost, but as he came more fully awake and felt Josh's warmth next to him, he snapped awake. Meg whispered, "I let you sleep as long as I could, but mom will be home any second."

Rob quickly slid out of the bed so as not to disturb Josh and tiptoed out of the room behind his sister. He gingerly closed the door to the converted porch. "Thanks, Meg. That was close."

"Yeah it was. You better watch it."

"I just lay down for a second."

"When I got home, I just peeked in to see how Josh was doing and saw you two."

"Thanks again. You're the best."

She smiled. "You're lucky I like you and Josh."

"You just don't want him thrown out before you can accidentally catch him in the shower."

Megan slugged her brother in the stomach just as their mother walked in. "Nice to see that some things don't change," she said in a voice she was forcing under control.

"Something wrong, Mom?" Rob asked as they turned toward her. Her face was set, her jaw clenched and even though she was trying to joke about the horseplay of her children, there was no joy on her face.

"I, uh, I am, uh . . . "

Rob took a step toward his mother. He couldn't tell if it was anger that was taking form. Meg stepped back as though from a strange dog.

"I was debating if I should tell you, but shit, after everything else that is happening, and you'd know soon anyway . . . I got fired today." Rob could tell from Meg's gasp behind him that she was as shocked as he was to hear a swearword from their mother. "I drove down to Marion to see the Warren G. Harding Memorial. I've heard about it since I was a kid and today I drove there. I just had to get away. It's a beautiful memorial to one of the worst presidents this country's ever had."

Rob had never seen his mother in this state. A spontaneous trip the Warren G. Harding Memorial was not something his mother would ever do.

"Fired? Why?" Rob asked numbly.

"On the drive I came up with a long story to tell you kids and your dad, but as I walked in, I decided you should know the truth as much as it sucks." Again Meg gasped at her mother's choice of words. "Do you want my version or his version?" When neither of her children answered, she said, "Mr. Trent's excuse was that I had missed too much work since 'the incident.' In reality, he got a few phone calls from some of his customers wondering why he allowed people to work there who harbored known homosexuals. People who go to—what was it you called it—that cracked-out church . . . "

"Whacked-out," Meg corrected without thinking. The incongruity of it caused them all to laugh.

"Oh my God." Josh's voice startled them all. He was so white, Rob wondered if he would simply keel over. "My God," he repeated. "This is all my fault."

All of their shoulders slumped as they watched Josh try to shoulder the guilt. His weak frame couldn't bear the weight and he staggered to a chair and sat down. In that moment, with time standing still, Rob realized he had never seen anyone in his family ever sit in the antique, high-backed wooden chair that had stood for the duration of his lifetime next to the fireplace. Rob wondered if they were even allowed to sit in that chair. He also wondered where that chair came from, if it belonged to his grandparents or great-grandparents. His mind was swimming with thoughts of ancient furniture because the one thought clanging in his head—and what his mother's news might mean for Josh—was too much to process.

"I need to leave. I'm causing you all too much trouble . . . " Josh said so quietly they could have passed for his dying words.

"No," she repeated. "I'm not going to blame the victim. I thought about this all day." Mrs. Wardell walked to Josh and put a hand on his shoulder, the weight of which seemed to cause his head to drop to his chest. "Think about what you just said. Do you really think he'd give me my job back anyway? Would I want it back? True, Mr. Wardell and I never asked for any of this, but now that it's here, we can't put things back the way they were. This town won't forget. It can't forget. I was an outsider here myself. Do you know how long it took me to get accepted?" Rob watched as his mother took Josh's head and pressed it to her stomach. "If Josh leaves, it's not going to be because this town forced him to," she said with such determination that even Josh couldn't question it.

Dinner was prepared by his mother with much more than the usual help from Meg and Rob and even Josh, who sought to spare her as much work as possible, although when they tried to insist she go sit on the porch and relax she said, "I have to do

something to keep from going crazy. Let me help or I'll be taking another trip to see Warren G. Harding."

Mr. Wardell took her news with a clenched jaw and just
nodded. It wasn't until after dessert—pudding made by Josh
and Rob—that Rob remembered Josh's things still scattered on
the backseat of the car.

Meg joined the boys on the trek to the car, parked out of
sight of the road, on the grass behind the garage. They were
now putting both Wardell cars inside and had started locking
the doors. Rob planned to clear space inside for Josh's car.

"What a mess." Meg shook her head at the heap of clothes
and other things scattered over the seat and onto the floor. She
folded each shirt as she picked it up and handed it to Josh.
Picking up one shirt sent a baseball bouncing to the floor of the
car. She picked it up and looked it over as she handed it to Josh.

"My lucky baseball!" he said as he handed the shirts to Rob
so he could take the ball. I can't believe Mat thought to pack
that."

"That is so sweet," Meg said. "Please tell me your brother
isn't gay. If I can't have one Schlagel, maybe I can have the
other." Meg picked up the next shirt and recoiled from it,
"Ewww!"

"What's wrong?" Rob asked, shouldering her away from
the open car door.

"There's something gross in there."

Rob carefully lifted the shirt. The remains of a now-melted
Reese's Cup slimed out. "Mat gave you a candy bar," he
laughed.

As the oozing mess sploshed on the ground, Josh said,
"Reese's. My favorite. I guess we should have emptied the car
sooner."

"Looks like. I hope mom can get the chocolate out of this
shirt. Let's see if it got on anything else."

Other than one dab of chocolate on the pair of jeans, the rest
of the clothes—some underwear, socks, and a pair of gym
shorts were all okay. At the bottom of the heap there was also a

photo of the Schlagel family, conspicuously minus the parents. Josh handed the baseball back to Meg to hold the photo. Josh's one good eye was fixed on the portrait. Meg made an effort to restack the clothes Rob was holding to have something to do to avoid embarrassing Josh with her stares. "Let's see, Brewers, Packers, Brewers. I see a pattern in these T-shirts," she kidded.

"My favorites," Josh smiled.

"You have the sweetest brother in the world," Meg said.

"Ahem!" Rob cleared his throat in protest.

Meg slugged her brother in the stomach. "Mine is okay and he does have the best taste in friends."

Rob handed the pile to Meg, "I'll pitch the candy bar in the trash."

By the time Rob got in the house, Meg had put Josh's clothes in the drawers of Nonie's antique dresser with the carved flower drawer handles and Josh was trying to find the perfect spot for the family photo on top of the dresser.

THIRTY-FOUR

It was the first day his tormentors were due back in school and Rob was walking with twice his usual wariness. As he entered the school the first eyes that met his were Danny Taylor's. Taylor turned and walked away. Rob negotiated the minefield of the hallway, now resolved to keep his head up so if he got hit he'd at least see it coming. As he met the eyes of Poulan, Brickman or the rest, it was they who broke eye contact for a change, not Rob.

He was almost to his homeroom when he heard, "Bobby!"

The name hit him in the back like a sniper's bullet. His heart stopped and then resumed beating. The voice was female. Completely unfamiliar. There were a dozen other Bobbys in the school; it must have been meant for one of them. He kept walking until he heard, "Bobby Wardell!"

He turned. Coming toward him was Brittany Burnside. Head cheerleader. Homecoming Queen. Volleyball star. And Corey Brickman's girlfriend. This was not good. He took a step back, looked for an escape route. He realized even though she was bigger than him—most of the girls at H-burg High were—

it seemed unlikely she would hit him. This was probably more about verbal abuse and public humiliation. But there was no public, just a handful of people at the far end of the hall, too far away to hear whatever insults she had to hurl unless she really screamed, and he didn't picture Brittany as a screamer.

"How is Josh?" she asked. "I think what they did to him is terrible. Josh sat in front of me in English Lit all last year. He is such a nice guy. I've been trying to find you to ask you. Is he going to be okay?" Rob still could not find his voice."I know what you must be thinking. Corey and all. I always knew he could be a bit of an asshole. But not this big. If it means anything, I dumped him. He's pissed. He wanted us to be homecoming king and queen again this year. He knows I'll be queen and that leaves him hanging. I'm tempted to ask Josh or you to be my escort. But we both know that would just cause more problems. I'm so sorry. Please tell me Josh is going to be okay. Is he?"

"Maybe. Not sure yet how permanent the damage is."

"I can't believe this. Would you please tell him I said hi. And I'm sorry."

"What did you do?"

"Nothing. I was just . . . I don't know. I feel guilty for even knowing those guys. Josh was always so nice in Lit I kept suggesting to Corey we should double with Josh and Jenny sometime and Corey always said no. I guess now I know why." Rob nodded. "Will you tell him that there are people at school who miss him and care about him? Tell him I said hi."

"Okay."

"Do you know who I am?"

"Of course. Everybody does."

"I wasn't sure since we've never really spoken before. I'm sorry for that, too."

"You knew who I was?"

"Of course. The cute loner. At the cheerleader table we had nicknames for everyone. One of the girls nominated you *most likely to go Columbine.*"

"How flattering," Rob said. "What do you mean, used to have nicknames?"

"I won't eat with them anymore. The topic of how unfair it is of Coach Hudson to cause trouble for their boyfriends kind of makes me want to throw up. I might not get to be Homecoming Queen after all, not that I care." She paused and looked at him. "Would you like to have lunch with me tomorrow?"

"I don't think that's such a good idea. The lower the profile I keep around here, the better."

"If your profile gets any lower, you'll disappear."

"That's my goal."

Brittany laughed and Rob laughed with her. She said, "It's good to see you smile and laugh. I don't think I ever saw you do that before." Rob smiled again. "Would you do me a favor?" she asked. "When we pass each other in the hall, give me a smile? I don't know that I'm going to be getting too many smiles these days."

"You're like Miss Popularity."

"I'm not supporting the popular position these days, so I'm not sure how much longer that will last." Rob nodded. "You know," she said, "I've had a crush on you since about sixth grade."

"What?" Rob blinked incredulously.

"Yep. Then I decided I had to go the popular route and could see you were going the social outcast route. I'm sorry. I should have gone for quality in my friends, not quantity." She leaned forward and kissed him on the cheek. "I hope someday we can be friends, if you can ever forgive me."

"Sure."

"I have to get to homeroom." She took a step away and then stopped. "I can't say as I'd blame you if you did bring a gun to school and wasted half the fuckers here. But I know you're too nice a guy to do that."

"Don't bet."

She touched him gently on the arm and then turned to leave. She stopped and turned back. "And you know what else?

You've gotten even cuter since sixth grade. Josh is a lucky guy."

Rob had barely settled into his chair in homeroom when Edward DeLallo appeared with a summons from Coach Hudson.

"How is it going?" Rob asked.

"No problems yet, but the day just started," Edward said.

"Let's be optimistic." Rob smiled and touched Edward on the arm as they parted.

It seemed odd to now be talking to more than one person a day at school. Hudson came out of his homeroom into the hall.

"How is Josh?"

"Getting a little better."

"When is he coming back to school?"

"I don't know if he is. We've talked about it, but he doesn't want to."

"He can't just drop out. Can I come see him? How is tonight after school?"

"Sure."

Mat had slipped Meg another note and they had set up another secret meeting and again Mat brought his brother more clothes and family mementos. As happy as Josh was to see Mat, the depression into which Josh sank afterward seemed twice as dark.

Although Josh's eye patch was off and most of the bruises had healed, Hudson was still a bit rattled by Josh's appearance. Rob left them alone and when Hudson reemerged from the sun porch after an hour he informed Rob, "He's agreed to let me tutor him so he can keep up his studies."

"You?" Rob asked.

"I'm not just a dumb jock. I am a teacher."

"I didn't mean it that way."

"Yes you did, but that's okay. I'll stop by tomorrow with some books if that's okay?"

"That would be great. Thanks for all your help."

Hudson was leaving as Rob's father and mother came in. She had been helping at the office more since she now had no other job. Rob did the introductions as they walked Hudson to his car.

Mr. Wardell stopped his son from returning to the house. "Bobby, we've got a little problem. When does Josh turn eighteen?"

"November fourth."

"About six weeks," his father said, doing the math.

"When your mother took Josh to the doctor today it occurred to her that if anything happens, we can't legally authorize treatment. We aren't his parents. I called my old roommate, Dave Jackson, today. He practices law in Akron. He suggested we adopt Josh or have Josh petition to become an emancipated minor."

"A what?"

"Have a court declare him an adult. But either of those things is likely to take more than six weeks. We'll just have to hope nothing happens before that."

His mother spoke up. "We've been debating whether to tell you, but you might as well know. We've lost some pretty big clients." Rob looked puzzled. "You know, Taylor Plumbing, some other business owners who have sons on the football team . . . "

"Wait? They're blaming you for . . . "

"There's something else," his mother said. "We may have to wait until Josh is eighteen since we can't authorize treatment, but we're thinking we should get Josh some sort of counseling. He's obviously not well mentally. He's been through a lot, and we're beginning to wonder if he's going to be able to snap out of it without help."

THIRTY-FIVE

Rob wheeled the shopping cart around the corner and almost hit a cart coming the other way. He stopped as did the other cart driver. When he looked up he was startled to be facing Mrs. Schlagel. She was just as stunned to see him, but recovered more quickly, backing her cart up to go around his. She glared at him as she passed him and when she was next to him said quietly but firmly, "You did this to him. You will burn in hell for this, too!" As more of a threat than a benediction, she added, "I suggest you read your Bible."

Rob was too stunned to say anything, but even more stunned to hear his mother's voice behind him, much louder than Mrs. Schlagel's, "I can't imagine having a child as wonderful as Josh and not wanting to have him with me."

Mrs. Schlagel hissed, "You might want to read your Bible as well. *If your eye offends thee, pluck it out. If your hand causes you to sin, cut it off.*" She looked at Rob.

Rob could hold his tongue no longer. "Maybe you should read the rest of your Bible. Like Psalms: *Though my father and mother forsake me, the Lord will receive me.* Or Matthew: *And a man's foes shall be they of his own house.* Since Leviticus also pro-hibits eating shellfish, are you going to go over to the fish counter and shoot everyone who's buying shrimp?"

His mother did a double take at her son then turned back to the other woman, "I may not know much about the Bible or being gay, but I do know how to be a parent, and I know it's wrong to throw your children out when they need you the most!"

Mrs. Schlagel gave a parting look that condemned them both and sped off.

"Way to go, mom!"

"Oh shut up!" she snapped as she grabbed the cart and wheeled it away.

Rob looked around and realized every shopper in the pro-duce section was staring at them. He hurried after his mother.

"I got the Pop-tarts," Meg said as she trotted up to them. Their mother snatched the box and flung it into the cart. "What's wrong?" Meg asked, confused.

"Don't ask," Rob said, giving her a look that reinforced that keeping quiet would be the best policy right now.

As they approached the checkout stands, they saw Mrs. Schlagel heading toward the line next to theirs, but the checker quickly flung the *Lane Closed* sign onto her conveyor belt before Mrs. Schlagel could place her first item. Mrs. Schlagel spun her cart off toward another lane. The clerk snatched up the sign and looking directly at Marilyn Wardell said, "I'll take the next per-son in line."

Rob smiled at the clerk and nodded thanks, but his mother was still too upset to notice what had just occurred. The clerk winked.

All the way home he was eager to tell Josh what had hap-pened, but as soon as he entered the sun porch and saw the look on Josh's face, all happiness and eagerness drained out of him and he just said hi and went to help his mother unpack the gro-ceries while Coach Hudson went back to his lessons.

Rob told his mother he was going out for a run until dinner. As he ran past the cemetery, he was surprised to see his father's SUV parked on the road that looped past the Wardell family plot. He ran in the gate and saw his dad on one knee on his grandfather's grave.

"Hi, Dad," he said quietly so as not to disturb the slumbering dead. Startled, his father turned. "Sorry, I didn't mean to scare you."

"I wasn't expecting anyone."

"Sorry. What's up?"

"I just needed a place to think."

There was an uncomfortable silence. Rob used to be accustomed to these gaps in conversations with his father, but now they seemed more awkward. Finally Rob spoke. "Mom wants to move doesn't she?"

"No, what makes you . . . ? No, she doesn't." Rob looked at his father. "No, she doesn't want to move. I was the one who brought it up, and we've talked about it, but no. I guess I came here to try to figure things out."

"The Wardells have lived in Harrisonburg for a long time."

"Yep. Your great-great-great-," he ticked off the greats on his fingers, " — grandfather came here after they lost everything in Virginia after the Civil War. He needed a new start."

"Do you think we need one?"

"We haven't done anything wrong. There's no reason for us to have to leave." His father stood. "Do you want to leave? Does Meg?"

Rob shrugged. "I'm leaving soon anyway. To college next year. I don't want to stay here. But I don't want to be forced out."

"How are things at school?"

"People mumble things now and then. But no one can be bothered bothering me anymore. Meg has lost some friends like Ashley, but she says they weren't really friends if they'd stop talking to her over this. Her real friends — Jesse, Stacey, Hannah — are still her friends."

Mr. Wardell nodded. "You want a ride home?"

"I'm sweaty."

"It's okay. Lots of stupid little family rules don't seem to matter anymore." The older Wardell put his arm around his son and steered him toward the SUV.

Rob stopped and looked back at the cluster of gravestones. "You said we have no reason to leave. We haven't done anything wrong." Rob jerked his head towards his great-great-great-grandfather's grave. "Did Francis Wardell own slaves?"

Mr. Wardell paused. "I assume he did. My grandparents never said. But the way they didn't say always made me think there was something they weren't telling. There are a lot of ugly pages to history."

THIRTY-SIX

The Mat-to-Meg-to-Rob-to-Josh handoff had worked again. Rob had taken grief for having skipped English at least once a week for the past few weeks and decided not to chance it again and sought out Coach Hudson for a hall pass. The meetings between Mat and Josh had become more routine now although all three of them always ended up crying. Not since the first rendezvous had Rob felt the need to pack protection. Rob tried to suggest that Josh could meet Mat alone, but the look of terror that came over Josh's face convinced him Josh wasn't ready to fly solo yet.

When Rob got to Hudson's homeroom Hudson looked up and said, "That's weird, I just sent DeLallo to get you and you're already here."

"I didn't see Edward. I came because I need a favor."

The coach nodded and Rob leaned in to whisper the situation. Hudson pulled out a pad of passes, wrote one out and handed it over. "Anytime," he said.

"Thanks. And you wanted to see me?" Rob asked.

"Yeah. I'm going to have to stop tutoring Josh."

"What? Why?"

"I'm starting to take too much heat for it. There are people saying that I'm visiting Josh at your place because he and I are doing it."

"Doing what?"

"Having sex."

"What?" Rob's raised voice caused everyone in Hudson's homeroom to look.

Hudson jerked his head toward the door and Rob followed him into the hall. "There's a rumor that I'm having sex with Josh and/or you. They say my 'shower at the gym' rule was so I can see you guys naked."

"That's crazy."

"Sanity has never played a big part in school proceedings in case you haven't noticed. Ordinarily I'd tell them all to go to the devil, but my wife is going to have our second child in a month — and that's part of it, too, I should be home more — but I don't have tenure. I already scalded the cat with Mr. Frost and he'd love to find a reason to can me."

"That sucks."

"There are teachers asking why I want to get so involved in a gay thing if I'm not gay. I try to tell them it's not a matter of being gay; it's a matter of right and wrong."

"It's so unfair that you're getting in trouble for trying to help."

"I'm not really in trouble, but I can't afford to let myself be. I'm not quitting the fight; I'm just going have to be less visibly involved. I've asked around and found someone else who's willing to tutor Josh until he comes back to school."

"I don't think he's coming back. He's afraid to leave the house."

"I understand." Hudson shook his head. "Well, I warned Tom Welke if he volunteered for this job he might be stuck with it for a while."

"Mr. Welke wants to tutor Josh?"

"Yeah. Go figure."

*   *   *   *   *

Mr. Wardell was coming in the front door of the house as Mr. Welke was leaving Josh's room after their tutoring session. Rob introduced his father to the teacher and explained that Welke was taking Hudson's place

"It's nice of you to do this," Mr. Wardell said shaking the man's hand again.

"I've seen my share of adversity so figure I should help out when I can."

"Bobby said you were in 'Nam?"

"Yeah, that's right," he said with just enough humility to make it sound like swagger.

"What outfit?" Mr. Wardell asked.

"The 334th."

"At Cam Ranh Bay? I was in the 349th. I was there in '72 and '73."

A look something like fear came over Welke's face. "'67 and '68," he said.

"Good outfit," Mr. Wardell said.

"We did our jobs," Welke answered.

They bid their good nights and Welke left.

Rob asked, "I thought you were in supply, miles from the action?"

"I was."

"So Mr. Welke's outfit?"

"Another quartermaster unit. Why?" Meg and Rob burst out laughing. "What's so funny?" their father asked.

"To hear him tell it, he single-handedly won the war. He was like a Marine or Green Beret or something leading dangerous patrols deep into enemy territory."

"The 334th was a supply group," his father said.

"That is too funny," Meg said. "I can't wait to hear what everyone at school says."

"They're not going to say anything," Rob said.

"They'll think this is hilarious!"

"No they won't. 'Cause you're not going to tell them."

"Sure I am. This is too . . . "

"Mr. Welke is sticking his neck out to help Josh. And I've read enough about Vietnam to know no one had it easy over there. So, please, for Josh, for me, don't say anything."

Meg stopped laughing and nodded, "Okay."

Her father put his hand on her shoulder, "Anyone who went over there and did what they had to do and came back to face what we had to, has my respect. I was no hero and I didn't do anything great, but I can tell you it was hell and if Mr. Welke wants to embellish a little and it gets some kids to think about Vietnam, I wouldn't say anything either."

When Rob explained why Hudson had quit and how bad that made Josh feel, his mother said, "Gay people are getting married all over the country and we're having the Salem witch trials."

*   *   *   *   *

Rob had just pulled down his sheets when he heard a knock on his bedroom door. "Come in," he said. His father and mother entered.

"I guess tonight was a mistake," his mother said.

"Yeah," Rob agreed. "You were just trying to do a nice thing."

"I thought since Josh got his cast off today he'd want to go out to dinner to celebrate."

"I know. Nice thought. You didn't know those people at the next table were going say anything to Josh."

"We just thought it was time we pushed him a little to go out, anyplace besides the doctors," she said. "But after tonight, he'll be more afraid than ever to go out. We should have known people in this small town would talk. I thought after all of his bruises healed and he got the cast off, he'd start feeling better, but even before dinner he seemed even more depressed."

"I know," Rob said. "I hoped he'd feel like doing something by now."

"He seems to be getting worse, not better," his father said.

"We talked about this before. About getting him counseling. I mentioned it to him the other day, but he got upset. Could you try to talk to him?"

"I've tried and he said, 'I don't need a psychiatrist. They're the ones that are crazy, not me.' But I'll try again. I've been checking into like gay youth groups and things."

THIRTY-SEVEN

Harrisonburg High School was doing a production of *The Headless Horseman* for Halloween with Megan Wardell in a minor role. Josh had declined to join the family in attending. Meg tried to persuade him, but Rob had reined her in. "If you were Josh, would you want to ever set foot in that school again?"

As they pulled into their driveway Mr. Wardell said, "Oh, shit!"

The front of the house was littered with broken pumpkins. Shattered glass glittered on the porch. DIE FAG was spray painted across the front picture window.

The Wardells burst into the house. All of them turned and looked at the closed door to Josh's room. The way it shut them all out left a low-pressure depression in the room. Rob was staring at Josh's closed door and could feel the eyes of the rest of the family shift from the door to him. He knew what was expected of him. In the car on the way home the depths of

Josh's misery had been the topic of conversation. Mr. Wardell had said, "We're going to come home some night and find him hanging from the banister."

Rob had turned his eyes fiercely on his father, and his father had apologized profusely, but the thought, which had laid coiled in everyone's mind, had now reared its ugly fangs and there was no recapturing the beast.

Now that same thought pounded in all of their brains, and Rob felt himself propelled by them to Josh's door. He knocked quietly and got no response. Rob knocked again and this time added a "Josh?" Rob wanted very much to walk away. From the outside they had seen Josh slumped in the chair, his head barely visible. The lamp and the television were on. If Rob didn't have the rest of his family leaning toward him, pressuring him with their eyes, he would have left it alone. He knocked again. "Josh, I'm coming in, okay?" He deliberately phrased it in such a way that Josh would have to answer to keep Rob out and getting no response, Rob grabbed the knob. Even though Rob knew there was no lock on the door, he half expected to find the door blocked. The only resistance he met was his own reluctance to push open the door.

Josh's eyes were wide, but he was seeing nothing out of the bleary orbs. The TV was on, with the sound down low, barely audible. Josh stared unblinking and said nothing when Rob again said, "Josh." Rob still had his hand on the door and pushed it most of the way closed.

"What are you watching?" he said, failing at sounding casual.

Rob wasn't really expecting a reply and Josh's voice startled him. "Dragnet." The sound of Josh's voice for some reason frightened Rob. Rob nodded, but the nod didn't indicate that he understood, in fact, quite the opposite. Without even looking up at Rob, Josh seemed to know this and added, "It's an old TV show. Detective Joe Friday was explaining to some lady that it was no good trying to deal with blackmailers. They get what they want and still ruin you."

Rob just looked in puzzlement at Josh's unseeing eyes — flat green now with none of their old luster. Josh was staring past Rob at the television.

"I gave them everything and they just took more."

"You told me . . . "

"I didn't tell you most of it. Not half of it . . . I couldn't tell anyone. They used me. They humiliated me. And every time I thought it couldn't get any worse . . . Danny took me over to Brickman's. He was being all nice to me and said he wanted us to be friends. I was so lonely, and I wanted . . . after all he had done to me, I thought it might still mean something if we were friends. Like boyfriends, even."

Rob knew he didn't want to hear any more. "Josh, it's okay, you don't have to . . . "

Josh was too mesmerized by the horrible video he was replaying in his head to pay any attention. He gripped the worn arms of Nonie's pink, flower-patterned chair as though bracing himself for what was about to happen on the TV screen of his mind. "He took me to Corey's and I couldn't say no. Part of me was afraid, but I still wanted so badly to be his friend. I couldn't believe he could treat me worse than he already had. I know it sounds crazy now. But I went. Not that I had any choice. I was so afraid of Danny by then anyway. We went downstairs. Supposedly to play pool. As soon I got down there, I knew things weren't right. Corey and Poulan were there. Pretty drunk. There was a rope lying on the pool table. Danny was behind me so there was no way I could run, even if I'd have had the guts to, when Corey said, 'So this is your little fag toy who wants to suck us all off?'" Rob felt his gut tighten into a painful fist and wondered if he could, or should, resist the urge to vomit.

"They grabbed me and tied me over the pool table. Each time I tried to resist they punched me, hard. By the time they had me over the table, I was choking on the blood from my bloody nose. They had my head hanging over the side and they yanked off my pants . . . "

Rob felt his head swimming and he wanted to let the wave of nausea carry him far away. He wanted to pass out and not hear the details that were thrust upon him about pool cues and rape and testicles beaten with pool sticks and sweet, innocent Josh being used by three punks and beer bottles and pool cues and the beating and he wanted to beg Josh to stop, to please stop, as though by stopping the retelling he could somehow stop the rape. But he knew he couldn't open his mouth without throwing up and he also knew Josh was very far away now where he would never hear Rob's pleas to stop.

A different voice, one not connected to the litany of crimes broke in. "Bobby?" it said. It took Rob a moment to find the voice in memory and recognize it as his father's. Once Rob realized whose voice it was, and how close, he could only hope his father hadn't heard any of Josh's story. Josh went on talking unaware of Mr. Wardell or anything beyond his pain. There was now something about being thrown out, shirtless, to walk home on a cold November night.

"Rob?" The voice of concern came again. Rob slowly got up, walked to the door and gently closed it without saying a word. He returned, like a dutiful zombie to continue listening to the recitation.

Josh seemed not to have noticed the movement and was now describing another trip to hell. " . . . they showed up at my house, the three of them. I don't know how they knew I was home alone. It was so . . . Danny always knew where to find me. Sometimes I'd let him find me, to use me, to beat me. To punish me for being the sinful faggot I was . . . "

"Oh, Josh." Rob could no longer contain the anguish, but his friend still wasn't listening.

"Sometimes Danny would just show up, and he'd make me take him upstairs and suck him knowing my mother was right downstairs. And they seemed to know I'd be alone and they'd all just show up. They'd open the door and walk right in, like it was their house not mine. Taylor slapped my face and asked me 'where's the beer, faggot.' I told them there wasn't any. My parents don't drink."

Josh was now wringing his hands reliving the fear of what sort of punishment being a bad host might bring from his uninvited guests. Fresh sweat was running down the frightened boy's face in spite of the chill of the porch.

"Danny said, 'Good thing we brought our own,' and he held up a six-pack. He pulled one off and shook it and opened it. The beer shot over the rug and the couch. I know it's crazy, but I knew what they were going to do to me, and still I was more afraid of what my mother would say if she got home and saw beer stains on the rug or couch."

Rob's mind again swam away only to surface unwillingly to hear of Josh being escorted to his parents' bedroom. Of being used repeatedly on his parents' bed. Of how even during the rape he was concerned about the stains on his parents' comforter. There were details of how they used his mother's lipstick to write *fag* on his stomach and chest and back and drew lipstick circles around his nipples and his navel, and on his penis, which Josh was embarrassed was hard while they were doing all of this and again instead of being worried about his personal degradations he was more worried about his mother noticing the damage to her lipstick.

Josh recited how he ran around the house, still in pain, blood trickling down his leg, trying to spot clean the couch and rug and comforter before his parents got home, before he would allow himself a hot shower and sank into the corner of the shower stall. Of how his family did come home and how his father yelled for him to get out of the shower, and he couldn't move, and how his father came in and yelled at him and dragged him out of the shower, and hit him.

"And the thing was I knew I deserved it. It was God's way of punishing me for being a fag. And I couldn't tell anyone. I could never tell. I could never say anything. I couldn't. Who could I tell? I just had to keep quiet. I couldn't tell . . . "

Rob realized Josh had become stuck—a wheel spinning in a snowy ditch, unable to free itself. Rob reached out and put his hand on Josh's shoulder. Josh recoiled, then recognizing Rob, grabbed his wrist and pulled Rob toward him. Rob knelt before Josh as Josh bent over him, sobbing into his hair, still repeating "I couldn't say anything . . . "

Rob stroked his cheek and said, "You can tell me. Anything. Anytime."

The tears continued until Josh had no energy left with which to cry and Rob helped him to bed and left the room, turning out the light and closing the door. He tiptoed upstairs. Light still seeped from under his parents' door.

Rob went into the bathroom and closed the door quietly. He slipped off his shirt and hung it neatly over a towel rack, then raised the toilet seat, knelt down and began retching.

Rob was still registering the knock on the door when it opened. Rob couldn't take his head away from the toilet, but from the corner of his eye saw his father's slippers and familiar sky-blue pajama bottoms. He felt a hand on his shoulder. "Are you all right?"

"No."

"Is Josh all right?"

"No."

"Bobby . . . "

"It'll never be all right." Rob fell to the floor, convulsing at his father's feet.

THIRTY-EIGHT

When he awoke the next day, Rob had only a slight memory of his father carrying him to bed. His head was still pounding and his stomach was a wrung-out rag. The taste of stale vomit still filled his mouth and sinuses. It only took a moment for him to remember the reason for his own pain and could only imagine how much worse it had to be for Josh. Without even checking to see if he was dressed, he leapt from his bed and sprinted down to Josh's room.

Josh was slumped in the chair again in front of the TV. On a game show network re-run, Bob Barker was telling someone the price was wrong. "Hey," Rob said as nonchalantly as possible, considering he was only in his briefs and was panting heavily. Josh tried to smile. It didn't work. "How are you?"

"Ok," Josh lied. "I'm sorry about last night. I didn't mean to dump all of that on you. It just sort of came out. I can't believe that a stupid TV show . . . I mean I must be pretty messed up if a TV show can make me lose it like that . . . "

"It's okay."

"Not really. I gotta get a handle on this. I can't keep freaking out on you and your family. Start crying if Bob Barker makes someone bid on a pool table."

"But that's a lot to keep inside you without telling anyone . . . "

Josh nodded. "But it just comes over me all of a sudden sometimes. Most of the time it's like something that happened to someone else and I just heard about it. Or like I saw it in a movie."

Rob said, hoping Josh wouldn't take him up on it but he knew had to offer, "Anytime you need to talk about it . . . "

"And I know now I deserved it."

"Deserved it?"

"They should've killed me for being gay. God hates homos. My parents said it so often, you'd think I'd have understood that."

"Oh stop it. If that's true, why doesn't he punish me?"

"He has. Your family has suffered. You've suffered and now you're stuck with me. It's God's will."

"A loving God would not let anyone suffer like this. Think about what you're saying. Do you really believe those assholes were the instruments of God? That's like saying God used Hitler to punish the Jews. I don't know much about religion and I've never read the Bible except to bullshit your mother, but I do know that if there is a God those assholes are not on his side. The devil's maybe, but not God's."

"Why else would God let this happen?"

"This had nothing to do with God. Ask yourself how Danny Taylor knew about you and me."

"He can spot a faggot when he sees one."

"He can spot one 'cause he is one. He has gaydar! He hates himself for being gay and since he can't beat himself up, he beats us up. Why else would he want to have sex with guys?"

"What about Brickman and those guys?"

"They would eat dog shit if Taylor told them it was cool. The biggest homophobes in history have all been gay. J. Edgar Hoover, Roy Cohn, Ted Haggard, Mark Foley . . . "

"Who?"

"Never mind. Too much history class and time on the computer. The point is they lash out at gay people to avoid being gay themselves. It reminds me of that thing little kids say about you point at someone, you have three fingers pointing back at you. Every time Taylor pointed me out for being a faggot, I kept thinking he was three times the faggot I am."

"You think Danny is gay?"

"Duh. I'll bet you twenty bucks he'll being hanging out in gay bars in San Francisco in five years!"

"Bobby?" Mrs. Wardell called from the living room.

"In here, Mom!"

"Are you okay?" She appeared at the door. "We didn't bother waking you for school."

"Thanks. And yeah, I'll be fine."

"Make yourself some breakfast if you feel up to it. And put some clothes on. You don't want to get really sick."

"I think I need to brush my teeth and let my mouth air out a bit first."

She smiled, "I have to go. I have a job interview."

"Job interview?" Rob asked.

"I'll tell you about it when I get back." She gave him a peck on the cheek, waved at Josh and left.

"Are you sick?" Josh asked.

"I was, sorta, last night. I'm okay."

Josh looked concernedly at his friend, but let it go. "I wasn't sure if I was dreaming it, but last night I thought your father peeked into the room while I was sleeping. The second time it happened, I knew I wasn't dreaming."

"They're worried about you, Josh. I'm worried about you."

"What a coincidence, I'm worried about me, too." Josh tried to smile at his own weak joke, but again his cute mouth wasn't in a smiling mood.

"Your parents don't seem to care how much school you miss any more."

"Neither do I. I do my work. I'll graduate. That's all that matters."

"Do people say things at school?"

The thought to lie to Josh crossed Rob's mind only fleetingly since he knew he was unlikely to get away with it anyway. "A little, not much. Sometimes. I need a shower." Rob started out of the room then turned back. "We have the house to ourselves. Care to join me?"

It was the closest thing to a real smile from Josh that Rob had seen in a month. The subject of sex hadn't come up since Josh had moved in.

They got in the shower together and Rob began licking the water off Josh's neck and chest. He moved up to kiss Josh, and Josh let him, but didn't kiss back. Rob pulled back. "Let me know when you are ready. I won't rush you."

"I think I told you that once," Josh said. "Then I rushed you anyway." Josh tried to kiss Rob. It didn't work. "I'm sorry," Josh said.

As they stepped out of the shower, Josh said, "I think I'm going to nap."

"Want me to join you?" Rob asked, grinning.

"Not today."

Without any recollection that he had made the decision to do anything, Rob pulled on some shorts and shoes and before he realized it, he was fleeing down the driveway, running. Running down the road, away from the house. And away from Josh.

Rob didn't return until sweat was running off his chest and back in the cool fall air. He got back in the shower. All of the thoughts from the run seemed to have been crowded together and now streamed through his head as the water streamed down his body.

He'd never had a friend like Josh and he might never have Josh or anyone like him again. If they didn't talk soon, the canyon opening between them would get wider. If they did talk, what Josh would want to talk about might be as painful as the previous night's conversation and Rob wasn't sure he was strong enough to listen to any more.

He had always been able to talk to Josh, and hated that now he didn't know what to say. Even little things used to be so easy, so fun. Even in a shared shower they now stood miles apart under the same spray of water. Rob wondered if now, while Josh was closer than he had ever been, he'd lost him forever.

When he came downstairs he peeked into Josh's room. A habit the whole family seemed to have developed. Soon they'd being placing bets on which one of them would discover the body.

"I'm sorry," Josh said. The voice startled Rob. It was the first time Josh had initiated a conversation since he had been there. "About in the shower."

"It's okay."

"No, it's not," Josh started walking towards him. "I guess you're right, I need to talk to someone. I can't keep dumping all of this on you. And I realized I want to be able to have you touch me again without feeling . . . "

Josh fell into Rob's arms and Rob held him. But Rob noticed Josh was not crying. The front door opening caused them to break their clinch.

"How'd it go?" Rob asked his mother.

"I didn't get it."

"I'm sorry," Josh said. Mrs. Wardell seemed a little startled that Josh's voice sounded almost normal. "Next week, when I turn eighteen and can sign the authorizations, I'll see a counselor. I promise."

Rob and his mother smiled.

THIRTY-NINE

Rob was climbing the steps of the school when he saw Danny Taylor about to go inside. "Taylor!" he yelled.

Taylor turned, saw it was only Rob, and went inside. Rob sprinted up the stairs, looked left then right, spotted him again and yelled, "Taylor!" This time Taylor stopped and turned with a smirk on his face. Rob walked up to him. "Stay away from my house."

"I didn't go near your house."

"Then you know who did. So tell them the next time they come by and they think the house is empty or Josh is there alone that might be what I want you to think and that I'm really just waiting in the bushes with my father's twelve-gauge."

"Yeah, right. Like you're going to spend every night in the bushes with a gun."

Rob leaned into Taylor so close Taylor took a step back until he was against the wall, jarring loose a poster about an upcoming dance. "I'd wait ten thousand nights in the freezing rain to blow your fucking head off. And it'd be that much sweeter to do it legally." Rob saw something he had never seen before on Danny Taylor's face: fear. Rob turned and walked to homeroom.

*   *   *   *   *

Whether it was the talking or the anti-depressants the doctor gave him, Josh seemed to be feeling better, doing better at his schoolwork and helping around the house. But Rob still could not shake the feeling that there was something different. Other than a small scar near his eye, he bore no outward signs of his ordeal, but he looked and talked and moved almost like a different person.

The counselor had suggested the same gay youth group in Cleveland Rob had found on the Internet, so Rob skipped out of school early with a pass from Coach Hudson to drive Josh there. Josh stared out the window nervously looking from the directions to the street numbers.

Rob said, "The gay center should be around here somewhere." As though the timing was rehearsed, a man in shorts so tiny they looked like hot pants came out of a doorway. "He's gay," Rob said, giggling. "You want to ask him?"

"I don't want to talk to him," Josh said through his laughter.

"If those shorts were any shorter they'd be a shirt."

Josh laughed then pointed in the next block. "There. The rainbow flag."

Rob flipped a quick U-turn into a parking place as a young white man with a multi-colored Afro walked by and went in the door of the gay center. Rob opened his door. Josh didn't open his.

A beautiful person of indeterminate gender entered the building followed by another cute young person, this one apparently male, but wearing large earrings, eye shadow and a silk scarf. Rob got out and walked around to Josh's side.

Josh looked up at him and said through the glass, "I can't."

Rob shook his head indicating he hadn't really heard. Josh rolled down the window. "I can't. I'm sorry, but I can't go in there with all of those fa . . . people. I just wouldn't belong."

"Do you want to at least walk in and see what it looks like? See if there are some more normal guys, maybe see what . . . "

"No."

Rob frowned and walked back around the car and got in. "Are you sure you . . . "

"Could we just go, please?"

*   *   *   *   *

Rob's job was to get Josh out of the house, which in spite of his mood improvement wasn't an easy task, but finally Rob got Josh to go with him to look at Cleveland State University. He had to lay the guilt on rather thick and added, "And who knows, you may want to go there."

"I doubt I'll go to college," Josh answered in a tone that said his depression was far from over.

When they came back Rob let Josh walk in first. Meg had done what she'd promised and in a few hours had decorated the house with more balloons and streamers than a typical Chuck E. Cheese would see in a month.

The shout of "Surprise!" worked and the Wardells, Meg's friends Jesse and Hannah, Coach Hudson and his wife, Mr. Welke, Josh's former girlfriend Jenny, and Brittany Burnside—head cheerleader, homecoming queen, volleyball star—all jumped up on cue.

A large bunch of balloons moved aside revealing Mathias Schlagel. "Hey, bro, happy birthday."

"We had to plan this at a time when everyone could come," Rob said.

"So the little family dinner for my birthday last week was just a fake?"

"No, we wanted to do something quiet with just us," Rob's mother said. "But we wanted to throw a party, too."

"This was the only day I could figure a way to sneak away," Mat said.

"You don't think those little gifts last week were all we got you for your birthday?" Meg asked.

"You've given me too much already," Josh answered.

As Josh opened more presents, Rob and Meg stood aside to watch. "I wasn't sure I'd ever see that grin again," Rob said tilting his head towards Josh. "Thanks so much. I think today helped a lot."

"I know it did. And it's worth it just to see that smile," she said. Rob put his arm around his sister as Mat put his arm around his own brother.

"I hate to rush things," Mat said, "But if we're going to have cake we ought to do it. I need to get going soon."

After the cake and ice cream, Rob volunteered to take Mat home; Josh and Meg wanted to come also. The Schlagel brothers rode in the back, talking quietly. Rob stopped the car a little ways down from the entrance to Quail Run. Mat would walk from there. Meg got out when Mat did. She put her arms around his neck and kissed him on the cheek. "Thank you," she said. "If they ever have a best brother contest, it's going to be a tie. I look forward to you slipping me notes and smiling at me between classes."

"You know when I can't talk it's nothing personal?"

"I know. It's cool. If you ever do manage to escape again, let me know."

*   *   *   *   *

They all knew the holidays would be tough on Josh and Thanksgiving dinner wasn't a joyous occasion. Josh's mood was still down as they finished dinner. Although Mrs. Wardell tried several times to insist that he didn't need to help with the dishes, Josh joined in clearing the plates and getting to work on the huge kitchen mess. Mr. Wardell was left alone in the living room in front of the TV.

"It's a good thing they made big kitchens back when this house was built," Mrs. Wardell joked. "The mess would be bulging out the door if this room were any smaller."

"Like I'm bulging out of my pants," Meg said, adjusting her waistband. "I ate too much."

They all laughed, except Josh, whose attempt at a smile was so feeble that it drew all of their attention. Mrs. Wardell grabbed him and hugged him. Her warmth and good spirits didn't seem to dent Josh's depression and as Rob moved to grab another stack of plates, she grabbed him and pulled him into the embrace. Rob knew he and Josh were not supposed to touch in the house but now he was shoulder-to-shoulder with Josh in his mother's hug.

His mother pulled them both closer so their heads were almost touching, and more to steady themselves than by choice they put their arms around each other's backs. She pulled them even tighter, cementing the embrace. Then she broke away, pushing them together as she left the circle. Josh was too weak to think or resist and fell into Rob's arms. Rob squeezed tight as though he could crush the pain with the power of his hug. He stroked the fine soft hairs at the nape of Josh's neck and whispered, "It's okay. It's okay." Only when he felt the tension break and Josh really returned the hug did he release his friend.

Soaking in what had just happened, Rob looked around the room to make sure everything was okay. His mother was smiling at them, her look far from disapproving. Josh started to pick up a plate, but Mrs. Wardell took it from him. "Now I really insist. You boys go watch the game. Meg and I can finish up."

Rob looked at Meg, expecting a blizzard of complaints, but instead she took Josh's arm and steered him toward the door. She rested her head on his shoulder and said, "Do you know what I'm most thankful for?" He looked down at her. "You." She kissed him on the cheek and shoved him out into the living area.

Rob smiled at her and followed Josh.

FORTY

Meg reached up, but even standing on tiptoes could not quite reach the nail above the doorframe. Her feet hit the hardwood floor with a loud *thump* as she jumped from the chair. The maneuver brought a disapproving look from the woman of the house. "Can you get this?" Meg asked Josh as she handed him plastic mistletoe with a red ribbon.

"Sure," Josh said as he stepped up onto the chair.

"You just have to feel for the nail that's up there somewhere," Mrs. Wardell coached as she hung another glass ball on the tree. "Bobby, could you grab another box, please?" She pointed to the stack of ornament boxes next to the archway.

Josh ran his hand along the top of the arch, found the nail, and easily looped the ribbon over it. He stepped off the chair just as Rob reached the boxes.

"Bobby, Josh is under the mistletoe," his mother said in a provocatively teasing voice—the same one she used to goad Rob into kissing her or his sister. Rob couldn't believe that his mother meant it the same way. While he tried to sort this out, she said, with even more encouragement in her voice, "You're not going to let him get away with that, are you?"

Rob hesitated then moved toward Josh. He paused again and looked at his mother for approval. She was smiling and nodding, so he kissed Josh lightly on the cheek. He was so self-conscious about it that he couldn't even enjoy a sensation that usually sent lightning down his spine to his toes. He looked back at his mother who was watching and still grinning. She lightly shoved Meg toward the boys.

Meg grabbed Josh in a hug and kissed him on the lips. "That's how you are supposed to kiss under the mistletoe," she said, slugging her brother in the stomach.

Rob was still trying to process all that was happening and again looked at his mother. She was still watching, smiling and nodding as though once again urging one of her young children to let go of the pool edge and swim to her. Rob hugged Josh, with not quite the ferocity Meg had used and kissed Josh lightly on the lips causing Josh's green eyes to flash like a traffic signal with a short circuit.

Rob pulled away and again checked his mother's reaction and it was still all-approving. He smiled at her as he slipped his arm around Josh's waist. "Want to help with the tree?"

"Sure," Josh said. His eyes now shone with the joy and color of the season as he grabbed a stack of ornament boxes and handed them to Rob, then picked up the remainder to carry himself.

"I want to have it all done by the time your father gets home," Rob's mother beamed like a child on Christmas morning.

The last note of the Bing Crosby Christmas CD ended. Meg went to the stereo. "Johnny Mathis, or . . . " she flipped through the stack of CDs, "Harry Connick, or . . . "

"Johnny is good," their mother said. "Every year I say this, but one of these years I have to get the Muppets one." They all looked at her and Josh laughed the loudest. "I know it is goofy, but I like it," she said. "And isn't that what the season is all about—being a kid again and enjoying yourself?"

They nodded and, with Johnny Mathis roasting chestnuts on an open fire, finished trimming the tree.

*   *   *   *   *

"You have to leave me alone for bit," Josh said when they got to the mall. Rob was just glad Josh was willing to go shopping. It was his first venture to a really public place since the disastrous dinner out months ago. Rob was even more surprised that Josh wanted to be left on his own. Rob agreed to meet him back in front of the Gap in an hour.

As soon as they got home, Josh reached into one of the big shopping bags. "Here," he said, handing a gift-wrapped shirt-size box to Mrs. Wardell.

"Oh, Josh, this is so nice, thank you. I'll put it under the tree. The first gift of the year."

"No, you have to open it now," he insisted.

"Okay," she said, taking the nearest chair and excitedly ripping into the wrapping. She pulled off the box lid and was greeted with a sea of tissue paper. Sifting through it she came up with a plastic CD case. Suddenly she shrieked. "The Muppets Christmas!" she said almost hitting her husband in the face with it in her haste to show it to him. "We have to put this on!"

"That's why I wanted you to have it now," Josh beamed.

"Thank you, Josh," she said, leaping from the chair. She hugged him hard and then grabbed Rob to join them. Meg and their father joined the team hug.

Soon they were all singing along to Miss Piggy's part in the *Twelve Days of Christmas*. The way they all camped up the da-dum-dums after the *five golden rings* had them all giggling each time it came around.

When the song was over, she again hugged Josh tightly. "Thank you, that was so sweet."

Rob bolted from the group and ran upstairs.

The knock on his bedroom door came softly and Rob waited, lying on his bed until it came again. He wiped his eyes as quickly as he could, but knew his eyes would be red if he opened the door. He asked through the closed door, "Yeah?"

"It's me, Josh." Rob swallowed during the pause. "Can I come in?" Rob hesitated, but knew he could never say no to anything Josh asked and slowly opened the door. "You're crying," Josh said. "What's wrong?"

"I . . . uh . . . "

"Are you unhappy with me because I got your mom a gift? I guess I should've asked you, but I thought . . . "

Rob pulled Josh inside and closed the door, "We can't keep this closed long. Don't want them to think anything is going on. You are so sweet to get that for my mom."

"You're not mad?"

"Not at all. I think it's great."

"But . . . "

Rob hesitated, then what he should say came to him and it wasn't a total lie. "I was crying because you were so happy. It's been a long time since I've seen you that happy, sure you're doing the right thing, relaxed around my parents. It was great!"

"But?" Josh pushed Rob away to look him in the eye.

"You never heard of being so happy you cried?" Staring at Josh was making it harder to keep up any pretense. The green eyes always cut like lasers into him.

"Not with you I haven't. I know you, Rob. You looked hurt. Did I do something wrong?"

Rob grabbed Josh and hugged him close. "You could never do anything wrong."

"C'mere," he said taking Rob by the hand and pulling him to sit next to him on the bed. "I know we can't keep that door closed long, so I have to make this fast, but I think I know. You realized what I realized a few days ago. That being without my family during the holidays is going to be hard, and being the sensitive guy you are, your heart is breaking." Rob's jaw dropped. "Is that it?" Josh asked. Rob could but nod. "Don't feel sorry for me . . . " Josh continued. Rob started to speak, but Josh touched his fingers to Rob's lips to stop him. "I've done enough of that. I cried myself to sleep Thanksgiving night feeling sorry for myself. Poor little Joshua thrown out. All alone. But Friday putting up the tree with your mom and Megan, I realized something. I'm not alone. For the first time in my life I'm really not alone. We never had family moments like that. Christmas at our house was all preaching. We didn't have Santa and Rudolph and the Muppets. It would all take away from the story of the Christ child. And God forbid that we might have *fun*. We had a tree, but we decorated it following orders. Mat would always break something. I think he did it deliberately just to piss my parents off, just to break the dullness."

Josh was crying now, but Rob didn't see any sadness there. "I'm not saying I'm not going to miss my brothers and sisters, and yeah, even my parents some. But I'm not going to miss that lame ritual my parents go through 'cause it's Christmas. I'll get to see Mat, I'm sure, and I got a few little things for the other kids. Mat can say they're from him, but we'll know." Rob reached up to wipe a tear from the scar on Josh's cheek. "And mostly, Rob, I decided I'm going to have my best Christmas ever. In a houseful of people who love me, and I love. And who would never hurt me. You don't know what it's like to just go to bed knowing you are not going to wake up with a fist in your face or a belt on your ass. Or being screamed at or threatened, and half the time you're not even sure why . . . "

"So you think I'm a wuss for crying . . . "

Josh grabbed Rob and kissed him hard. "I ought to slug you the way your sister does when you do stupid shit. No, I don't think it was lame to cry. I'm very touched that you care so much for me that you'd feel my pain if you thought I was hurting." Rob took his hand from Josh's face to wipe one of his own tears. "It seems weird to me to use the word love, 'cause I usually had it directed at me while I was being hit. But, you have to know I do."

"We ought to get back downstairs, before they think something's up." Josh nodded and smiled. Rob stood and opened the door. Josh started out, and Rob grabbed his arm. "You have done wonders for my family. All this closeness, all the lovey-dovey stuff you see down there? A lot of that is because of you. We hug all the time now. We didn't that much before. And . . . "Josh looked at Rob, puzzled and Rob went on, "We were never that close. I never really talked to them that much. I talked to Meg some, but was too afraid to talk to anyone for fear my big secret would slip out. Now that it's out, I can talk. And amazingly, they talk back. 'Cause of you, I've talked to my parents about things I never thought we'd talk about. You sort of made us come together. And I never dreamed my mom would actually encourage me to kiss you!" Josh smiled. "So, thank you, Joshua Lawrence Schlagel. In your own sneaky way, you've really made us a family." Josh was beaming now. "And another thing," Rob checked to make sure the hall was empty and planted a small kiss on Josh's wet cheek, "I love you. And I never doubted you love me."

"C'mon," Josh said and dragged Rob toward the stairs.

"You guys work out whatever the problem was?" Rob's dad asked when they reentered the living room.

"There was no problem," Rob said.

"None at all," Josh agreed, grinning with a tear-filled dimple.

Mr. Wardell looked at his wife, but she shrugged.

"Everything is great," Rob said, his nose still twitching from crying.

Josh looked at Rob and Rob could feel the love and warmth wash over him. "But not quite perfect," Josh said.

"It's not?" Rob asked, concerned.

"No. It's not. We missed the rest of the Muppets."

"More Muppets!" Meg yelled.

"Muppets! Muppets! Muppets!" everyone began chanting, except Mr. Wardell, who was too busy laughing.

"And we need popcorn," Rob said "Then it would be perfect."

"It would be," his mom said as she threw herself on the couch forcing Josh to scrunch over against her son. She put her arm around Josh and looked up at her husband, "Make some!"

"Anything else?" he asked with mock offense.

"Uh, hot chocolate would be good," Josh said. They all looked at Josh. It occurred to Rob, and he wasn't sure if it did to the other members of the family, that it was the first time that Josh had ever asked for anything or made any sort of demand upon the family.

Apparently Mr. Wardell did take note, because he offered none of the playful resistance he would have if another member of the family had asked. Instead he said, "Hot chocolate and popcorn, coming right up!" The rest of the family could hear his voice carry from the kitchen as he sang along with Miss Piggy.

FORTY-ONE

After another below-freezing night selling Christmas trees at Greiner's, Rob and Josh were huddled under one blanket on the couch in front of the fireplace drinking hot chocolate. They barely had time to break their embrace at the sound of footsteps on the stairs when Mr. Wardell appeared and they both greeted him in voices that gave away their guilt.

"Your mom wanted a nightcap," he said and headed for the kitchen.

The boys let out nervous giggles once he was out of the room. "I thought they were in bed," Rob whispered. His father reappeared and they both smiled sheepish smiles again.

His dad put one foot on the bottom step then turned back. "It's not as though we don't know you guys sneak into each other's rooms after we're in bed."

Rob swallowed. "I, uh . . . I'm sorry, I just . . . "

"And it's kind of hard to say we approve, but it's not like one of you is going to end up pregnant."

"Are you saying it's okay?"

"Not really okay, but it's happening. And that porch never did get much heat out there. Good night, you two,"

Rob looked up. "Thanks, dad."

"Merry Christmas," he said as he continued up the stairs without looking back.

*   *   *   *   *

Josh walked into the kitchen ahead of Rob. "Well, I guess that's it for a few months."

"Yep, cleaning up and closing up Greiner's the week after Christmas seems kind of sad."

"It's not sad that we won't be freezing our butts off any more."

Rob leaned in to pin Josh against the kitchen counter. "The fun part of that was warming your butt afterwards." Rob kissed him but stopped suddenly when he heard a stifled scream. He turned to see Mrs. Jackson fleeing the kitchen.

Rob walked into the living room where Mr. Wardell's old college roommate, Dave Jackson, and his wife along with Rob's parents were reacting to the scream.

"What's wrong?" Rob asked.

"You were kissing that boy!" Mrs. Jackson yelled. Josh walked into the living room. "Him!" she said, as though pointing out her assailant to the police.

"This is my boyfriend, Josh," Rob said, amazed that it was the first time he had ever introduced Josh that way and that it sounded so simple and right.

"That's disgusting!" she roared. She looked to her husband and then the Wardells.

"Karen, calm down," Mr. Wardell said.

"You knew this was going on under your roof?"

"Yes, of course."

She looked at her husband and started for the door. He looked at the Wardells then back to his wife, "You might want the car keys so you can keep warm out there," he said.

She turned. "You're not coming?"

"We just got here. And Marilyn promised us lasagna. She's not going to get out of it that easy." His attempted joke fell flat.

"We're leaving," she said.

"I told you about Josh months ago," he said, "When Bob called me for legal advice."

"You said a friend of Bobby's, not a boyfriend!"

"Same difference." He got up and extended his hand to Josh. "Hi, I'm Dave Jackson. And I believe you've met my wife, Karen."

"Nice to meet you," Josh said, taking the offered hand.

"And how are you doing, Bobby?" The man offered his hand again.

"Fine and you?"

Jackson turned to his wife. "Are you going to calm down?"

She was still clutching the doorknob. "I just get so tired of this. Every time you turn on the TV or open a newspaper, there is gay this and gay that. I never expected to see it in this house."

"Frankly, Karen, neither did we," Marilyn said, "But now that it's here, the world hasn't ended. In fact our world has sort of expanded. We didn't lose a son, we gained one."

Meg came downstairs. She said her hellos to the Jacksons then turned to her mother. "Dinner smells great. When do we eat?"

"We're going out to grab something," Rob said. "We can leave the adults alone to talk."

"What?" His mother stood up.

"The atmosphere here isn't really conducive to digesting food. We'll go out," he said.

"What about the lasagna?" Meg asked.

"We'll have leftovers for lunch tomorrow. It's better the day after, anyway, when it gets a little crusty on top."

"What about . . . ?"

"Come along, Megan," Rob said firmly.

She followed him and Josh through the kitchen. Josh got into Mr. Wardell's SUV next to Rob. "I didn't want to say anything inside, but after what happened last time we went out . . . "

Rob nodded. "There's a new pizza place in Strongsville."

"That's a bit of drive."

"That's the point — to get the hell out of this town."

"Are you guys going to tell me what's going on?" the female voice in the backseat demanded as they drove off.

*   *   *   *   *

The first warm day of spring found Edward DeLallo standing next to the teacher with a pass. Rob got up and followed Edward out. "How's it going?" Edward asked as they walked the deserted halls of the school while the morning announcements leaked out of each door they passed.

"Good and you?"

"Okay. I haven't been slammed into a locker in months."

Rob laughed. "Me neither. Makes life almost dull, doesn't it?"

"You and Josh still together?"

"Yeah."

"He's a lucky guy," Edward said. "I know this is bad, but I keep hoping you guys will break up so I can date you. I hope you're not offended."

"I'm flattered. But Josh and I are still together. He sleeps in my bed every night."

"That lucky bastard."

"I'll tell him you think so. Thanks, bye."

Edward kept walking past Hudson's homeroom. The coach came out into the hall. "Wardell, you weren't at practice yesterday," Hudson said by way of greeting.

"I'm not going to be on the team this year."

"Why not?"

"I'm busy working at Greiner's and with school and stuff. I never played anyway."

"You would this year for sure. We're short a lot of guys. Beechler, Rydell, Renko and Acosta graduated and we're minus

Schlagel. Taylor, Poulan, Brickman and the rest didn't come out. Of course I made it clear I didn't want them. We'll have lots of holes. And a pretty lousy team. I'd love to have you back. In fact I was going to make you captain."

"Captain?"

"You're one of the most experienced guys I'd have and you are more of a leader than you think."

"I'm not that good."

"Do you think I forgot that you saved Schlagel's no-hitter? The team needs you and I'd like to have you back. You've got a good head for the game. You'd make a great coach."

Rob smiled. "I was never really that into it, Coach. I only stuck with it last year to be near Josh."

Hudson smiled. "Please think about it. I really could use you."

"Thanks Coach, I will, but I doubt it'll happen."

"That's too bad. You look like you've put on a few inches and a few pounds since last year."

"We both know I couldn't play college ball anywhere anyway. And somehow it doesn't seem right without Josh."

"I understand. Speaking of which, I need to talk to him. Will he be around this evening if I stop by?"

"He's working tonight. Tomorrow would be better."

"Okay. One more thing, Wardell. Of all of the lousy Coach Hudson imitations I've heard over the years, yours was the best."

*   *   *   *   *

"What did Coach Hudson want?" Rob asked as he entered what was still Josh's room although he rarely slept there.

"He wants to try to get me a baseball scholarship. Says he knows some people."

"Awesome."

"I told him no."

"Why? With your arm, there are lots of schools that would pay you to go there."

"I'm out of shape."

"You're looking at your personal trainer. I'll work you back into shape so fast, I'll make your sorry ass sweat . . . "

Josh smiled. "You really think I can do this?"

"I know you can. I'm gonna make you."

*   *   *   *   *

Rob knocked on the door of Hudson's homeroom and motioned the teacher into the hall. Hudson smiled when Rob told him he had changed Josh's mind.

"He's going to have to work hard for this to happen," Hudson said.

"He knows. I'm going to kick his ass."

"You would make a good coach," Hudson smiled. "Where are you going to school next year?"

"I don't know yet. Money is a little tight these days, so I'm looking at state schools. We looked at Ohio State last month. The size of it kinda scares me."

"You could get lost in a crowd that size."

"That might not be a bad thing," Rob smiled. "Or, since it's thirty times bigger than this school there could be thirty times more Taylors and Brickmans."

"It still frustrates me that all those guys got was a small suspension. They should have been expelled and prosecuted."

"One thing I have already learned, Coach, is that life isn't always fair. I was so mad for so long, but what did that prove. I just have to put it behind me and get on with my life. I just wish Josh could."

"I do, too. You've grown a lot this past year, and I don't just mean in inches. You know there are scholarships for private schools. You'd be an asset to any college."

"I'm getting A's this year, but overall my grades weren't all that great." Rob was used to getting B's so as not to draw attention to himself, but now that he had the attention anyway he had decided to get straight A's and did.

"There are other types of scholarships. Let me do some checking for you." The coach patted him on the shoulder. "Are you willing to learn to catch?"

"I can catch."

"Behind the plate."

*   *   *   *   *

Hudson met them as promised after regular baseball practice and for the first time in his baseball career, Rob donned the tools of ignorance which Hudson had borrowed from the school. The chest protector and mask and shin guards made it hard to walk let alone squat or catch anything. The first day's practice turned out to be more coaching for Rob than for Josh.

As they walked off the field, Josh smiled. "I had forgotten how much I missed throwing a baseball. I've never told anyone this, but sometimes I would go out to a baseball diamond—didn't matter which one—and just lay on the pitcher's mound with my head on the rubber and stare at the clouds. The mound was the only place I felt at home and happy until I moved in with your family."

*   *   *   *   *

Rob and Josh were already on the field with Josh stinging Rob's hand with every throw when Hudson walked up to home plate. He handed Rob some papers. Rob stood from the crouch to look at them as the coach said, "It's a scholarship application for the Point Foundation. Ever hear of Oberlin College?"

"Yeah, sure."

"Nice little school. Very open-minded. Check it out."

Before Rob could thank him, Hudson trotted toward the mound. "I saw those last three pitches, Schlagel. On every one you weren't bringing your leg around. You need to use your whole body . . . "

*   *   *   *   *

"The drive to Oberlin isn't that bad," Josh said as he drove back from the campus tour with Rob. "You could commute if you had to."

"I'd like to go away to school if I can. If the scholarship comes through, that will cover most of my tuition so dad will just have to pay the rest and room and board. Or student loans. Kind of ironic—a year ago I wasn't gay and now I'm applying for gay scholarships."

"I have a feeling you'll be president of the gay group or the student body in a year or two."

Rob smiled, "Yeah, right."

"If Hudson comes through, I'll end up at a school with a good baseball program in Florida or Arizona or California. I thought I couldn't wait to get out of Ohio, but now that I might be leaving soon, I realize how much I will miss it. Well not Ohio, just you and your family."

FORTY-TWO

Tickets to the Indians' home opener were always hard to come by, but against the rival Detroit Tigers were even more of a challenge. Rob's persistence had paid off and when he surprised Josh with the tickets he thought Josh was going to knock in his teeth with the power of the kiss.

Josh and Rob crossed the street toward the stadium and started down the sidewalk. Horns blaring behind them caused the boys to turn and see a man coming at them doing a broken field run through moving traffic. "Josh! Josh!" the man was yelling.

Rob looked at Josh for some sort of an explanation. The man grabbed Josh and held him by the shoulders to look at him at close range. Rob tensed, not sure if he should be doing something to protect Josh from the crazed intruder who asked, "My God, it really is you, isn't it?"

"It's me," Josh said, surprised by the depth of emotion coming his way. "Hi, Mr. Hood."

"You're alive!"

"Uh, yeah," Josh said, confused.

Mr. Hood hugged him tightly then released him to look at him again. "It's really you! I'm so relieved you're alive!"

"Why wouldn't I be?"

"Because your father told me you were dead."

"What?"

"Last fall. He told everyone at work you had been killed in a motorcycle accident. He said your body was so badly mangled they weren't even going to have a funeral."

"He what?" Josh began shaking.

"He said you were dead. We had the whole family over to offer our condolences. Oh my God, I have to call Ellen and Katie. Katie is going to be so happy . . . " Mr. Hood pulled out a cell phone.

Josh grabbed his hand. "He told you I was dead?"

Mr. Hood let his hand with the cell phone in it drop to his side. "He told me you were dead?" he said again, but now it was a question not a statement.

Rob reached out to put his hand on Josh's shoulder. He could see a meltdown coming.

"Why would he do that?" Mr. Hood asked.

Josh shook his head and looked at Rob instead of Hood when he answered, "He'd rather have me dead and mutilated . . . he'd rather kill me to the world than . . . "

Rob grabbed Josh as Josh crumbled into his shoulder.

Looking over Josh's shoulder, Rob could see Hood slowly nodding as things fell into place. Hood reached out and turned Josh from Rob and let Josh now have his body for support. The baseball crowd gave them odd looks as the man tried to comfort the boy. From inside the stadium, they could already hear the rhythmic thumping of the drum.

"I'm so sorry," Mr. Hood said. "I've known your dad a long time. We worked together before you were born. He always could be an ass, but since he found God he's gotten much worse."

"You don't know the half of it."

"They threw him out," Rob said quietly, trying to control his own tears. Two of them crying was already drawing enough stares.

"Josh, I'm so sorry. I guess he had to explain your absence at family functions so they . . . "

As Hood hesitated, Josh finished the sentence, "Killed me."

"I don't know what to say. I'm just so glad you're alive. Really, our family is going to be so happy. Katie was distraught for months. I'd like to kick your father's ass for putting us through that." Hood turned to Rob. "My daughter is a year older than Josh and has been in love with him since even before they started school." The man extended his hand, "Hi, I'm Rob Hood."

"Rob Wardell."

They shook.

"You're his . . . ?" Hood searched for a word.

"Boyfriend . . . and brother," Rob answered. "My parents pretty much adopted him."

"I'm glad he's safe and taken care of. I'm sure the shock will sink in later, but right now . . . " Hood again hugged Josh, "I'm just so glad you're okay." He looked at Josh again. "Are you okay, Josh?"

"Yeah. Most of the time. They take good care of me."

"Do you still have our number?"

"I don't think I've had it at all since the move to Cleveland."

Hood patted his pockets. Rob pulled out his cell phone. "What is it? I can put it in here."

Hood rattled off the number then said, "Call if you need anything. You're still family to us, Josh. I know Katie and her mother would love to see you. Would you guys come to dinner?"

Rob looked at Josh, who was still in a daze as though he'd been struck in the head. "We'll give you a call," Rob answered.

The opening notes of the National Anthem were now drifting out of the stadium.

"You guys should get going, you'll miss the game," Hood said. He again hugged Josh with a force Rob thought might break ribs. He then turned and shook Rob's hand again. "Take good care of him. I sometimes feel like I'm his uncle, so I want to know he's in good hands. With the name Rob I know you have to be a good guy." With a final hug, Hood hurried off, putting his cell phone to his ear.

Rob looked at the devastated young man in front of him. It was as though he really had been mangled in a motorcycle accident. "Do you want to go home?" Rob asked as gently as possible.

"You paid all that money . . . "

"I did it because I love you and I want you to be happy. You won't be happy at the game. So if you want to go, we can go." Josh pulled Rob to him and held him tight. Rob was aware of more strange stares, but was past caring what anyone thought. "We can go home," he whispered in Josh's ear.

He felt Josh's head nod and they turned to walk away from the stadium as a cheer went up from the crowd inside Progressive Field.

At the car, Josh opened the passenger door of his car then handed his keys to Rob. "Will you drive?"

Rob went around and got in the driver's side.

"They're never going to stop ruining my life are they?" Josh asked. "Every time I think I've accepted how things are, they can still make it worse. And what sucks most is that they manage to ruin your life, too. You plan this wonderful day, you get us tickets, and I think I might just be able to be happy again . . . "

Rob grabbed Josh in a tight clinch and Josh mumbled into his neck, " . . . how could he do this to the Hoods? They've almost been family. I know it's crazy, but as much as I hate them and after all they've done to me, I still miss them. I can't tell you how much it hurts to know they killed me to everyone I know."

"You're right. I can't imagine how that would feel. All I can do is tell you that I love you. And you have a home."

As they exited I-71 onto Route 303 Josh looked at Rob. "Could you stop for a minute?"

"Sure. What's up?" He pulled off onto the wide dirt shoulder and stopped the car.

"I just don't want Meg to see me like this. I feel like I've let her down so much."

"She understands. We all do."

"Maybe you shouldn't. Maybe you should tell me to take my problems and my scared little faggot ass and get out."

Rob grabbed Josh and turned him to face him full on. "I don't ever want to hear you say that again. Ever. You're not leaving, you're not a faggot, and you have to stop thinking that way." Josh recoiled as though he had been slapped. "I'm sorry," Rob said quietly. "I just hate to hear you do that. You are still Meg's hero. And my hero. Now let's go home."

Their entrance into the house where the family was watching the game on TV caused puzzled stares, but Rob's warning look silenced any questions as he escorted his patient upstairs.

When Rob came downstairs later he was surprised to see his father still in front of the TV with the volume low. His dad immediately switched off the set and turned to face Rob.

"Still up?" Rob asked.

"Yeah, wanted to see how the game came out. Your mom and sister gave up and went to bed."

"Thanks, dad."

"For what?"

"Staying up for me."

"Are you okay, Rob?"

Rob shrugged. His dad motioned to the seat next to him. Rob said, "I came down for a drink. I'll be right back."

Rob went to the kitchen, returned with a Gatorade and took the seat next to his father. Rob sighed. "It just seems like so much work sometimes. Like it's never going to end." His father nodded and Rob went on, "I know this is selfish, but I just want to have fun again. It seems like everything is work now. I want to be a kid again."

His dad put his hand on his shoulder. "You've grown up a lot in the past few months."

"Sometimes I feel like it's too much. Like I'm Josh's father instead of his boyfriend. Here to catch him after one crisis then another."

"That's an interesting description of parenting. But that's kind of what it is. You try to help your kids through each crisis, but at the same time try to help them be strong enough to handle things themselves. At some point they have to learn to fly on their own."

"Your little bird leaving the nest." Rob smiled even though he could feel his already-drained eyes swelling up again.

"What you've done for Josh is amazing, but at some point he's going to have to make his own way in the world. That's not selfish. That's life. I'm so proud of you and it'll hurt a lot when you leave for school next year, but it'd be selfish of me to want you to stay here and stop growing and learning. At some point Josh will have to leave the nest, too. You can't always be there for him."

Rob nodded and frowned.

FORTY-THREE

All of Rob's powers of persuasion could barely get Josh out of bed and there was no way he could talk him into baseball practice. Josh was on the sun porch watching TV when Hudson entered. "Get up, Schlagel," Hudson ordered.

Josh looked up, but didn't stand. "Okay, then I'll come down to your level," Hudson said, spinning a chair in front of the television. "Do you have any idea how many phone calls I made, how many strings I pulled to even get you tryouts with these schools in Florida?"

Rob watched, leaning against the doorframe, as Josh stared at Hudson. "You're lucky to even have a shot after not playing your senior year. Most schools wouldn't even give you a tryout. Now, I'm sorry all this happened, but you can either suck it up and get on with your life or just sit here and wallow in self-pity, but don't try to drag Wardell down with you. Even if you can't see your future, he's got one."

Josh looked over at Rob. Then Hudson did. Apparently Hudson hadn't known Rob was there. There was a question in Josh's eyes. Rob answered it, "I want what is best for you, Josh.

You have to know that by now. Even though it means losing you for a while, this is the best thing. You can't live the rest of your life on this porch. I'm not staying here. My parents are going to sell the house as soon as Meg graduates. You need to get a life. We both know it's a long shot that you'll make the pros, but it can at least pay for college. Please. Grab your mitt and let's go throw a few."

Josh got up, grabbed his hat and glove, but said nothing. Rob had no great hopes for it being a very good practice.

The next day's practice wasn't much better and Hudson was having a practice with the team so Rob was on his own. Rob knew Hudson had lots of extra work to do given the lack of experience among the players he had this year. Between school, the team and coaching Josh on the side, Rob wondered if Hudson ever saw his children.

Rob had his hands full just with Josh. After yet another sloppy pitch that was way too high for him to even try to jump for, Rob pulled off the mask and stood up. "I'm not chasing those. You can run around and gather them up." Rob pointed to the collection of balls that had accumulated in the net behind the garage. Rob had built a pitcher's mound and laid down a home plate sixty feet, six inches away, using the back of the garage, strung with a net as the backstop. His dad had helped so it would be finished in time to surprise Josh when he got home from work one day. Rob still marveled at how well he got along with his dad now and that they could really talk.

"If you don't want to practice today, that's fine," Josh said and started to walk toward the house.

"Where are you going?"

"You said you wanted to quit."

"No, you said *you* wanted to quit," Rob corrected. "Do you think I like sweating my ass off, having my hand hurt so bad at the end of the day I have to stick it in ice before I can do my homework?" Josh couldn't hold Rob's eyes any longer and stared out at the cornfield. "Now, if you're willing to work, I am, but if you're not I've got other things to do."

Josh studied the tiny green stalks. "I guess not. Why bother?"

Rob walked toward the mound. "What do you mean, 'why bother?'"

"What's the point?"

"The point is to get you to practice so you can ace a tryout and get into a decent college."

"Is that what you want?"

"Do you think I'm doing this for me? Yes, it's what I want. And I want you to start caring about something again."

"Why? If I do, they'll just find a way to ruin it."

"Is that what this is about? You're the only one who can ruin this. I'm willing to do the work, Hudson's willing to do the work, but we can only do so much. You have to pitch. And if you do, no one can take that away from you. You can call your own shots; make your own decisions."

Josh looked down at his friend, then back at the corn.

"You really think some college would want me?"

"Would I be sweating to death in this stupid outfit if I didn't?" Josh turned back to face Rob. "I'm going to get the balls, I'm going to throw them to you and then you're going to pitch them to me. PITCH THEM. Not give them a half-assed toss over my head. Are you ready to work?"

Josh gave a slight nod and Rob trotted back to home plate. Rob threw the balls to Josh then crouched down. He held up a hand to stop Josh from pitching and stood back up. "Every wild pitch or pitch you don't bother to put anything on will mean a lap to the cemetery and back."

"How will you know if I go all the way?"

"Cause I'll do them with you to make sure you really run. I can still run rings around you, Schlagel, but I'll be there for you every step of the way."

Josh smiled and then jerked his wrist to warn Rob that a curve ball was coming.

*   *   *   *   *

Rob headed towards his locker and was surprised to see someone leaning against it. She turned and he saw it was Brittany Burnside. Head cheerleader. Homecoming Queen. Volleyball star.

"Hey, Bobby," she said. "How are things?"

"Okay, and you?"

"Good, but I want to make them better. And I need your help. You got a minute?"

Rob looked at the giant hall clock. "I have six until the bell rings. Shoot."

"Jenny and I were talking. We want to go the prom, I mean, we're only seniors once, so we really want to go. But when we look around at the prospects—well, she wants to go with Josh. That is, if he wants to. And if you're cool with it. I mean, it's not a date obviously—he'd just be her escort. And you have to admit, he'd look great in the pictures that she'll have for the rest of her life."

Rob smiled. "True. Maybe I should rent him out for proms."

"Yeah, start pimping your boyfriend," Brittany laughed.

"So, you want to borrow Josh?"

"Well more than that . . . " she began.

"You want me to ask Josh for Jenny . . . "

"Yes, but I also want you to be my date."

"Huh?"

"I want the four of us to go. You as my escort, Josh with Jenny, but if the four of us all end up dancing together, hey, shit happens."

"You want to go to the prom with me?"

"Yes, if you would."

Rob laughed; she didn't. "The homecoming queen and the king of the dweebs—you don't think that's a bit funny?"

"Not at all. I can't think of any other guy at school I would care to date. If you were me—do you see any other candidates? Anyone who isn't a total jerk or likely to try to get me drunk and rape me? Danny Taylor asked me, if you can believe that. And I told him he didn't know how to date a girl, only rape one."

"So I'm like your last resort?"

"Oh, no, Bobby, I didn't mean it like that," she said touching his arm. "I just know I'm not exactly your type." She smiled. "I would consider it an honor to go with you. You aren't a dweeb. I'd want to date you if there was anything in it for me."

"You don't care that you are like what, two inches taller than your date?"

"Probably four. And, no. I look up to you. And I promise not to wear heels."

"You don't care what anyone will say when they see who you brought?"

The bell rang, but neither of them moved. She waited until there was silence to answer. "Yes, I very much care. I want to be seen with the cutest, bravest, most thoughtful guy in this school. I want my prom to be special and I can't think of anyone more special. These memories have to last the rest of my life and for once I want to make the right choice."

"I never even thought about going to the prom."

"Please do. I can't imagine anyone bothering us. It's been so long and there'll be so many people there."

She tore a page out of her notebook and scribbled. "Here is my number and Jenny's so Josh can call her if he wants. Please think about it. It can be yours and Josh's prom with us just along for the ride." Rob took the paper. "I'll even make my dad spring for the limo," she added, flashing the famous Brittany Burnside homecoming queen smile.

"I'll talk to Josh."

"Thanks. You know the other nice thing about only having a few weeks of school left — we don't care if we're late for class." She kissed him and hurried down the hall.

FORTY-FOUR

They heard the limo crunching on the gravel drive and a moment later Meg scream up the stairs, "Rob! Josh! Your ride is here!"

"Just a sec!" Rob yelled back. "How do you put this on?" Rob asked Josh, holding up his cummerbund. "And what's it for?"

"To make you look even more handsome than you already do," Josh answered as he slipped the strange item around Rob's waist and buckled it for him. While Josh still had his hands there, he kissed Rob.

"You know what I keep thinking?" he asked with his lips still almost touching Rob's. "What it would be like to be marrying you." Rob swallowed. "Us both in tuxes like this, you looking so wonderful. Us walking down the aisle together . . . " He kissed Rob again.

"We should go," Rob said. "Can't keep our dates waiting."

"I love you, Rob."

"And I love you."

Rob turned away from Josh and pulled a tuxedo jacket off a hanger on the bedroom door. "Turn around."

Josh did and Rob helped him on with his coat. "Your turn," Josh said as he slipped Rob's jacket off its hanger and onto his boyfriend. Rob started for the door, but Josh said, "Wait." Josh held up a boutonnière.

"Shouldn't we let the girls do that?" Rob asked.

"I'd like to."

Rob smiled and walked back to Josh who pinned on his flower. Rob returned the favor and Josh kissed him again.

"I could just stand here and look at you all night," Josh whispered.

"I'm not sure that was the plan for the evening." Rob took Josh's hand and led him into the hall.

Rob's parents, Meg, Jenny and Brittany all turned and their faces lit up as Rob and Josh came down the stairs hand in hand.

"Wow!" Mrs. Wardell said.

Meg said, "You both look so beautiful." She kissed them both. "Where's your camera?"

"Oh shoot, I left it upstairs."

Rob turned back toward the stairs, but Meg said, "I'll get it" and darted out of the room.

"We have to swing by my house and Jenny's," Brittany said, "Our parents want pictures, too."

"The first picture here has to be of Bobby and Josh," Jenny said. "This was a bad idea, Brit, our dates are better looking than we are."

"The boys don't look bad, but you are both beautiful," Mr. Wardell said.

"I don't think I was this excited at my own prom," his wife said.

After many photos in all possible combinations of couples and with and without family, they left. As they walked to the limo, Brittany took Rob's arm and said, "Thank you. I'm so happy right now."

"Thank you," he answered. "I never would've thought to do this. But it's going to be a wonderful night."

*　　　*　　　*　　　*　　　*

Maybe it was only Rob's imagination that everyone turned to stare when they entered the ballroom. As he felt the stares of Danny Taylor, Corey Brickman and their cohorts and dates he tightened his grip on Brittany's arm and she squeezed back. A flash went off in their faces blinding Rob for a moment. When his vision returned, he saw a friend of Brittany's was smiling behind the camera.

Ryan Tattorelli came toward them, his large body looking very odd in a tuxedo. Rob braced, he wasn't sure for what or why. Ryan extended his hand. "Glad you could make it," he said, welcoming Rob then turned to Josh. "Good to see you again, Josh. You look great." Ryan guided them to a table on the far side of the room away from Taylor and company.

*   *   *   *   *

Rob tiptoed upstairs, but Meg's light was on. She came out into the hall. "How was it?" she asked in a whisper.

"Great. More than great," he whispered back.

"Where's Josh?"

"He had a few too many sips from Ryan's flask. I put him to bed downstairs."

"Are you tired? Should I wait and ask you about it in the morning?"

"I won't sleep. It was too awesome. On one of the last slow dances, Jenny came over and cut in—not to dance with me, but to let me dance with Josh. My head against his chest, his head on my shoulder. It was incredible. I don't think I will ever be that happy again. Ever."

"Wow."

"And when the song ended," Rob swallowed, choking before going on. "People applauded. Not just Brittany and Jenny, but Ryan and Summer and Ronnie Hicks and lots of people. This whole circle of people. People I don't even know. They were clapping for me and Josh. It was the best night of my life. But then I realized something. It was the worst night of my life."

"Why? What happened?"

"No, nothing like you're thinking. Nothing bad happened. The few assholes were so outnumbered they just left us alone and after a while I forgot they were there. I just realized as incredible as Josh looked tonight—he did look incredible didn't he?"

"No. Incredible doesn't begin to describe it. I got goose bumps—look, I'm getting them again—you both looked so great."

"As great as the evening was, I realized something."

"That you aren't in love with Josh anymore?"

"How'd you know?"

"I could tell. The last month or so. Something changed."

"Was it that obvious?"

"I'm not sure anyone else knows. I don't think Josh does."

"And I can't tell him. He asked me to marry him tonight. How can I say no? I'm all he has."

"You can't spend the rest of your life with him out of pity."

"It was such a strange night. How I could be so happy and so sad at the same time. I mean I still love him. I always will."

"How could you not? But you just aren't in love with him anymore."

"I'm tired of having him leaning on me all the time. I'm not that strong to carry both of us."

"You're a lot stronger than you think."

"I know it makes me a terrible person, to want out."

"No, it makes you human." Meg hugged him again and said, "I think we're both a little disappointed he isn't the hero we both once thought he was."

"How did you get so smart?"

"I learned from my big brother."

Rob smiled. "You ought to get to bed. I'm not going to be able to sleep. I need to go for a run."

"In your tux?"

Rob smiled. "It's a thought."

Meg turned back towards her room, and Rob said, "Wait."

She turned around. He unpinned his boutonnière and presented the flower to her. "Here. Thank you."

"For what?"

"Being a great friend. I also realized tonight, my days at home are numbered. I'm going to miss you."

"You're not leaving yet," she said, slugging him in the cummerbund.

"Is it possible I'm going to miss that when I go away to college?"

"Maybe you'll get a cute roommate who can keep you on your toes."

Rob smiled then pulled his tie off and unbuttoned the first button of his shirt. He reached behind his neck and undid a clasp. He handed Meg her gold cross. "Thanks for that, too."

"You wore it tonight?"

"Yeah, for good luck."

She placed it back in his hand. "Keep it. Good night, Rob."

She kissed him and went into her room. Rob went into his room, took off his jacket and cummerbund, traded his dress shoes for his Nikes and went out for a run.

FORTY-FIVE

Josh's fist was in Rob's face before either of them knew Josh had swung his arm. Rob staggered backwards, reeling from the blow. The punch registered as much fear and pain on Josh's face as it did on Rob's. Rob was too shocked to feel the physical damage. Josh stepped forward to touch Rob, the look of horror still carving itself in Josh's features. Rob instinctively drew away and that motion caused Josh to recoil and say, "Oh, God. I'm so sorry!"

Rob couldn't bring himself to speak. He stared in amazement at Josh, afraid to even blink for fear of what might next happen. He was oblivious to the red rising on his cheek, the cut on his lip oozing a tiny slice of crimson, or his frozen eyes swelling up.

"Rob, I don't know how that happened. Robby, please say something."

Again he tried to move toward Rob and again Rob backed away. Rob turned and started walking. He could hear Josh's footsteps behind him. Without turning or looking back, he held up a hand to stop Josh. The gesture worked. The footsteps stopped. Rob kept walking until he found something to support himself. He looked around at the beautiful surroundings of Josh's secret spot, the gurgle of the waterfall in the distance still filling his ears, and he wondered if he could ever enjoy this place again. He leaned his head against the tree and closed his eyes as he fought for some notion of what had just happened.

He shouldn't have yelled at Josh. He should have known how vulnerable and fragile Josh still was, but Josh had a lot of nerve telling him he was leaving next week. He thought they'd have the summer together. He thought Josh would've have given him some notice. Josh should have called from Florida the minute he knew he'd have to start for the summer session to make the team. After all Rob and his family had done for him, Josh at least owed them that.

"Rob?" Josh's voice grew closer. "Please don't run away. Please let me talk." Rob stiffened but didn't move away from the tree. "If I say I'm sorry again, I know it's still way too little. But I am sorry. I don't know what happened." Josh paused. "Actually I do. You never yelled at me before. I snapped. I'm sorry, but, oh God. This is how my father was. Someone pisses you off, you hit them." Rob didn't turn around. "I know it's not right, and I pray that I'm not really wired that way. I think I scared me more than I scared you. I'm sorry. You have to know I didn't mean that." Rob took a breath. "Please, Rob, say something."

"I want to go home."

FORTY-SIX

Rob put a suitcase into the backseat of Josh's car. "That's the last bag. You're WTW," he said. He tossed his baseball glove in on top.

Josh looked at Rob. "Your glove?"

"Yeah. I'm not going to need it again and you've worn it more for the past few months than I have. Maybe it'll bring you luck."

Josh hugged Rob again. "How many more times can I say thank you?"

Rob opened the door and Josh got in, looking up awkwardly at his friend. Rob closed the back door and looked down at Josh and said, "I once said I couldn't go on living without you. Now I know we're both strong enough to make it on our own."

"I'm only strong enough because I know you're here for me," Josh answered.

"And I always will be." Even as he said it, Rob knew that the promised phone calls and emails would soon dwindle.

A chapter in his life was closing as he closed the car door.

DEDICATION

If you're a reader who likes to skip ahead, this is at the back of the book instead of the front because it makes reference to some incidents in the story and I would hate to spoil any surprises, so you may want to wait to read this until after you've finished the book. Just a suggestion.

*   *   *   *   *

This story is basically true. Although this book is a work of fiction—that is, the Wardells, Schlagels, the rest of the characters and the town of Harrisonburg are all figments and fragments of my imagination and any resemblance otherwise should be regarded as coincidence—all of the major incidents, the beatings, the pool table rape, the suicide attempt, the harassment, the parents telling the world their son was dead—are not fiction at all. Some of the major events in this story happened to me— for instance, there were frequent fights at my high school and I did spend my high school years cowering in the background so as not to be pummeled and I sprinted many miles running away from the demons that pursued me. But don't assume it is all autobiographical or which parts happened to me.

The other incidents actually occurred to young men I know in Ohio, Pennsylvania, Missouri, Texas, Maine, Nevada, Oklahoma, California, Florida, North Carolina, Virginia, Illinois, West Virginia, South Dakota and Oregon—the reason for this list is to show that things are very much the same all over.

This book is dedicated to those brave young men who survived such hardship to be able to share their stories with me. I thank them and dedicate this book to:

Chad, Chad, Oren, Ryan, David, Davey (the Zugrat), Tommy, Sean, Craig, Jeremy, Victor, Josh, Zack, Jason, Cole, Josh, Chris, Kevin, Scott, Bill, Greg Congdon (about whom I wrote in *Hero Magazine*, November, 1999), and Coach Eric "Gumby" Anderson and his brave track team at Huntington Beach High School, California, 1993.

The suicide rate of gay teens is seven times that of straight youth and in spite of huge strides forward, most kids are still afraid to come out. The average high school student hears the word "fag" or the phrase "that's so gay" dozens of times a day. So far none of the tragic school shootings have been committed by anyone who self-identified as gay, but a common theme in most of them has been that the kid or kids who finally snapped had been called "fag" often.

The flippant reference Brittany makes to Columbine is not meant in any way to minimize the tragedy in Littleton, Colorado. Rather, it's really the way kids talk and it's meant as a reminder that seemingly small slights can add up to very big tragedies as happened at Santana High School in Santee, California not far from where I live. I have talked to several of the kids who survived that school hallway full of bullets.

In speaking at my old high school in 2004, I was shocked to learn that in a school of almost 2000 students, there was only one kid brave enough to be openly gay. This book is dedicated to him and another young man, Bobby Sosnowski, who was brave enough to be out at Maplewood High School in the tiny town of Guys Mills, Pennsylvania; and to Allan Acevedo, about whom I wrote in the May, 2005 issue of *Out* magazine who took a leading roll at Hilltop High School in Chula Vista, California; and to the many other courageous young men and women, fragile minorities in their schools, who risk daily abuse—both physical and psychological—to be honest about who they are.

In the many stories I have heard over the years, it seems that those who came out fared far better than those who are outed. Incidents of sexual extortion such as Josh suffers in this book are not uncommon, but it's not possible to blackmail someone if they are already out.

If you doubt the underlying truths of this story, watch the news: a young man in New York beaten by his parents with lead pipes to drive out his gayness; a young man in Pennsylvania murdered by his brother for being gay—and the parents sided with the murderer, not their other son, the victim. This is not ancient history. Those incidents occurred in 2003 and 2002. If Josh's father's treatment of him seems excessive, in 2005 a man beat his three-year old son to death for acting gay—that is not a typo, yes, he thought a three-year-old was acting gay. Experts say that 40% of homeless teens are gay; the hell on the streets is preferable to the hell they left at home. In 2009, a group of high school students in Florida were charged with repeatedly raping another student in the locker room over a period of months.

And this book is dedicated to the memory of my high school crush.

SOME THANK YOUS . . .

Although writing is a solitary task it is made infinitely easier by the support and input of others. For their help on this project I would like to thank, in no particular order for reading the manuscript or providing background information, or suggestions: my friend and mentor, Martin J. Smith; Bob Frick; Moises

Ventura; Margie Mingione; Ann Smolen; Dan, Joe and Debbie Cybulski, Ethan and Ray Meyer, Dan Manes, Jennifer Schumaker, Bryan Munson and Brent Hartinger.

*   *   *   *   *

And thank you to my parents. Phil Reed, another writer friend, after reading the first few chapters of the book said, "I'm learning a lot about your dad." As a good writer himself, Phil knows writers often borrow from their own lives for their books. And I would be lying to say that there are not elements of my father in Bob Wardell, but not the ones that Phil assumed. The main part of Bob that I preserved from my father is his confusion of how to handle a rather eccentric son. Give a shepherd a goldfish and he's likely to be a little confused of how best to handle it. Even if he is the best shepherd in the world, he's going to be a bit out of his element. The reflection Bobby has that "His father was like that. Quietly doing his duty" is an accurate description of my father.

I often felt sorry for my parents, who were clearly puzzled as to what to make of their son, and how to handle his rather strange mood swings, but I was in no position to help them with their own confusion; my confusion was even greater. I thank them for their patience and understanding, because like the Wardells, when the chips were down, they came through.

Walter G. Meyer began his writing career when he won a short-story contest while in elementary school in Bethel Park, Pennsylvania. He turned pro when he started freelancing for the local newspaper when he was in ninth grade covering topics ranging from the JFK assassination to the high school baseball team while he was a member of that team.

He wrote for the *Daily Collegian* at Penn State and created such a name for himself that some of his work was printed in a book celebrating the first 100 years of the school paper. Shortly after graduating, he was asked back to speak at his alma mater — a rare honor for a 21-year old.

He went on to freelance for numerous newspapers and magazines including the *Pittsburgh Press, Pittsburgh Post-Gazette, Pittsburgh Magazine, Kiplinger's Personal Finance, Orange Coast, Westways* and the *Orange County Register*.

After his own coming out story was published in the *Los Angeles Times Magazine* it was reprinted around the world and he received hundreds of emails from people whose lives it touched. He has written for the national gay magazines *Hero* and *Xodus* and he has penned numerous articles for the two largest: *The Advocate* and *Out*. His interest in baseball continued and he did a story for *San Diego Magazine* about college baseball.

He has co-written two nonfiction books. *Going for the Green: Selling in the21st Century* is a business book in the form of a novel which teaches the right way to sell. *Day is Ending: a doctor's love shattered by Alzheimer's disease*, was optioned to be a movie based on his script. Meyer has appeared before many Alzheimer's groups and care facilities to talk about that tragic disease.

He has spoken on other serious topics like the environment, but has also done stand-up comedy. A comedy play that he co-wrote, *GAM3RS*, was produced to rave reviews in New York, received a fantastic reception at MIT and in other performances around the country. It is being considered as the basis for a television sitcom.

He has volunteered for AIDS Walk San Diego, as well as the GLBT Center and Hillcrest (LGBT) Youth Center in San Diego, Gay Pride and the Marriage Equality Project.

His own experiences on his high school's baseball team and his work as a mentor with gay youth inspired much of the story of *Rounding Third*.

Walter G. Meyer can be contacted at:
Myspace.com/sandiegowriter
Facebook.com/walt.meyer

*   *   *   *   *

To find out what happens next to Rob and Josh,
read excerpts of *Unassisted Triple Play*,
the sequel to *Rounding Third*, at
waltergmeyer.com